A PLUME BOOK

SYLVAN STREET

DEBORAH SCHUPACK is the author of a previous novel, *The Boy on the Bus*, as well as many short stories and newspaper and magazine articles. She lives in the Hudson Valley with her husband and daughters.

Sylvan Street

A NOVEL

Deborah Schupack

A PLUME BOOK

PLUME
Published by the Penguin Group
Penguin Group (USA) Inc., 375 Hudson Street, New York, New York 10014, U.S.A.
Penguin Group (Canada), 90 Eglinton Avenue East, Suite 700, Toronto, Ontario,
Canada M4P 2Y3 (a division of Pearson Penguin Canada Inc.)
Penguin Books Ltd., 80 Strand, London WC2R 0RL, England
Penguin Ireland, 25 St. Stephen's Green, Dublin 2, Ireland
(a division of Penguin Books Ltd.)
Penguin Group (Australia), 250 Camberwell Road, Camberwell, Victoria 3124,
Australia (a division of Pearson Australia Group Pty. Ltd.)
Penguin Books India Pvt. Ltd., 11 Community Centre, Panchsheel Park,
New Delhi – 110 017, India
Penguin Group (NZ), 67 Apollo Drive, Rosedale, North Shore 0632, New Zealand
(a division of Pearson New Zealand Ltd.)
Penguin Books (South Africa) (Pty.) Ltd., 24 Sturdee Avenue, Rosebank,
Johannesburg 2196, South Africa

Penguin Books Ltd., Registered Offices: 80 Strand, London WC2R 0RL, England

First published by Plume, a member of Penguin Group (USA) Inc.

First Printing, June 2010
10 9 8 7 6 5 4 3 2 1

Copyright © Deborah Schupack, 2010
All rights reserved

 REGISTERED TRADEMARK—MARCA REGISTRADA

CIP data is available.

ISBN 978-0-452-29628-2

Printed in the United States of America
Set in Sabon
Designed by Leonard Telesca

PUBLISHER'S NOTE
This is a work of fiction. Names, characters, places, and incidents are either the product of the
author's imagination or are used fictitiously, and any resemblance to actual persons, living or
dead, business establishments, events, or locales is entirely coincidental.

For Patrick

ACKNOWLEDGMENTS

Heartfelt thanks to my editor, Denise Roy, a beacon of wisdom and encouragement; my agent, Maria Massie, a skilled navigator of many waters; and my thoughtful readers, Rosalyn Bodycomb, Kathryn Davis, Patrick Dias, Matthew Goodman, Linda Schupack, and Kate Walbert. A debt of gratitude to Blue Mountain Center for the gift of time and space, and to Rose and Ida for being such good girls.

Sylvan Street

Prologue

Eclipse

June nights came pleasantly late on Sylvan Street, fully round the bend of day. This night, after dinners were eaten, baths taken and the earliest bedtimes accomplished, a dozen neighbors meandered onto the cul-de-sac to watch the partial eclipse of the moon.

As the moon rose bright and full, talk among neighbors was at either extreme of the general or the particular. Generally pleasant weather, generally unpleasant economy, on the one hand. Geocentric coordinates of tonight's moon and details of impending bedtimes, on the other.

A couple of children waved flashlights while adults chatted, or didn't. Light beams sharpened then dimmed as they touched surfaces then set out into the great night sky. Sylvan Street was as dark as any rural outpost. One was always reminded—whether by a loved one or by darkness itself—to carry a flashlight, even if one was only embarking on a simple trip to make inquiry of a neighbor or look for a pair of children's shoes left on a dampening lawn.

"Oh, here it comes," someone said at the first sign of the moon passing into the earth's umbra.

Everyone who hadn't yet done so extinguished their flashlights with a certain collective understanding.

"It looks like someone's erasing the moon," a girl whispered to her mother, who nodded.

Indeed it did, a smudge taking the edge off the moon's crisp, perfect circle.

"Supposed to last about a half hour," someone reported.

The shuffling of anticipation gave way to a hushed silence. There was a tensile, near-perfect feeling of community. For the time it would take a planetary shadow to pass, everyone would witness the exact same thing, and with no earthly consequence.

The moon reddened as it grew obscured. It was now more in shadow than not.

"Why is it red?"

"Volcanic dust," came one answer.

"The glow of the penumbra?" came another, although as a question.

A few clouds drifted into the celestial drama.

"Pretty," someone said.

"Better than fireworks," someone else said.

The group rippled with wordless assent.

After a time, a husband said to a wife, "Dramatic, huh?"

The wife understood. "You want to head in?" she said.

Similar domestic duets—nods to the wonder of it, followed by self-dismissal—and the crowd was down to seven . . . four . . . finally, two: the young mother who had always been awed by celestial spectacles and the retired calculus teacher who knew the parameters of the eclipse's totality and was committed to waiting it out.

Janic Levlovic, the retired teacher, could not have told you whether this eclipse was pretty or not, whether it stoked a communal feeling of goodwill, whether it kept children up past their bedtime. He could tell you, however, the geocentric conjunction, the P. radius, U. radius and Gamma. He could tell you the eclipse's umbral magnitude: 0.81, or 81 percent obscured, which was quite impressive and probably did translate to the layperson as "pretty." He could tell you that in another eighteen years, eleven days and eight hours (one complete 6,585.3-day Saros cycle), a similar eclipse with similar geocoordinates would pass over Sylvan Street. If it was a clear night and if all was still relatively right with the world, especially Ashley-on-Hudson as it homed in on Sylvan Street, a similar collection of people might well drift out to a similar spot on the street and, hushed, gaze skyward.

ONE

1

Pool Party

Sally Levlovic tipped her face to the sun and watched out of the corner of her eye as Billy Cane dipped his foot into the pool. Meanwhile, Maggie Cane was doing all the setup, running around laying out the food, making drinks, schlepping towels and more towels.

Sally suspected her own husband was falling for Billy in the same way Maggie had, seduced by a transparent sensual charm that you'd think would wear off pretty quickly for smart people like Maggie and Janic. Billy was lanky, sultry, beautiful to behold and easy to envy. But to spend a whole afternoon with him, as Janic was doing these days, let alone a lifetime, seemed dull to her, and a bit of a deal with the devil.

"Yes?" said Shoshanna Yaniv, who was sitting in the chaise next to Sally. "Is there something I should know?"

Sally had inadvertently been squeezing her new neighbor's arm at the elbow.

"Oh, my, no," Sally said. "Just so happy to have you here. A new neighbor on Sylvan Street."

"I thought you wanted me to notice something about Billy Cane."

"No, no, the whole scene," Sally said, thinking fast. "I just wanted you to take in the whole Sylvan Street scene. This is as good as it gets."

"Is that good or bad?" Shoshanna asked.

"Beautiful blue sky, all of us gathered for the annual pool opening party at this beautiful house . . ."

"Yes, nice," said Shoshanna. "We feel lucky to be here. It feels like the country, but at the same time, Daniel's commute to the city is really quick."

"Ah, commuters," Sally said. "When we first moved here, the city was as far away as Atlantis. We talked about it like a distant, golden place. Now, so many Ashleyites commute every day. What brings your Daniel into the city?"

"Advertising," Shoshanna said. "Technically, it's 'branding,' but I've never gotten a satisfactory answer about how the two are different."

"All these newfangled careers," Sally said. "We were teachers, Janic and I. Period, end of story. How about you?"

"Me?" Shoshanna said. "The title, I suppose, is stay-at-home mom, but the kids are barely home anymore. Soccer, day camp, gymnastics, piano, martial arts. Not to mention school."

She gave a quick bio: born in Israel, came to the U.S. for Penn Law School, her father's alma mater. Then five years at a big Manhattan firm. Once the kids started arriving— she supposed she had expected more than two; that was the ancient Israelite in her—she left work. They left Manhattan for Brooklyn, where they were for seven or eight years. And now Ashley-on-Hudson.

"That's hardly nothing," Sally exclaimed.

Billy Cane was taking pool toys and equipment out of the shed. He wasn't quite sure how this tradition had started, the annual pool opening party for the neighbors. He certainly didn't come up with it, but neither did it sound like an idea of his wife's—all the neighbors gathered at once, thinking how easy life was for Maggie and Billy Cane.

Let them judge. Let them hold an outsider's notion of Maggie and Billy Cane. He knew they thought he wasn't good enough for Maggie. Which was a fine way to keep people out of his marriage.

Maggie. Look at her! Her long black hair was shiny from an earlier swim; her green eyes could light the way in the dark. Maggie in summer. Maggie as he met her. Tan, freckled, windblown.

She caught him looking at her and couldn't help a smile. He squinted privately, almost a wink, and she, if he wasn't mistaken, pursed her lips in a small suggestion of a kiss, freeing them to go their separate ways, united.

He took out a couple of rafts. He reached behind the shed door for the backup skimmer, which he'd leave on deck in case any of the husbands—as often happened at these gatherings—wanted a chore. He pulled at the skimmer, but it was stuck, the end pinned behind a black briefcase. What a strange place for a briefcase, especially one that he'd never seen before.

"Okay, who's moving in?" he said, hauling the surprisingly heavy case out to the deck.

No one looked up.

"This isn't yours, is it, Mag?"

She looked over then back to the hors d'oeuvre table, where she was rearranging fruit and iced coffee and juice boxes.

Billy unlatched the case but clapped it shut almost immediately, with a *whap* that caught Ash Flemming's attention, made him look up from his cell phone.

"What?" Ash said. "A body?"

"He's kidding with that face, Ash," Maggie said. "Right, Billy? What's in there?"

Billy shook his head, tried for nonchalance.

Keith Margolis, who'd been digging through his wife's jammed pool bag, looked up. Billy held out his palms, as if to show a dog, *It's nothing*, and backed a few steps toward the shed.

Janic Levlovic looked up from the Sunday *Times* crossword puzzle.

Sally Levlovic propped her oversized sunglasses on her head and squinted. "What is it, William?"

Shoshanna Yaniv sat forward in her chair. Daniel Hansen stopped trying to detangle the pool thermometer from the pool ladder. The Yaniv-Hansen kids stopped waiting for their father to detangle the pool thermometer from the pool ladder.

"I don't really know what to do," Billy said.

Jenny Margolis looked up from her *Vanity Fair*. Her twins looked up from the pool. April Margolis looked up from putting sunscreen on her bikini-exposed belly.

Only Tiger Margolis, who was three, carried on, running

around the yard naked and on his tippy-toes like he was in *Hair!*

"Who says the economy's in the tank?" Billy said. He unlatched the case and tipped it toward his neighbors. Not a single bill shifted. That's how tightly the money was packed.

2

Lobbying the Levlovices

Sally was beginning to feel like she and her husband were sitting shiva, as the Jews do. One by one, their neighbors trickled over, bringing muffins, children's drawings, greetings, good wishes. Now here was Billy, toting a chessboard, bringing the game to Janic for a change.

"Only fair," Billy said. "You've come up to my house so many times."

Yesterday, after Billy found the money, someone—Sally remembered it as Keith Margolis; Janic remembered it as Ash Flemming—said, seemingly as a joke, "Hey, let's split it five ways."

No one laughed.

"Some kind of prank on the new neighbors?" Daniel Hansen had said.

"Right," Billy'd said. "We all decided to pitch in our loose hundreds and pack a million bucks into a briefcase."

"Is that how much you think it is?" Jen Margolis asked.

"I don't know," Billy said, trying to wedge a hand in, as if he could count it that way.

"Shouldn't touch it," Keith said. "Fingerprint Evidence 101. I'll call my guys, figure this thing out, if you want. Unless you want to go to a lawyer or something."

"Why would I go to a lawyer?" Billy said.

"Right," Keith said. "He'd take half of it as a fee." He laughed.

"No, really," Billy said. "Why would I? I haven't done anything wrong."

"Of course," Keith said. "But clearly this is ill-gotten gains. Even if you're not the one who ill-got it in the first place, you got it now."

That's when Ash—it was Ash—said, "Think about it. If we do split it, dole it out five ways and hide it under our mattresses, whoever it belongs to is going to, what, call the cops?" He looked at Keith. "No offense, man. *Um, Officer, I lost my stolen money.*"

Shoshanna had the presence of mind to round up the children, hers and the Margolises', keep them out of earshot, have them take one last swim, then help clean up the buffet table.

"My point is," Ash said, lowering his voice, "what if this money disappears? Whatever it is, drug money, a bribe or ransom. What recourse does that kind of criminal have?"

"*What recourse?*" Maggie said. "Recourse that begins at the end of a gun."

"Let's not argue first," Daniel said. "First, let's count it."

"That's your take?" Shoshanna tucked back in among the adults. "That's your moral take on this?"

"It's not a *moral take*, honey," Daniel said. "It's a practical suggestion."

"Can't count it without implicating yourself," Keith said. "Fingerprint Evidence 102."

"Maybe you should count it," Ash said to Keith. "You're the cop. You'd be counting it as evidence."

"Ever heard of a little thing called procedure?" Keith said. "I'd have to, for instance, file a report, log evidence, conduct an inventory."

"Inventory?" Billy said.

"You have to inventory the place after an incident, account for what was stolen, defaced or damaged," Keith said. "Or added? Boy, never had that before."

"You all can keep it if you'd like," said Sally. "But we want no part of it." She looked at Janic. "I, anyway. Perhaps my husband's no longer with me. I don't recognize him half the time, since he retired."

"I didn't even say anything, Sal," he said.

"Are you with me," she said, "or with your felonious neighbors?"

"Sally," Maggie said.

"Margaret," Sally countered. "You of all people."

"We're just talking," Maggie said. "Doesn't make us criminals. This is such a crazy thing, and we're all trying to get our bearings, sort out our thoughts."

"Talk isn't harmless," Sally said. "You should know that. You're a smart girl, probably the smartest one here. Besides, you of all people don't even need the money. I can understand if the poorer folk among us—"

"That's not fair," Jen said.

"I was meaning us, the retired high school teachers with plummeting pensions," Sally said. "Not you, Jennifer."

"Of course you were meaning us," Jen said. "And Ash, probably."

"Hey," said Ash, looking up again from his phone. "I'm just sitting here minding my own business."

"What if I was?" Sally said. "Count yourselves in if you'd like. Nothing wrong with being poor and proud. I'm all for it."

Jennifer had been the first one over this morning. Yesterday, everyone had agreed that the plan—whatever plan it was— would only work if everyone was in on it. *If we don't hang together,* Daniel said at the pool, *we'll hang separately.* Advertising, indeed.

"As one poor, proud mother to another," Jen began, when she came to lobby the Levlovices this morning, "would you at least think about it? If we could figure out a way to make the criminal part of it go away, would you think about it?"

"Oh, Jennifer," said Sally. "Little Jennifer Hotten."

Jennifer could cast Sally back to her own days as a young mother, when she was pregnant with Byron, and her neighbor Ellen Hotten was pregnant with Jennifer. This was back in the day when pregnant neighbors were shy around each other at first, until the shared indignities and downright obviousness of their condition created an inescapable, though not always durable, bond. In those final months of pregnancy, they'd sit on Sally's back patio or Ellen's screened-in porch, have a glass of white wine or something stronger, depending on the day, and talk about how they couldn't wait to trade the bowling balls resting on their bladders for actual ten-fingered, ten-toed little babies.

"It's a meaningful amount of money," Jen said to Sally, "if it's bundled hundreds. Which Keith is sure it is. God knows, we could use the money. Keith's overtime has been cut to nothing. But the twins still need braces, and Kelli probably needs glasses. And they all need computers. That's not even a luxury anymore. The kids need the latest things just to keep up with their schoolwork. I don't know how April gets through high school with half the things she doesn't have."

"We could all use the money," Sally said. "That's not my point. That's entirely beside my point. I'm just saying—and I can't believe I have to spell this out to my neighbors, fine people all—it's not our money. And if whomever the money belonged to were to give his blessing and turn it over to us tomorrow, I still wouldn't want anything to do with it. There's no way, Jennifer, just no way this money could pass down to us through clean hands."

"But if it did—"

"But, but, but," Sally said. "Goats butt, birds fly, to quote Mary Poppins."

"Can I tell you how much Keith makes a year?" Jen said.

"Please don't," Sally said. "I may be dating myself, but I come from a time when people didn't talk about salaries. Besides, Janic and I were public school teachers all our lives. We can go paycheck stub to paycheck stub with your husband. We're all doing much too good work for much too little money, Jennifer. But this isn't going to change that."

"Well, what is?" Jennifer asked, as if she honestly expected to find out.

"Work hard, fly right, good will out," Sally said. "That's my suggestion for the day."

As the day went on, Sally would dispense that wisdom to Ash, who ostensibly came to give them a *Times* review he'd clipped about the Whitney Biennial; to Daniel Hansen, who came to see if the calculus teacher had a scale rule he could borrow; and to Maggie, who dropped off blueberry corn muffins, which, in fairness, she did whenever she baked more than she and her husband, not an ounce of fat between them, could eat.

Sally would have dispensed that wisdom to Keith, too, but she grew exasperated with him before she could get a word in edgewise.

"Boy, I bet we're all telling you what we need for our kids," Keith said, after he had indeed just gone over a laundry list of needs. "But then I think to myself, Wait a minute. The Levs have grandkids who could use a thing or two, four little orphans from around the world. I can't think of any better cause than the Lev family."

"Careful with the word 'cause,' son," Janic said, rising from his chair and speaking in his too-soft voice. "That's our family you're talking about, not some civics project."

Byron and his wife, Bianca, had over the last two years adopted Lazlo from Guatemala, Jaq from Vietnam and two sisters, Renata and Ulaht, from Kazakhstan. Byron and Bianca were humanitarian aid workers by whose mailing addresses you could map the last decade's geopolitical strife. Burma, the Balkans, Kazakhstan, Afghanistan, the Sudanese-Chadian border. Now they were settled in Astoria, Queens—one of the most diverse places on earth, according to Bianca—with their new family.

"They're no longer orphans, Keith," Sally said. "You're missing the central concept of adoption."

"I'm quite sure I understand what adoption means," Keith said, his neck reddening. "I'm just saying it's a noble thing to do, even if other people think it's no different from raising your own biological children."

This was the kind of day it had been for Sally and Janic.

And now Billy. She'd let Janic handle this one. She excused herself and went out back to the garden. She extracted a few weeds from among the colorful portulacas, her favorites. She loved their bursts of hopeful colors: yellow, pink, white, red, orange and a surprising neon salmon.

Janic was the garden's original architect, but over the years killing frosts and grazing deer had opened up space for some of her choices. Pansies, daisies, black-eyed Susans and the delightful portulacas. Hers were humble flowers, while Janic chose the more hubristic ones: irises, peonies, lilies and even, God help them, gladiolas when she wasn't looking.

How was Billy lobbying Janic right now? She had no idea who held sway over whom in that pair. She didn't even know who was the better chess player, who had the edge in games. She'd have guessed Janic, anyone would, but several times he had remarked on Billy's surprising skill. Afternoon after afternoon, Janic would amble home from the Manor House at the end of the day, relaxed as a man returning from the beach, and he'd give no indication of who'd won. Little indication of anything, really. Occasionally, he'd relate a snatch of conversation—"They're getting dry rot in their basement, too"—or something Maggie had said as she walked by. Or even a word or two about April Margolis, who was apparently up at the Manor House as often as Janic.

April was a good girl, always polite, which was surprising for a girl who was starting to look like that, ripening in a way that made Sally glad she hadn't had girls. Trouble. April had the definition of milky skin, full lips that were sure to earn her a nickname and, as they said in Sally's day, *legs up to here*.

Sally could just picture the two men inside, Billy and Janic, brows furrowed (Billy's under that ski cap he wore, even though it was summer), elbows on the chess table. Better Billy than me, she thought. Janic had tried to coach her in chess, but she wasn't interested enough to present him any kind of challenge. It's more than a game, he'd said, expounding on life lessons that could be drawn from this Napoleonic exercise in measured aggression.

Perhaps between moves, Billy was mounting his case, as the parade of neighbors had done throughout the day. Or maybe (one could hope, couldn't one?) Janic was making their case, his and Sally's. Billy and Maggie had apparently spent last night in the city, too apprehensive to sleep in their own home—shouldn't that be a sign that what they were doing was wrong? They were all decent people, Janic's argument might go (if he'd been listening to his wife at all over the last twenty-four hours), and what decent people did when they found a briefcase packed with money was go to the police.

Give it to Keith Margolis—he'd put it in the right hands. Then again, the hands that Keith Margolis wanted to put it in were his own. He was as decent as anyone, but Sally knew he must be overwhelmed with expenses. A family of seven!

Sally's grandchildren needed plenty, too. Byron's children, anyway. Not Blake's Lila, who had too much and was spoiled rotten.

That *Scarsdale*. (Blake said some of Lila's friends had not only their own room but their own wing; one had her own house, the "children's cottage.") But Byron and Bianca were trying, on his lone nonprofit salary, to raise four kids who had an international array of health problems. What if Sally and Janic could help pay for experts to find out why Lazlo kept falling asleep in his chair at school, at the dinner table, on the subway? Or help send Ulaht to the orthodontist for those teeth, and Renata right behind her?

If Billy could convince Janic that they and their hardworking neighbors—and even their nonhardworking neighbors— deserved something extra, that maybe this was some kind of sign from above that they were deserving people . . . If Billy were to convince Janic, then Sally would have to listen. Janic was, after all, the voice of reason. That was why she married him.

She went into the living room, found the two men indeed furrowed in concentration, as she'd expected. The board was untouched. Billy made a gesture with his chin, and Janic nodded. More staring, then Janic pointed a finger at the board, and Billy nodded.

They were taking turns without moving pieces.

The silence held Sally at bay until Janic noticed her in the doorway. "You rang?" he said. This, the Addams Family's Lurch, was one of Janic's three imitations. He also did a remarkable James Cromwell (whom everyone said he looked like) and Sir Winston Churchill in his first speech to the House of Commons: "I have nothing to offer but blood, toil, tears and sweat." On the latter, Janic was impressively stentorian, though there were few, if any, who could judge his accuracy.

"What's this?" Sally said. "Imaginary chess?"

"Something like it," Billy said. "It's our warm-up."

They were warming up brain muscles, he explained, before getting down to the thought marathon that is a chess game. Before they began play, they would take turns without actually moving pieces. The challenge of holding that many dimensions of time and space in your head couldn't help but sharpen mental acuity. They would play like this until one or the other, or usually both men at once, lost the full mental picture, then they'd start the physical game.

They were getting better each time, Billy said. They could now keep as many as seven moves in their head before the mind's human frailty revealed itself and the exercise fell apart.

"I'll leave you to your game, then," Sally said. "Before my own frail mind reveals itself."

She continued about her day, fixing a chicken, changing a load of laundry. She was playing out imaginary moves of her own. A friend of hers who was a realtor had a new listing in Ashley and had called to ask if Sally knew anyone who was looking. "I know, I know, not you," said Ruth Simon, Ruth Simon Realty. "I know you're in love with your house and your Sylvan Street."

The listing was on nearby River Rise, a midsize bungalow with four small bedrooms, a reasonable yard and a crazy amount of charm, according to Ruth. As compared to a 750-square-foot two-bedroom and God knows what that other room was—walk-in closet—that the boys slept in. And the crowded, dirty, hot streets of Astoria, Queens. Even if Bianca was right and it was the most diverse place on earth, ethnically speaking, mightn't a backyard and plenty of bedrooms be more what the doctor ordered, after all those kids had been through?

Sally checked on the men in the living room again. They had moved from imaginary chess to actual chess. The frailty of the human mind must have revealed itself.

Still, they were silent. Perhaps that was what Janic liked about Billy. Silence. While Janic Levlovic, after forty-four years of marriage and as many in the public schools, had put in enough conversation to deserve a break from it, Billy was young and so was his wife. Good, clever Maggie, a vibrant woman with no children and no job to speak of, must be craving conversation. The alliance of marriage was all wrong, Sally thought. Maggie and Sally would be well suited to passing the time together, talking about anything and everything, while Janic and Billy, silently moving—or not moving—chess pieces around a board, could not have been happier with each other.

Sally changed another load of laundry. As she hung a couple of cotton sweaters to dry over the back railing, she was struck by the transformative power of fresh air. She took a deep breath. Her shoulders relaxed, her collarbones spread, her lungs expanded. Ah, Sylvan Street. She took this air for granted. Maybe Lazlo kept falling asleep in the middle of everything because the poor kid wasn't getting enough oxygen. And how about Jaq, the little monkey who more than once fell out of that ridiculously narrow top bunk, the only thing that made it possible for two boys to sleep in a walk-in closet.

She'd call Ruth, at least take a look at the River Rise place. Inquire a little more—the neighborhood? the boiler? storage space?—and ask what kind of deal a person could get in this soft market if a person were to put, say, fifty percent down.

3

The Formula

To judge from the apprehensive entries—as opposed to the eagerness last weekend: *pool's open!*—everyone was thinking of the pool as a sacred spot. Or a crime scene. There was a collective sense of misplaced intimacy, like someone had walked in on someone else in the bathroom, or bedroom.

There was no summer buffet spread, although there was a bouncing array of pool toys. The kids were to think it was a pool party, but for the adults, this was a working session.

Sally was still not sure how it had happened. She and Janic had separately—then, somewhere along the line, together—moved from *terrible idea* to *maybe not such a terrible idea*. Janic was dispatched to break the news to the Canes, who in turn broke it to the others. During a chess session, Billy and Janic had counted the money, a move that seemed to be all right with everyone. At least, no one was complaining. No one seemed to know how much say they had in all of this.

Once everyone arrived, Billy went into the shed, waltzed right in like anyone else could have done if they were looking to redeem their case full of cash. Last week, Keith had come up with an idea that all the neighbors signed on to: leave the money just where they'd found it, unlocked, seemingly undiscovered. If it was something illegal, which everyone assumed it was, either the lowlifes would come back for it in the first few days or they wouldn't because they couldn't, meaning they were dead or locked up. Every day that went by, it became safer to assume that whoever knew about the money was not coming back. Keith had been convincing, and everyone was eager to be convinced.

Jen and Maggie shepherded the kids to the other side of the pool, where the ladders and rafts were. The parents, Keith and Jen and Daniel and Shoshanna, had been asked to tell the kids that the grown-ups were having a boring neighborhood meeting, a tax issue, zoning. Something they needed to talk about as a group.

One by one, the Margolis children slipped into the pool. Brittany, Bethany, April. No sign of Kelli, and Tiger was in the garden again. Daniel and Shoshanna's kids sat by the ladder, dangling their feet.

Billy stepped back outside, pulling the case on its little wheels. He propped his foot on it like a conquering hero. "One million, two thousand, five hundred," he said, his voice probably not as low as it should have been.

"Divided by five families . . . ," Ash said.

"What do we do?" Jen whispered, though loudly. "Deal it out like a hand of cards?"

"Wait a minute," Keith said. "We're seven mouths and this

guy"—he thumbed toward Ash, who happened to be reaching for his cell phone on the side table next to Keith—"is one mouth."

"I get penalized because I don't have a hundred kids I can't take care of?" Ash said.

"Who has a hundred kids they can't take care of?" Jen said, dropping a drink right out of her hand, plastic cup and ice clattering onto the ground.

"I don't mean literally," Ash said. "I just mean that I have a lot of expenses, too. People with kids always think they're the only ones with responsibilities."

"Want 'em?" Keith said. "One or two, anyway?"

Jen looked up from the ground, where she was trying to corral spilled liquid and ice in her hands. "That's a terrible thing to say, Keith," she said.

"Jenny," Maggie said, hopping up, "let me get you something for that. You don't have to use your hands. My God."

Maggie headed toward the house but stopped before getting to the door, turning around like Lot's wife. "Better yet," she said, "leave it. It's ice and juice on flagstone. Who cares?"

"And vodka," Jen said.

"Good for you," Billy said. "Drinking at three in the afternoon. Good. For. You."

"It's a crazy weekend." Jen sounded indignant, as conversation with Billy Cane could turn a Margolis.

"Let's figure out our formula," said Daniel. "Maybe something like each household is worth a certain percentage, then each adult's worth a certain percentage on top of that, and each kid, another, smaller percentage." He turned to Janic. "You should probably call the shots. You're the math professor."

"High school teacher, my friend," Janic said. "Retired high school teacher."

"But back in the game," Daniel said.

"This guy?" Billy said. "Never out of it."

"Then let's get to work," Daniel said. From what was masquerading as a pool bag, he pulled out a legal pad and two mechanical pencils.

"You come prepared," said Maggie.

"Recovering Boy Scout," he said. "Always prepared."

"I thought that was the Post Office," Billy said.

"Nope," said Daniel. "Boy Scouts. Prepared in mind, body and spirit. *C'est moi.* Troop 381. Great Neck, Long Island, circa 1974. Den Mother, Mrs. Rita Goldfarb, mother of Josh and Seth."

"Great Neck, meet Bethpage," Sally said, patting her chest.

"Okay, Great Neck," Janic said. "If we're going to work, let's work." They excused themselves and headed to a small cocktail table at the far corner of the pool, taking the working atmosphere with them.

Maggie went over to the kids' side, sat next to Allie Yaniv-Hansen and gave her a warm, potentially maternal smile. Allie looked to her brother. Caleb shrugged. Maggie sat down next to them, dangling her feet, too.

"What do you think of all this?" Maggie said.

Surely it was not her responsibility to consider other people's children. Where were the parents? Jen and Keith were sunning and splashing, like it was any other day at the pool. Daniel Hansen, the recovering Boy Scout, was happily working on a math problem. And Shoshanna wasn't even here.

"Of all what?" Caleb said.

"I don't know," Maggie said. "Of the pool? Of the party? Of your new neighborhood?"

"I like it," Allie said. "He doesn't."

"Why not?" Maggie asked Caleb.

He shrugged again.

"He misses his soccer team," Allie said.

"*Traveling* team," he clarified. "Plus, there are no boys on this street."

"Aha," Maggie said. "He speaks." She got a smile out of him.

"There's that baby," Allie said, pointing to Tiger. "He's a boy."

"There may be, shall we say, a limited population of boys on this street," said Maggie, "but there is a pretty awesome pool, right?"

"We can't go in without Mom or Dad," Allie said.

"Your dad's right there," Maggie said.

"But he looks busy with the tax stuff."

"Where is your mom?" Maggie asked.

"At temple," said Allie.

"I'll watch you," Maggie said. "So you guys can go in if you feel like it."

Caleb dove into the pool. Allie looked to Maggie, who nodded. "Go on, sweetie," she said.

Allie jumped into the pool, knees locked, hands stiff at her sides.

Jesus. Maggie didn't even know whether these kids could swim. Allie Hansen was seven years old. *Go ahead, jump.* What the hell kind of mother would she make?

Glassy with pool water, Allie surfaced on the other side. She was a perfectly capable swimmer. Maggie knelt by the side of the pool. Allie shook her little seal head and rubbed a hand over her face. "It's not too hot and it's not too cold," she said gleefully.

"Goldilocks!" Maggie called, but Allie had already wriggled back under.

"Hey, folks," Ash called over to the math table, too loud for the confluent lull in conversation and splashing. Everyone looked at him. "I should tell you mathletes that Suki might be coming back. So if you could keep that in mind—"

"Oh, Ash," Maggie said. "That's great. I love Suki."

"It's up in the air," Ash said, "but maybe."

Daniel came over to the nonmath side of the pool. "What did you say?" he said. "We can't really hear over there, we two old men."

"My girlfriend," Ash said. "She might be moving back. So we'd be a household of two."

"What does your formula do with dubious girlfriends?" Billy asked.

"Suki's not here," said Daniel. "So that might be one way we categorize."

"Your wife's not here, either," Ash said.

"That's different, Ash," Maggie said.

"She's not *not here*," Daniel said. "She's doing an errand and will be back in a couple hours."

Temple—an errand? That wasn't lost on Maggie.

"As opposed to never," Billy said under his breath.

"We'll try to be fair," Daniel said. "Maybe an adult who's not here can receive a smaller percentage or something. Same as a child."

"You're valuing Suki's life the same as that kid?" Ash pointed to a bare-bottomed Tiger Margolis, who was over by the fence waving his penis at the Canes' poor old dog. Barclay, in the earned repose of the elderly, moved his head this way and that, trying not to look.

"My word, Asher," said Sally, who after more than forty years of formality in the classroom (*Treat them with respect, and they'll treat you with respect*) always reached for the most formal name she could find, even though Ash's complete given name was Ash. "Nobody's valuing anybody's life. Nobody's dead."

"It's for potty training," Jen said. "It's a proven fact that kids are more tuned in to their needs down there when they're naked."

Daniel held up an index finger, as though he were going to say something, arbitrate or scold someone. But he excused himself and went back to the math table.

After no more than fifteen minutes, Daniel and Janic returned with their results.

"What took so long?" Ash said. "A million divided by five—wham, bam, thank you, ma'am."

"Where's the fun in that?" Daniel said. "We had mechanical pencils and everything. Give two systems guys pencils and paper and . . ." He held up the paper with his scribblings.

"I just want to say—" Ash started.

"Not to worry, my friend," Janic said. "I think you'll be happy with this."

"I hate when they say 'my friend,'" said Ash. "Like when Orrin Hatch calls Ted Kennedy 'my friend.' You know you're about to get slammed."

"Orrin Hatch?" Janic said. "Bite your tongue."

"Slammed with . . . ," Daniel started. He looked down at his paper then back up. "Slammed with a hundred seventy thousand, four hundred and twenty-five dollars."

Ash couldn't help but smile.

The clamor came up. *Who else? What else?* And Billy, the joker: "Is that before or after taxes?"

Daniel held up a hand. "Let us explain," he said. "Professor?" He looked to Janic, but Janic demurred.

"Okay," Daniel said. "Let's begin at the beginning."

Dutifully, everyone studied the arrows and circles, names and numbers that Daniel had drawn on his legal pad. But none of it registered. It was raw, unprocessed thought, not language.

"Translation, please," Jen said finally.

Three-quarters of the money, Daniel explained, would be divided evenly among households. The remaining quarter would be divided per head, with adults counting as a whole, and children counting as a half. As discussed.

"Not discussed," said Ash. "As pronounced."

"Fair enough," said Janic. "Mathematics is not exactly a participatory sport."

"How come he got to participate?" Ash said, indicating Daniel.

"Don't really know," said Janic. "He seems to get things done."

It was true about Daniel. He was the closer in his office, which was filled with creative and renegade types, aspiring novelists and playwrights and artists who had learned this generation's lesson: make money first, then pursue your artistic dream. He was the one who could be trusted to read the client, to shift direction if need be or sum up key points and show the creative before doubt surfaced. Everyone always felt better, he knew, once they had seen the creative. His business sense had come as quite a surprise to him, and now others had come to expect it of him.

Daniel walked his neighbors through the scribblings:

Per household

¾ of $1,002,500 = $751,875
$751,875 divided by 5 = $150,375 per household

Per person

9 adults = 9 heads
7 children = 3.5 heads
Total: 12.5 heads
¼ of $1,002,500 = $250,625
$250,625 divided by 12.5 = $20,050 per head
$20,050 per adult, $10,025 per child

Total payout

Cane (2 adults): $190,475
Flemming (1 adult): $170,425
Margolis (2 adults + 5 kids): $240,600
Levlovic (2 adults): $190,475
Hansen/Yaniv (2 adults + 2 kids): $210,525

"Practically a quarter mill." Keith smiled broadly at his wife.

"Braces for Brit and Beth," said Jen. "And glasses for Kell. Where is Kelli?"

"How about Suki?" Ash said.

"Ash," Maggie said, brimming with sympathy, "maybe you guys will get back together. I really hope so, for both your sakes. And for mine. I'd love to have her next door. But she's not here now, and that's what we have to base this thing on. Today. The moment."

"Since when are you so Zen?" Ash said.

"Hey, don't pick on my wife," Billy said. "We're giving you a hundred and seventy friggin' thousand dollars—"

"Janic?" Ash appealed.

"It's a good formula," said Janic.

"The voice of reason," Sally said, looking up from the *Sunday Book Review*. "I have a question, too, for the voice of reason."

"Yes?" Janic sounded like he was bracing himself.

"What about *our* children?" Sally asked.

"Children?" Janic said.

"Byron and Blake," she said. "I believe you've met them."

"Sal, they're thirty-three and thirty-seven years old."

"We have grandchildren, too."

"They don't live with you," Daniel said. Didn't anyone understand how unassailably neat this formula was? To be working fractions into large, odd numbers and come up with *12.5 into 250,625*, which yielded the graceful *20,050* when it could have been so much more cumbersome or chaotic . . . The numbers signaled to Daniel he was on the right track.

"You're not exactly putting glasses and braces on those kids and food in their mouths," Keith said, pulling himself out of the pool. "Never mind hundred-dollar sneakers on their feet." He gave a mock disparaging splash to the twins.

"Part of last weekend's lobby," Sally said, "and I don't know what else to call it, was, *Oh, think of your poor grandchildren, all those immigrants—*"

"'Orphans,' I believe the word was," Janic said.

"Yes. It was 'your son the hero,'" Sally said, shifting in her chaise. "Taking in impoverished children from around the world."

"It's true, Mrs. Lev," Keith said. He hopped on one foot and banged his head to get water out of his ear. "I wasn't saying anything that wasn't true."

"Neither am I," Sally said. "You all worked pretty hard to convince us. And once Janic and I agreed with you—or, more accurately, figured our family would be better off with the money than without it—now you're dropping our concerns like flies."

"Okay, Sal, come on," Janic said, as privately as possible. "We have our pensions, we have a paid-off house—"

"Nobody else has children they're not counting," she said, talking over the voice of reason. "And nobody else has grand-children who contracted some kind of bugborne neurological disorder in Guatemala and fall asleep in a kindergarten class-room. Or little girls' teeth that spent their first twelve years on some kind of sugar-water gruel, which was all, apparently, the orphanage wanted to spend on girls who were only going to be sold into some kind of sexual slavery when they were old enough."

"Sally," Maggie said, "that's terrible. Is that true?"

"The point is," Janic said, "they *didn't* get sold into slav-ery. They're comfortable fourth- and sixth-grade girls who are attending a wonderful U.N. school in the city."

"Not for long," Sally said. "They have a one-year scholarship. After that, Byron and Bianca will never be able to afford it. I was thinking we should bring them here, to Ashley. Which requires a little bit of money."

"A hundred ninety thousand and something will go a long way," Janic said softly.

"Whose side are you on?" she said.

"Right now, I'm on the side of moving on."

"Put a little money in the bank and move on," Billy said.

"We can't put this in the bank," Janic said. "The questions it raises . . ."

"We can't really spend it, either," Maggie said. "No conspicuous consumption."

The kids were traipsing back, dripping, from the pool.

"Girls," Jenny said to the twins, "I'm afraid we might have to go shopping."

"Jenny," Maggie said.

"Those tax breaks," Jen said. "From the zoning thing."

"Oh, Mom, do we haaave to?" said Brittany, hamming it up.

"What good is money if you can't spend it?" Jen said.

April closed her eyes and put her fingertips to her forehead like an old woman. "Mom," she whispered, "don't be the shallowest one here."

"Get over yourself," Jenny said, swatting playfully at April. "The *pool's* the shallowest one here."

"Don't worry," said Bethany. "We'll buy you something, too. If you ever come home."

"Yeah, how come you're never home?" Brittany said.

"That's two kids now that they can't find," Ash muttered.

"Get over it, buddy," Keith said. "Money's not going to bring your girlfriend back. And if it does, she's not worth it."

"It's a good question." Jen to April. "How come you're up at the Manor House all the time?"

"Don't you love us anymore?" Bethany said, pretending to pout.

April sneered and stuck out her tongue. Maggie was glad to see April acting like a little girl for a change, free of the responsibility that came with having an irresponsible mother. Maggie knew. Maggie'd had it worse. Jen was a lovely person, just immature and often overwhelmed. Maggie's mother was not a lovely person. Alice Stoughton McKenzie was a raging alcoholic who had lost a young daughter to a urinary tract infection that arguably a mother should have caught. While no one, apparently, was looking, seven-year-old Catherine McKenzie's condition progressed into a fatal kidney infection.

And now Margaret McKenzie, Maggie Cane, was here by the side of her luxurious pool, adding money to her mother's family's money and getting no closer to what she wanted. Maggie could caution her neighbors against conspicuous consumption because her plan for the money was as far from conspicuous as you could get.

"Do I have something on my face?" April brushed a finger over her cheek.

"Hmmm, sweetie?" Maggie said, coming back to the present.

"You were staring, I think," April said. "I thought I might have some sunscreen un-rubbed-in or something."

"No, no, my mind was just wandering," Maggie said. *Caught*. She had been staring at April, imagining her to be hers. A daughter like that. Smart, polite, pretty. Whatever Jen's faults, she had raised a daughter Maggie would love for herself. Forget imitation. Longing was the greatest form of flattery.

"What's this obsession with sunscreen, all of a sudden?" Jen asked.

"Maggie says to," April said. "Because of global warming. The sky is thinner, and the sun is more dangerous."

"Then why are you the only one who should put it on?" Jen said.

"Probably everyone should," April said. "I'm just the only one who listens."

"True, baby," Jen said. "Maybe that'll get you into trouble in the long run. Or maybe it'll save your life."

4

No Rest for the Wicked

Dating back to an era when proximity had greater real estate value than privacy, most of Sylvan Street's houses crowded up to the road's edge, which gave the street a certain old-fashioned charm. It looked as if the houses themselves were eager for company. At the top corner of the street was the Manor House, a 1910 farmhouse that sat just feet from busy Deveau Hill Road. The stately white clapboard had been added on to several times, elegantly and in keeping, creeping over its double lot. Forty-four Deveau Hill Road—that was the formal address, but the house belonged to Sylvan Street—was a bucolic acre, a graceful and somewhat misleading foyer to the rest of the street, which was hardly so grand.

Tonight in the 1910 farmhouse, Billy Cane was sleeping uneasily. He was mired in a terrible dream: a shoot-out around his pool. His neighbors were there, as well as Keanu Reeves and Johnny Depp, both of whom people said Billy looked like. Billy was searching desperately for Maggie, until he realized she was right next to him. In the same here-and-gone clarity of dreams, he realized that he was dunking her under the water. He woke with a wrenching gut.

Maggie lay curled on her side, facing away from him. Billy could not say whether she was asleep or pretending to be.

Maggie had left it to him to secrete their portion. She didn't want anything to do with it. She didn't want to bump into it accidentally when she was doing laundry (so he couldn't put it in the basement), using the computer (so not the study) or getting a coat (not in the front closet), sweater (bedroom closet), sheet (linen closet) or towel (bathroom closet). There were the two guest bedrooms, but they were so little used Billy didn't even think of them.

Margolis had gotten a safe. He'd been tempted, he said, to pick up a shovel and bury it in the backyard. But they had a saying in the department: if someone looks guilty, look in his backyard.

Billy opted for hiding in plain sight. Leave the bills in the original case (which felt incumbent upon him, the original discoverer), put it in the mostly empty cabinet under the sink in his studio—where Maggie was sure not to bump into it—and let the chips fall where they may. He was evolved enough not to fight with an armed robber. *Don't protest. Give the guy what he wants.* If some lunatic comes back for his money, escort him to the studio, no questions asked.

What about the case being more than eight hundred thousand dollars light? Billy must have believed that, honestly, the lunatic was not coming back. Billy, like everybody else, must have opted to believe Keith Margolis.

* * *

Next on the street came one of two century-old workmen's houses, simple brick four-rooms built by the Italian masons who came to town at the turn of the century to lay the great Ashley Dam. The two houses had gone in very different directions. This one had changed hands every few years and was a patchwork of frequent turnover. The bricks, chipping and spalling, had been painted gray, and the house looked like an elementary school. The old slate roof had been replaced over time with asphalt shingles, and the original windows replaced with Home Depot specials. The mishmash of a house and mishmash of a street reminded Ash Flemming of his beloved Williamsburg, where he'd missed the real estate window and could not afford, with the small inheritance from his mother, to buy a place.

Tonight, in Ash Flemming's century-old house in Ashley-on-Hudson, he was doing what he did when he couldn't sleep: painting. He had just gridded his canvas for a large horizontal called *Multigression of Light*, which would explore the cycle of light, darkness and clarity. He had ground tarnished silver into various calibrations, from essentially atomized (*weaponized* came to mind) to a rough confetti, and suspended each calibration in an indigo pigment. He began to lay down the finely ground silver and indigo. Through gradients, he would play with expectation, locating clarity somewhere other than trending toward light.

He had painted through the night many times, but only rarely because he was inspired. Mostly it was when he couldn't sleep because a mortgage payment was coming up, or the oil bill, and he had nothing coming in. Over the last several months, all he had was one pending sale of a small work to a friend's parents. Now, in this economy, it would probably never go through. He did have a moment of glory three years ago when his oil and malachite on canvas, *Breathtakingly Simple*, was included in the Whitney Biennial. Before the Biennial had apparently come to disdain painting entirely. These days, he was getting nothing but rejections.

How long could he keep it up? That was usually what he calculated when he was up nights. He would move some paint around on the canvas, but what he was really doing was thinking about how much he could reduce his prices in this market—$30,000 down to $18,000 for outsize works or for a series; $9,000, not $14,000, for midsize canvases; and for small, $7,500 down to $4,000. Four thousand was probably where his only market would be. If that. He was weighing these figures against the sands of time. It was too early to tell whether the Biennial marked the pinnacle from which he was on the descent or was a sign of great things to come from Ash Flemming.

Instead of sales figures, what he was really counting were the sands of time. How long could he live off ego, hope, memory or mention of the Biennial, and an inheritance that was receding to the vanishing point?

A hundred seventy thousand, four hundred something dollars! Less than everyone else. But, in the privacy of his own home, plenty. He wouldn't even bother to calculate how many sales that added up to. Now he could put off the question, could continue to paint no matter his success or failure, just like those rich housewives to whom he used to teach portraiture when he was in art school.

Finally, he'd be liberated from that penurious artist's calculus of time invested versus eventual remuneration.

He put down his brush and headed downstairs, even though

he was not at a good stopping point and would have to paint back into seams.

The canvas messenger bag was in the basement, sandwiched amid the cartons of still-unpacked dishes, books, bedding, winter clothes. He'd stopped settling in the instant Suki left, four months after they moved here. The cartons, and now the messenger bag, huddled together in the middle of the room, touching no walls. Ash, a renter by nature, worried that the basement's cinder-block walls would leach water, mold, lead paint, asbestos or whatever else basement walls could leach.

He took a packet of bills from the bag. There was a wonderful texture to the money, fragile and fibrous. What if he pulped it, made a rich, dense paper? How was that for commitment to his art?

Keith Margolis, who left the Canes' with Ash this morning, had rambled on about the finer points of household safes, finding the right combination of fireproof and theftproof. Ash nodded, figuring he wouldn't be here long enough to drill a safe.

Despite a pact they'd all made at the pool, not to go anywhere or do anything too soon, Ash planned to head right back to Brooklyn. Sell his house and resume his old life, only this time he'd have some cash. His *new and improved* old life. He would no longer worry about the next Biennial, the next show, the next sale. He would have time because he had money.

He slid back the paper wrapper and thumbed the bills like a flip-book, half expecting some movement. An animated Ben Franklin flying a kite, say, discovering electricity. But each bill was exactly the same. They did not animate into a narrative. Hundred-dollar bills revealed nothing more in the aggregate than they did in the singular.

* * *

Across the street in the other workmen's house, well maintained, with repointed brickwork and the original slate roof, Sally Levlovic was awake with worries old and new. First, the old. The grandchildren. What if doctors discovered something was really wrong with Lazlo, that there were crossed wires in the poor child's brain, that his nerves didn't connect properly at the synapses, or that worms had indeed eaten through his insides? There were some terrible possibilities for the near-silent little thing. Worse, what if the doctors never discovered what was wrong? Poor Byron and Bianca, throwing good money after bad just trying to get those children up to the baseline where most parents start.

These familiar worries ran headlong into new ones. Who had come onto their street? What kind of terrible thing had such a person done for this money? And what would they do now? Or what about the very slim chance that the money legitimately belonged to someone? Then *she* was the thief, along with her up-until-now-law-abiding neighbors.

She buttoned another button on her nightgown and went to one of the original double-hung windows in the bedroom, from which she could see the Manor House and, behind it, a corner of the pool shed. Her neighbors had certainly put them in a bind. If Sally and Janic had refused to go along, they would have thwarted the wishes of everyone else. That was no way to live in a neighborhood where they'd lived, generously and happily, for more than forty years, amid a changing cast of characters. She thought of the Riccis, the big Italian family who used to live in the Manor House. Eight or nine kids, if you can imagine. There were kids everywhere on the street in those days, playing Capture the Flag or some other suburban dodge-and-dart game, dashing out from behind bunkers (houses and cars) and in and out of foxholes (leaf piles, drainage ditches). There had been at least ten couples or small families in Ash Flemming's house over the years. Most were pleasant, a few were odd. But they were Sylvan Streeters, minding their manners and tempering their volume, which was all you could ask of neighbors.

The house Shoshanna and Daniel had just moved into also changed hands frequently, especially since the old one was torn down about fifteen years ago and replaced with this modern one. The latest to move out were the Ilionescus, immigrants from Transylvania. Occasionally, one could hear the father, Gavril, ranting in Romanian. If Sally had to say, she might implicate him in the money. Something, good or evil, had earned him a lot of cash, and where better to store his earnings than back on the old street once he and his family had (ostensibly) moved back to Romania?

Gavril Ilionescu's ranting echoed in her night-memory. She began to recall him as definitely a little crazy, indeed capable of such a thing.

Out her other bedroom window, Sally saw the Margolises' front floodlight come on. Was someone going out? Coming in? In any case, Sally was thankful for a cop on the lookout.

Next door, in a 1960s bungalow that Jen's parents—worried about their youngest, her police officer husband and those five kids—had practically given to Jen and Keith when they, the parents, moved to Florida, Jen Margolis was sleeping soundly. Her usual anxieties, always about money, were not keeping her up.

Keith had gotten out of bed a minute ago and, in a "better safe than sorry" frame of mind, turned on the outside flood-light. He was back to bed now and sleeping like a cop, as he'd come to think of it. His body was at rest, but his mind was on guard, on watch, sifting through details of the day to see if anything seemed out of the ordinary. That was the first thing he learned when he started at the department (and had since passed on to class after class of rookies): the real job of a small-town cop is observing patterns of daily life and noticing when they are broken.

He was picturing his family and neighbors around the pool, each of them staring at the money as though they were expecting a show to begin (everyone but Tiger, who was squatting, bare-bottomed, in the flower garden, and Kelli, who'd gone AWOL again). Money, however, is an inert thing, especially bundled like that. They could wait a lifetime, and there'd still be no show. He'd been to crime scenes, he'd seen bundled money. It never moves. Doesn't even *appear* to move, because it doesn't catch or hold light. He'd seen guns jump in the light, and diamonds. Cocaine, too, and certain cuts of meth catch light. But not money.

On the uphill side of the Levlovices, in the only modern house on the street, Shoshanna Yaniv sat at the top of the stairs, which looked steeper and narrower in the dark.

Daniel said that Keith Margolis said (*hearsay, Your Honor*) that if money like this isn't retrieved immediately, it's because whoever knows where it is is dead or locked up. That was meant to appease and seemed to work for Daniel. But Shoshanna thought, *We know where it is.*

Even though she hadn't been there when the money was doled out, she knew she'd given her tacit consent. She couldn't hide it from herself as she sat in an unfamiliar temple, among strangers. Although they were Jews, the congregation was no more kin to her than fellow shoppers at the A&P, moviegoers at the theater, passengers on a Metro-North train.

Her community, for better or worse, was these neighbors bound together on the other side of the law.

She went on her nightly rounds of the kids' bedrooms. Caleb had his hard, curved back to the door, sheets kicked off. He was as fitful asleep as he was awake. Next time she checked, he would be in a new position entirely, maybe even upside down, feet kicked under his pillow. She hoped his upcoming soccer camp would burn away some of his energy and frustration, which the night could not seem to do.

Her daughter lay on her back, chin and nose pointing heavenward. Since she was a newborn, this was Allie's nighttime repose. Shoshanna used to stare at her sleeping baby girl, face open, beckoning, angelic, and imagine a butterfly alighting on the nose or chin. Fine little butterfly point to fine little Allie point.

Allie was going into second grade and already was consumed by clothes (and, my God, *brands*: "Are you wearing your Mad Milo or your Abercrombie?"), hair and soon, to be sure, boys. Their recent move to Ashley had given her a jolt of popularity—the exotic new girl from the city, with the hyphenated last name, almond eyes and deep olive skin.

Now and then, Shoshanna caught Allie looking at her with a certain scrutiny. Shoshanna imagined her daughter was trying to figure out in what ways she, Allie, would grow to look like her mother. Neither Allie nor Caleb looked particularly like either parent. The family looked no more related to one another than any four people caught in crosshairs.

As a girl, Shoshanna had longed for the breeziness of the beautiful Israeli girls. The skimpy tops and sun-kissed shoulders, the nothing little gossamer skirts that to her spelled freedom, happiness. She had been consigned to a life of good grades and hard-won worldliness (her own parents, who each spoke five languages, had her and her brothers learn a new language every few years). She never got to wear the barely there Greek-goddess sandals that laced up the leg. The popular girls, the beautiful girls, wore those sandals out in the sun until their skin tanned in rings around the laces into a sort of reverse henna tattoo, which they displayed with the pride and loyalty of gang colors.

Shoshanna went downstairs to double-check the doors. The front door had a straightforward lock—*check*—but the garage and back deck doors had newfangled magnetic locks, which took three steps to secure. Disengage, lock, reengage. She once said to Daniel that she felt like she was locking a weapons cache, a degree of protection that made her feel *less* safe, not more. She remembered this from her days in the Israeli Army. The weight of the gun over her shoulder and weapons belt on her hips reminded her how slight and finite she was, rather than how powerful. The camouflage uniform reminded her how poorly camouflaged she really was.

Daniel Hansen didn't have the luxury of sleeplessness, of checking the house against demons real and imagined, of weighing danger and safety, past, present and future. He had to get up in the morning, catch the 6:53 and face the daily grind.

5

Trapped

Maggie lay awake, eyes closed, and, in her head, paced out her home. Traverse that great big foyer—six, eight, ten steps—much too big for them, like the rest of the house. Turn left into the formal dining room, which they hardly ever used. Nine steps, from chair to chair to chair, circling around the nine-foot-long butterfly-groove Nakashima table and eight matching chairs, for which they'd traveled to Pennsylvania early in their home-owning days and selected a black walnut that would be cut down for them, aged and sculpted into this beautiful, barely used table.

Counting steps, counting furniture—essentially, *counting your blessings*—was the reproductively challenged's version of counting sheep. "So much of infertility focuses on what you don't have," said Dr. Hachsacher, her reproductive endocrinologist. "When you can't sleep, which is quite a common side effect, focus on what you *do* have."

For Maggie, that meant the house. The dining room led into the kitchen, her favorite room. She could spend an entire afternoon cooking dinner, especially now that she was teaching someone, April Margolis, to cook. From the kitchen to the TV room. Ten, twelve steps if you were Maggie. Eight, maybe, if you were Billy. *Focus on what you have* also meant Billy, didn't it?

So finely calibrated was her empty body that as she lay there unable to sleep she swore she could feel the swirl of hormones, even though so far it was only the Pill, the counterintuitive first step in fertility treatment. She was back to the beginning now, this long after the miscarriage. Quiet the ovaries, regulate the cycles. If she blurred her mind, her daily encounter with the little flesh-colored disc, popping the tiny pill out of its foil, could make her feel young again, back when life was long and options were endless, back when she was taking the Pill to pause fertility before what she imagined would be its onrush.

She half sat up, leaning on her elbows, and tried to determine whether she was awake for the night. Billy was sound asleep, so this would be yet another moment that she wouldn't have to tell him about the Pill, about her—forgive her—*baby steps*. Pinned by moonlight, he looked so vulnerable and pretty, his fine-boned face, his long eyelashes. Pale skin and dark hair like her, some Black Irish in him, too. How much of life was perspective? If she saw Billy only in moonlight, could she ever be disappointed?

Maggie knew everyone thought Billy wasn't good enough for her. All her life, she'd been adjudged too good for things she wanted. For her alcoholic mother. For Downeast Maine and later for Ashley-on-Hudson. Even for Brown University, since she had also been accepted at Harvard. Leave it to Maggie McKenzie to turn down Harvard, said her parents' friends.

The only surviving child of the prominent Downeast McKenzies, Maggie kept rising to the top, whatever she did. She finished her first marathon as the top female in her age group. She apprenticed with a Maine potter her senior year in high school and helped the potter invent a now widely used glazing process. She took one writing class at Brown and ended up publishing a short story in *The Paris Review*. She started a catering business in the city and quickly became *the* caterer in certain Upper West and Lower East Side circles.

She met Billy on a vineyard-to-vineyard bike tour through France when she was thirty-one. It had been the perfect trip for her, physical challenge by day, five-star inns by night. Because the trip was so expensive, she was surrounded by midlife wealth. Maggie and the moguls, couples in their forties and fifties, looking for ever more exotic ways to both pamper and challenge themselves.

Twenty-six-year-old Billy Cane, the only one anywhere near her age, was a guide, not a guest. Endorphins from the biking, lust from the drinking, a beckoning from the deep, warm king-size beds, and soon, for Maggie McKenzie, the trip was all about Billy Cane, trying to ride next to him or, in the inns' overstuffed living rooms, sitting near enough to him that she could lean a knee or a shoulder against him as the moguls retired to their rooms two by two or, as the trip went on, one by one.

They were encouraged to have mantras, either verbal or visual, to help on long climbs. Maggie's became *Billy Cane*. Breathe out *Billy*, breathe in *Cane*. She sprinted to catch up with him or lagged behind to see if he would lag (he would). She gave him little nods of her helmeted head and, soon enough, unabashed I'm-yours-if-you-want-me smiles.

* * *

Billy took a rough inhale, which meant he was about to head into a snoring jag. At first, Maggie thought the crashing sound had something to do with Billy's breathing. But no, it was outside. Chaos, clatter. Raccoons in the pool area? Deer?

The money! She sat bolt upright. She knew this would happen. *Knew* it. And let herself be lured anyway. By her husband, by her neighbors. Really, by her own desires: a hundred ninety thousand and some-odd dollars would surely guarantee success (although everyone in the fertility process cautioned against guarantees).

She went to the window. Of course someone would come back for the money. It was not a matter of if. It was a matter of when.

From what she could see, the shed was innocent of activity. A couple of chaises lay on their sides. The damn featherweight titanium things, expensive as they were, tended to blow around in a stiff wind. But the sky was clear, and the night was still.

How had she missed it? It seemed like an optical illusion at first, a painted backdrop. At the far end of the pool, a deer stood in eerie silhouette. How could such a peaceful thing be responsible for all that havoc? It flinched and shook, like it was having a seizure, then tugged its leg. It must have gotten itself stuck somehow at the edge of the pool.

She should wake Billy. He was the pool man. He was snoring now, loudly enough that on another night she might have left for another bed. She pulled on a pair of shorts and went downstairs.

Let sleeping dogs lie. E.g., Billy. And e.g., Barclay, who had grown hard of hearing and would have kicked himself with his good leg if he knew there was a deer trapped in the pool and he was slumbering away on the front-hall rug.

She tiptoed past him—"sorry, Barc"—and inched the door open. Maggie sensed a bittersweet regret in Barclay as he aged. Oh, the things he was missing out on! Barclay, more than either of his masters, loved to be in the thick of things.

Maggie was glad Billy was not here to make the joke out loud, that it looked like a deer in headlights. It did, but she could no longer bear when Billy said or did something she knew he was going to say or do.

Once she got closer, she saw how the animal was trapped. Something was wrong with the cover. The other day, Billy was complaining that the new thousand-dollar cover didn't fit exactly right.

The deer tugged its trapped foot again, shimmying the half-moon's reflection in the damp pool cover. The free front leg crumpled, and the deer looked like it was bowing to a deity, or to the mistress of the house. This was a young deer, white spotted, unweathered and taut. All shiver and heartbeat. Nothing like her Barclay, cuddle and muscle and a rich chocolate coat.

Come on, Maggie thought. *Free yourself. It's a man-made pool cover. You're a wild animal.*

It tried to yank the leg again. More shuddering, more tugging. A muscle memory of horses came back to her, of stroking the broad bone of the nose, the damp, tapered muzzle. She didn't remember wildness in her horses, but they had been largely handled by staff. Although she liked riding well enough, she had no passion for horses. It had been her mother's idea of how a well-to-do little girl should grow up in the wilds of Maine, to which her Boston Brahmin mother had run off to marry the genial country doctor who was all-consumingly in love with her. Ah, the romantic beginning to the story of two sisters, Margaret and the late Catherine McKenzie.

Maggie and the deer stared eye to eye, unfathomable to one another. She realized why God had created man in His image: so He would know what to do with him.

Come up in front of the animal, present yourself at its eye level, open your palms. That was from a middle-school field trip to a large-animal veterinarian. She could still remember the young, nervously handsome vet explaining to eleven-year-olds how to calm a horse or a cow, how to give it a vaccine, how to help it give birth.

Forget what she'd learned. Staying visible, staying *presented* was getting her nowhere. Maybe invisible and absent would work. Despite the dampness, she crouched onto the pool cover, guaranteed for a thousand dollars to hold about three times her weight, and slithered on her belly. She cut a high arc away from the animal until she was far enough from it to be safe yet still within reach of its trapped leg. She fished for the hoof and, in an instant, flicked it free.

The deer light-footed away, right over the fence, as though she'd encountered it midflight rather than trapped.

She wanted to go inside and cuddle with Barclay to regain the animal familiar. She was damp and cold on this humid night. It took her a while to notice drops of blood on the pool cover. She hadn't thought the deer was injured, so gracefully had it run off.

Wait. It was her blood. Now she felt the sting. The hoof had sliced her wrist straight across.

* * *

She climbed into bed as quietly as she could, trying to keep her wrist, which she'd wrapped in gauze and tape, above her heart. She had foregone waking Barclay for comfort; he couldn't be trusted not to reopen a wound.

She raised her good hand to wake Billy, but something stopped her—the same thing that had stopped her from waking him when she first heard crashing at the pool. Everyone had their theories about the money, and Maggie's, inchoate as it was, revolved around Billy. A friend of Billy's? A scheme of Billy's? There was a certain falseness, wasn't there, to his surprise when he opened a strange briefcase only to discover, *voilà*, bundles of cash.

It was hard to square Billy with the sheer volume of money. One thing he was *not* was hard-boiled. Soft-boiled, she'd say, if pressed.

The moon had passed to another window of the house, another quadrant of the sky. Billy, snoring and unaware, had lost the moonlit amnesty of earlier in the evening.

Her thoughts resumed their nighttime ramble, through her empty house, her empty body. It was not Billy's fault. He had gotten a girlfriend pregnant in college, which Maggie learned only during their initial screening. The doctor ticked through preliminary questions, starting with Have you ever conceived before, which seemed to Maggie the troubleshooting equivalent of Is it plugged in?

After her "No, that's why we're here," Billy, to her surprise, said, "Yes." Matter-of-factly, like he was answering any other question. *Did you lock the car? Are you ready to order? Can you see the screen from here?*

"College girlfriend," he told the doctor. "Abortion."

Maggie clamped a hand over her bandaged wrist, which was throbbing. What was she chasing? She had just raced downstairs because she thought her windfall was threatened; money that she didn't want, didn't need, and put her on the wrong side of the law.

The money changed nothing. They had spent tens of thousands already. The problem wasn't money. The problem was endpoint. Four years of on-again-off-again treatment, constant monitoring, temperature taking, peeing on a stick. Graduating to the serious stuff, the needles in the upper thigh until she felt like a piece of meat. Two IUIs with Clomid, five cycles of IVF, three pregnancies, three miscarriages. When do you stop? The question was originally Billy's, but once he asked and Maggie couldn't answer, it became her question, too.

And suddenly a million dollars drops into their laps? Even at two hundred thousand dollars, *that's* an endpoint. She didn't know exactly what their share of the money would buy her. But she'd get started again and see. If she didn't have a baby after that, she'd accept that she wasn't meant to. The money changed everything.

6

Hero's Ransom

Keith wouldn't let Jen touch the money. "There's this little thing called fingerprints," he said, rubbing his thumb and index finger together. "I just want you to stay as far away from implication as possible."

He was on his knees, jiggering the new safe into place, into the hole he'd excavated in the cement floor at the base of the cellar stairs. She sat on a lower stair with her sleepy Tiger, just up from a nap.

"If you're trafficking—drugs, guns, whatever—you must find yourself counting money all the time," Keith was saying, talking not really to Jen but as if he were narrating a movie. "Once you cross that line, counting money is no different from any other bean counter counting beans."

"I don't like this," Jen said. "Guns, drugs, all this money, armed and dangerous, in my house. Around my children, to be exact." She gave Tiger a squeeze, which seemed to wake him up. He wriggled out of her lap and ran into the basement.

She went to the doorway, watched him go into April's part of the basement. It wasn't even a real bedroom, as some basements were. A bed, yes, and a bureau, night table. But it was surrounded by the rest of family life that gets stored in basements. Bikes, winter clothes, washer/dryer in the corner. The first thing they should do with the money was build April a real bedroom, especially now that there was a maniac on the loose and a quarter million dollars of the maniac's cash in their basement.

What were they doing, trading their children's safety for shopping?

"That issue, that whole armed-and-dangerous thing," Keith said, "that's taking place in some warehouse somewhere, some safe house, with some lowlife getting wasted by some better-armed lowlife because the first lowlife couldn't hold on to the money. Even if someone was still alive enough to come back for the money, they're only going as far as that pool house where they left it. Not snooping around in our basement."

"Still, not a hundred percent," she said.

"Nothing's a hundred percent. That's why you need a cop around." Keith gave her that dopey smile, which half embarrassed her, half hooked her every time.

He turned to the floor, began drilling the anchoring bolts. Metal shrieked through concrete.

Jen squeezed her eyes closed and visualized the chaos and confusion of motherhood being poured into a whirring blender. Money and ear infections and potty training and teenage scorn and what-ifs.

The drilling stopped. The sudden quiet unnerved her. The chaos and confusion of motherhood had not been frothed into a summer drink.

Keith ripped the tape from the contractor bag, which made her shiver. Then a crash from the other room.

"Tigey!" She jumped up, rushed to the doorway.

He was squatting on the floor, ramming two souped-up toy trucks into each other.

"Your new safe is ready." Keith was sweeping off the face of the safe. "A quarter mill," he said. "At your service."

"Tige, don't touch that." She planted herself between her son and the seductive door-in-a-floor, which only made him more desperate to get in there. "He shouldn't be down here. What if he tells the other kids?"

"Who's going to believe him?" Keith click-click-clicked open the safe. It looked like a movie, a display. Full of green paper. She couldn't quite register it as money.

"Take him upstairs," she said after a minute. "I need to switch the laundry. And this whole thing is making me nervous."

"Here's your hat, what's your hurry, as my grandfather used to say," Keith said. "Come on, buddy. Looks like your mother's trying to get rid of us. I hope she doesn't run off with our money."

"Cabo, here I come," she said.

After the boys went upstairs, she reached into the open safe and, just like that, took out ten thousand dollars, one pack of a hundred hundreds. She would never again have to say no to her children. No more weighing braces for one against glasses for another. No more weighing college for April against everyone and everything else. No more Payless. No more Marshalls.

No more apologies from Keith each birthday and Mother's Day, when it was flowers instead of diamonds. She didn't care about diamonds, but she knew he wanted to *give* them. Whoever said it was right: all arguments between married couples are essentially over money.

Maybe they'd take a family vacation—airplane, hotel, like a normal family. Finally get to Cabo San Lucas before Keith retired and they were both too old to enjoy it. The last time they talked about it and decided yet again that they couldn't afford to go, she said, "Just bury me there when I'm dead. It'll last longer."

She shut the safe and spun its lock. The *tick tick tick* of the wheel pack sounded like a bomb. She wished she could have called their accountant to handle the money, like an actual rich person would do.

She thought about how much Keith deserved to be rich. Her? Maybe, maybe not. The children? Of course; all children do. But really, Keith Margolis was an old-fashioned hero, whether he looked the part or not.

7

Welcome to the Neighborhood

"Tonight he lasted all of ten minutes," Shoshanna said. "And that's an improvement, believe me."

After trying to read with Caleb for what was supposed to be the third half-hour session of the day but was only the first, Shoshanna retreated in search of easier alliances. Allie was sleeping at a new friend's house, and Shoshanna found Daniel in the basement, cleaning the inside of her *zayde*'s steamer trunk. The now-familiar black trash bag lay next to him.

"What would Zayde say?" Shoshanna said, shaking her head.

The trunk had belonged to Shoshanna's grandfather, a World War II fighter pilot who had helped found the State of Israel and was an adviser to Moshe Dayan. Shoshanna had used the trunk during her own army service, back when she had a purpose without question, then shipped it to the States with her, hauling it from home to home, Philadelphia, Manhattan for a time, Brooklyn, Ashley.

"WWZS?" Daniel said. "I'm sure he'd say, 'Holy shit,' or some more dignified, Yiddish version of it." He opened the mouth of the trash bag.

"Did they just split it five ways?" Shoshanna tried to look only casually but found herself staring. It looked surreal; it looked like a movie; it looked fake. All the things you might think. She felt like she was watching her life from a distance, something happening in someone else's house, to someone else.

Not so Daniel. He was *in it*, picking up bound packets one after another, weighing them in his palm. "If you're so interested," he said, "why did you skulk off to, of all places, temple? Which everyone there just accepted, but where I happen to know you haven't gone in your entire adult life."

"I wouldn't say 'interested.' It's more like watching a car wreck. Can't look away. How did they decide who got what, anyway?"

"Not *they*," he said. "Me. I came up with this great system—"

"You? Why on earth—?"

"I happen to be pretty good with numbers."

"I don't doubt that," she said. "But you've been here all of three months. And your disappearing wife didn't even come to the grand unveiling party, or whatever we're calling this felony."

"Please don't say that," he said. "You sound like Sally Levlovic. Where's your sense of adventure?"

"Ran off with your moral center."

"Very funny," he said. "Never mind. Talk is cheap."

He got to work, packing bound hundreds into the trunk.

She squinted at her kneeling six-foot husband, who looked small and greedy. Unfamiliar. Un-Daniel-like. When they met, he was in journalism school, and she admired his simple, do-good priorities. She herself had taken the unreflective path after law school, heading to the corporate firm, logging the requisite hours, doing what she was told. When she decided to stay home with the baby, Daniel decided to take his skills as an underpaid reporter over the divide. Advertising. He was good and moved up quickly in the indie-hip agency. The title on his business card read HEAD BRANDING GUY.

She brushed her hands and crossed the room. "I don't even want to touch it," she said. "I'm taking up Sally Levlovic's case for her. This isn't right and it isn't safe. Don't you—and these neighbors of yours—see that?"

"What do you mean, *of mine*?" he said. "This town, this house, this street was your idea. Need I remind you?"

He needn't.

He had wanted nothing more than to stay in the city. But its dangers had finally caught up with Shoshanna, in the form of a break-in at their unlucky neighbors' and in the form of Caleb's miswired brain. First, the easy one: their downstairs neighbors' apartment had been broken into. Midday. Shoshanna was probably home when it happened, and, although the burgled apartment was directly downstairs, she didn't hear anything more than the general milling about of neighbors. Door jimmied open, valuables stolen. Computer, stereo, jewelry. Only thing they didn't take was the behemoth old television. Too outdated even for robbers, she overheard their neighbor Mark say to the police, as he was enumerating their losses. Thank God,

Shoshanna thought. At least she didn't overlook the sounds of someone stealing a *television*.

Then there was Caleb. At the beginning of this past school year, when he started second grade, he was diagnosed with a language-based learning disability. That explained the halting reading. That explained the frustration with schoolwork, with organization, with time. The school responded swiftly and accurately. Then came the news, first as a rumor, then as a letter from the New York City Department of Health, that they were investigating a cluster of language-based learning disabilities at his school, in particular among second-graders—who would have been infants during 9/11. The study was following Lower Manhattan–Brooklyn wind patterns, airborne toxins and any chemicals that might have any possible connection to the developing infant brain.

Now, from what was until a moment ago the safety of her capacious basement, she said, "Maybe this is God's way of saying I made the wrong decision. To move here."

"Your God's awfully vengeful," Daniel said. "Maybe this is His way of saying you were right, I was wrong. Ashley-on-Hudson *is* the place for us."

He held a packet of money aloft, dangling it like a just-caught fish whose life hangs in the balance of this particular fisherman's moral code. *To eat or to throw back?*

"You know what I want to do with the money?" she said, the idea taking form as she spoke. "Give it away."

"Oh, come on—" Daniel started.

"No, I mean it. Create some philanthropic something. I need to go back to work now that the kids are in school, but I don't want another meaningless job. Certainly not law. A foundation—maybe that's why the money came into our lives. We're no Bill and Melinda Gates, but I'm sure we could do some real good for a couple hundred thousand dollars."

"Or you could get *a job* with a foundation," he said, "and we could keep the cash."

"Who are you?" she ventured.

"Keep saying that," he said, "and you're going to make me wonder."

8

The Uncle Richard Theory

Billy had, like everyone else, first thought *crime*. But couldn't there be a benevolent source of the money—for instance, someone in Maggie's moneyed family giving her yet more money, wanting so desperately for her to find happiness, even if she had to buy it? (How much money would it take?) Uncle Richard, Maggie's favorite uncle, came to mind. He was terminally ill and had been quite public about the unworthiness of his heirs.

This past winter, Richard had stayed with Maggie and Billy on the way to the city for a last-ditch attempt at treatment, a Chinatown herbalist. Richard hadn't seemed like a dying man, a little pale, perhaps, but present and eager to engage. He kept Billy up until one in the morning. Maggie had excused herself—never could stay up past eleven—and the two men headed out into the balmy December night. Richard ostensibly wanted to look at Billy's sculpture, but once he got walking, he didn't seem the least bit interested in the rocks. He confessed that he just wanted to be outside. This unseasonable weather, he said, tricked him into feeling that this whole depressing terminal-illness bit was over with. A shred of warm air would touch his skin, his hair, and he felt like he had lived through the worst of it, made it to spring.

"It's apparently a common symptom of my illness," he said, "this physiological need to be outside. When I'm inside, I feel like I can't breathe. But sometimes, in certain weather—especially in surprising weather, like this perfectly equatorial December night—I step outside, and—" He took an exaggerated breath, which actually undercut his point; this was the first time that Billy saw him struggle. "*Ta da.* I'm cured. Like Thomas Mann and that goddamn Magic Mountain, getting sick in order to get well."

Richard seemed to have talked himself angry, despondent. Billy caught a glimpse of Richard looking longingly at the pool and steered them there. Change of scenery and, he hoped, change of mood.

Billy scrambled to be a good host, ducked into the pool shed for a couple of chaises. How cold would the titanium ones be in this weather? Not bad, it turned out. The fine mesh really held no temperature. He set them up next to the drained, covered winter pool.

Richard began talking again, about everything and nothing, rubbing his hands together absently like a man with plenty of time left to live. "You know, this is one thing I never did, a pool," he said. "Had the room for it—"

"And the money," Billy said.

Richard laughed heartily. "Ah, money," he said. "Who the hell needs it?"

And they both laughed, Billy following Richard's lead.

"But no pool," Richard went on. "Kids would have loved it. And you know what? I think that's why I never did it. I kept waiting for a moment of generosity to seize me. To seize *them*, and then sweep us up in a familial goodwill. Never, ever felt it." He looked toward the house, back to Billy. "We never quite got on track with the kids. Has to be the parents' fault, doesn't it, if all four kids, each and every one of them, turn out wrong?"

"I'm afraid I wouldn't know about that," Billy said.

"Come to think of it," Richard said, "what are you two beautiful people still doing in this world with no children?"

"Haven't gotten around to it?" Billy tried.

"Nonsense."

"No, I know," Billy said, tempted to tell all. "We want them. We will. Just waiting for the right time."

"No such thing," Richard said. "There's never a right time to have kids. Only the wrong time. So, damn it, go in there and procreate."

Billy took a deep breath. "We're trying. Maggie had a mis-carriage right before Thanksgiving."

"Oh, I'm sorry." Richard's breathing turned audible, fast and shallow. "But *trying*—that's what I like to hear. There's nothing a dying man likes to know more than that his favorite part of the family will carry itself on. There's too damn much money in this family to not have worthy heirs."

The third miscarriage after five years of treatment. That would have done it; that would have put an end to the conversa-tion, if that was what Billy'd wanted to do.

"You don't make a very good case for them, you know, sir," he said. "For kids."

Richard waved a hand dismissively. "Ah, they're wonderful. At first, anyway. Just keep them on track, so they're not all fighting over your money like buzzards before you're even in the grave."

Thank God Maggie was not here for this conversation. Billy could just picture her, folding herself tighter and tighter, willing herself to sleep in medias res. These days, she seemed to sleep at anytime and anywhere but bed. Often, she'd curl into a ball on the couch and fall asleep. Sometimes Billy woke her to go upstairs; sometimes he didn't. He didn't know which was right.

"You keep trying, son," Richard said. "You have a wonderful, warm house there, and my favorite woman in the whole world. If I could, I'd leave it all to you."

Billy sat with him for a long time, long enough to grow uncomfortable, then to pass through to the other side, until they were two men—father and son, perhaps—sitting by an empty, covered pool, on the shoulder of Richard's last winter, quite probably the last time they'd ever see each other, confessing secrets and longings and a great goodwill. They sat until Billy felt sleep overtake him.

He broached the idea of going inside to bed, which felt strange, almost rude. There had been something eternal to the evening.

"If you don't mind, I'll stay right here," Richard said, "maybe even sleep right in this chair, contented as I've been in a long time."

Billy offered blankets, pillows, a good stiff drink. A hot chocolate. Tea, maybe?

"I am, as only a dying man can say, truly and utterly without want," Richard said.

"The perfect guest," Billy said.

"Dying to be."

Billy felt the urge to say something profound, that he loved him or thought him a wonderful, worthy person, that he would miss him and so would Maggie, that they would name a son after him.

"Good night, sir," Billy said.

"Good night, sir, yourself."

So it wasn't outside the realm of possibility that a dying Uncle Richard, in love with the potential family that Billy and Maggie would create, would bequeath them at least some of his considerable wealth. In the form of a briefcase full of cash? That's how Billy would do it if he had kids squabbling over inheritance while he was still alive, thank you very much. Pull the rug right out from under them.

Billy could picture it to the last detail, Richard wheeling the case from his car to the pool house, stopping now and then to catch his breath but spurred on by the feeling that his plan was ingenious and served everyone right. The moon, Billy remembered now—with plenty of romantic hindsight—was full, or at least gibbous in its brightness, lighting Richard's way.

Had Billy in fact divvied up his wife's inheritance among their neighbors? He found the notion benign enough. The last thing he and Maggie needed—and he was sure she'd agree with him on this—was more money to separate them from those around them.

Billy had given up his circle of friends bit by bit, through the social atrophies of marriage, of moving to the suburbs, of being without children year after year, which was hollowing out his wife and separating them from other couples deep into their thirties.

This cul-de-sac of a street, such as it was, was his life. There'd been something both adversarial and communal about those two afternoons at the pool—finding the money, then divvying it up—when he was driven by, truth be told, a simple desire to be liked.

9

Grand Plans

Tasmin "Toomer" de Silva was the only guy still wearing a hat. Shit, he thought. It's spring. Wasn't it just yesterday they were kicking around in big-ass American hunting coats? Ducking and sliding around in fifteen fucking inches of snow. *Frojones*, they called to each other. Frozen balls.

How the hell was it spring? Nothing ever happened. And still, time moved on.

He stood at the edge of the Stop & Shop parking lot, kicking mud with the other *foráneos*. Younger guys, four, five of them, the ones without families, the ones who stood in the back and rarely got hired on jobs. They'd bum cigarettes as the morning dragged on. Talk about the cold. Or the snow. Rain. How the weather was changing. What they did the night before.

By ten, ten thirty, other guys gone, either to jobs or back home to try again tomorrow, the *foráneos* would start kicking around escape plans.

Here was today's: Haitian named Batista knew some guys who were moving oxy and Demerol. Had a prescription pipeline from Canada. Easy on, easy off the thruway. Batista was going to get in on it. Not run pharma—that wasn't Bats's style. But to double-cross. Get hold of that money. Make his move.

Bats, making a move? That was a good one.

—And I'm going to win the lottery.

—I'm going to take over goddamn ICE, let all you guys in.

—My mama's going to come back to life.

—And I'm going to be president of the United States—

—No, ha ha, *Bats* is.

—T's right.

Bats's voice was all island music, stories no more real than a song. No one believed him, and that was the beauty of Bats. No surprises. Sitting on that cement barricade on the south side of the lot. Just sitting.

—*Jai*, listen to what this guy Batista's planning to do.

But Toomer's *jai,* his cousin brother, didn't understand escape plans. Didn't need to. Nishal had a job. Had the bed in the one-bedroom. Toomer had the couch. The couch, a hat and nothing else.

—Kid's either blind or crazy. Outrun runners? You're crazy, too, for believing him.

—Tell me what else, then. What else?

Again, Nishal promised. He'd get his *jai-titi,* little cousin brother, a job at the quarry. He would. Just let him settle in a little longer, win over the boss. Then he'd ask. He would.

Where Toomer and Nishal came from, everyone lived

crowded along the coast. The rest of the country, the inland center, was all rock. Toomer had his escape plan: learn to quarry, steal some tools, and go home to quarry the fuck out of the center of his country. Own all the land. *Rey de la montaña.*

—Just wait. Little longer, little brother.

—I'll turn to fucking stone waiting on you and that quarry.

—Good, *titi.* Keep you out of trouble.

Nishal pictured going home, too. Not as *rey de la montaña.* His dream was even more impossible. Going *home.* To his mother and father, his brothers. To the cramped cement house and the smell of his mother's cooking. A pot on the stove all day, poblanos, polenta, hominy, *sopa.* Rich smell of protein and a mother who loved her boys, even though she had too many. Five, six, seven . . . Each year, each new boy, his father stayed out longer and longer on the ocean, fish haul growing leaner. Until his heart gave out when he was fifty-one.

Foráneos attracted gaga girls. Gaga, meaning their mouths were hanging open, ready to do anything to anyone. And meaning that they were little more than babies. Fourteen, fifteen if you were lucky.

Natasha said she was eighteen. Probably not, but close enough. She was different. She reminded Toomer of his twin sister. Stronger than him, clearheaded. Said what was on her mind. The mirror image of Toomer. The better half.

He wondered what the hell she was doing there, kicking around the side of the Stop & Shop with the gaga girls and *foráneos.*

Afternoon turned to evening. Evening to night. Four or five

guys to two or three. Then just Toomer and Natasha. Sitting on a concrete barrier. Nowhere.

She put her hand on his chest.—Your heart.

He pulled his wool *tope* off his head. Felt like he might burst into flames.

—Want to go get some dinner?

—You buying?

—You bringing?

He didn't even mean anything by that. *You bringing?* She laughed, all nervous and sexy, and he was glad he was holding his hat on his lap.

They went to Toomer and Nishal's usual rice and beans place. The Truck. It was an actual rice and beans truck and a few aluminum picnic tables, wrapped in that clear plastic tenting with slappy plastic doors.

Place was better now, winter gone. Those slappy plastic doors do dick against this frozen tundra. Upstate. Rippeskill, New Fucking York. Toomer had stopped complaining to Nishal about Rippeskill. (—You don't like it, leave.) Where the hell else would Toomer go? So, by night, it was the couch, which sank in the middle. And by day, back aching like an old man, the Stop & Shop parking lot.

But now, right now, he felt as young as he was. His girl!

—Get anything you want.

Tasha laughed. But he wasn't joking. He'd swiped a twenty and a five from Nishal's wallet.

—I'll have the lobster thermidor.

His eye went to the menu posted outside the truck. —What number is that?

—Number one million. As in millionaire.

She tapped him on the forearm. He was still staring at the menu, confused.

—I'm just joking. Saw it in a movie one time. Lobster thermidor is what the rich kids, spoiled brats, ordered in a restaurant. Don't think they have it here.

An image gathered in his brain—him and Tasha at a restaurant like the one she'd seen. He'd seen movies, too. Seen white tablecloths and rich kids and rich adults, stiff-fitting clothes that they never wore more than once.

No reason he and Tasha couldn't live like the movies. Have a couple kids—*whoa, there, movies*—let the kids order whatever they wanted.

He brushed her hand with his. Pretending to be shy.

Worked every time. They shuffled through the line, holding hands, until it was their turn to order.

—Number six for me, the platter, with a Coke. And the lobster thermafare for my girl.

—What number is that?

Poor shit-for-brains girl in the truck leaned outside to look at the menu.

Tasha touched his skin. Right at the top of his jeans. At the private hip. His balls tightened. He swore his cock could feel the twenty in his pocket. He was full of anything she wanted tonight.

—Number one million.

Shit-for-brains looked down at her register again. Back up at

Toomer. Down, up, down, up. A bobble-head doll the *chuco-chas* sell on the street.

—Aw, give her a break, T. I'll have the number six, like you. And a Diet Coke.

—Okay, T.

Tamed for a moment, Toomer was happy.

10

Cash Offer

Turns out that if a person were to put fifty percent down on a medium-sized house in Ashley-on-Hudson, a person could get a pretty good deal. Asking: $405,000. Purchase: $350,000.

Sally wasn't exactly sure how to translate the cash she had—one sturdy contractor bag (offered by Keith), folded over and taped to hold nineteen packets of one hundred hundred-dollar bills—into the cash she needed to buy the house. As a start, she drove thirty-five miles to a Hudson Bank in Poughkeepsie with the bag in her trunk.

What would she say? How would she act? Was ignorance best? Or confusion? *I'm just a poor old woman* . . . Conspiratorial? Or bullying? These were her choices. Her usual—honest, straightforward and a little prim—was off the table.

She waited at the front of the bank until she was called to the cubicle of Harriet Merchant, a kind-looking, dowdy woman around Sally's age.

"Harriet," Sally said, "I've found myself in a strange situation. My husband and I are retirees, and we've recently come into a bit of money with the death of a beloved aunt. On my husband's side."

Harriet nodded.

"She was a child of the Depression, this aunt," Sally heard herself say. "Kept her money under the mattress. In a hollowed-out box spring. This, honestly, was a lot of cash. She had no kids, it all came to my husband, and now we want to pass it along to our son. He and his wife work in the nonprofit sector, bless their hearts, all over the world, and they've gone and adopted four children from different underprivileged countries."

The last part, the true part, sounded the most made-up.

"Good works," Harriet said. "It takes all kinds, doesn't it? Now, my question to you is, Just what can Hudson Bank do for you today?"

"Can I trust you?" Sally said.

"Funny you should ask," Harriet said and pointed to a pamphlet on her desk that said HUDSON BANK: TRUST US.

"I mean you personally," Sally said. "Woman-of-a-certain-age to woman-of-a-certain-age." Oh, what the heck. She'd go for conspiratorial.

Harriet, fortunately, smiled. "I don't know quite what I'm getting myself into, but I'd say, Of course."

"I have the cash in the trunk of my car. I'd like to deposit it and write a check over to my children."

Harriet nodded again. "Let me just talk to the manager about this one. I'm sure it can be done, but we do have procedures in place for cash deposits."

"Of course," Sally said, talking over her nerves. She tried to read fraternity in Harriet Merchant's bustling walk as she disappeared through the back "Employees Only" door.

This, this right here, was why Sally had resisted the money. The jangling nerves, the shortness of breath, the hearing her own heartbeat. By choice, starting with her choice of Janic, Sally had led an uncomplicated moral life.

Honestly, she had expected Janic to put up more resistance when she suggested they consider taking the money. *What if we helped the kids out with a house in town?* she'd said, just floating the idea. She expected him to give her a better version of the moral veto she'd been giving herself. Instead, he pronounced it a damn good idea to help the kids out with a house in town.

Hadn't everyone agreed, no conspicuous consumption? Now she wondered, just how conspicuous was the house? How big, and how far up River Rise? She remembered it as closer to the bottom of the hill, but maybe it was higher up than she was remembering. River Rise was Ashley's great symbolic street where wealth and prosperity climbed the hill. Houses at the bottom were urban-narrow, a jumble of one- and two-family homes with no yards, laundry lines across the front porches and the occasional rooftop antenna. These houses were the first to flood, being at the base of the hill and right off the Hudson, and it showed in their frequent warp and two-tone paint jobs. Every storm—and Ashley got its share—littered the lower part of the street with tree limbs. Point your nose uphill, and you climb to the grandest houses in town. Tudor mansions and Adirondack-style great homes, dating back to the robber barons who once summered here. Sweeping river views. The hill culminated in the Pinnacle, a stone tower that one robber baron or another had built as an observatory so his children could stargaze. It was now semipublic property—no one knew for sure; people talked of an "easement"—that had a great view of the river, was a frequent stop on the Ashley tour when houseguests came to town and served as the local lovers' lane for teenagers.

As soon as Sally left the bank, she would drive by the house, recalibrate the level of conspicuousness she and Janic were getting themselves into. Why wasn't Janic with her now? Or Byron? Why hadn't Byron asked more questions about the source of this down payment? A little prodding, and Sally would have told him. It had all gone a little too smoothly, now that she thought of it. The kids had seen the house, a midcentury bungalow, and Bianca pronounced it and its warren of small bedrooms perfect. "Don't you think, By?"

Thinking or not, Byron nodded.

"But we could never afford it," Bianca added quickly.

"Byron, didn't you tell her?" Sally said. "Honey, we're giving you half as the down payment."

"What?" Bianca said, stunned. "Oh, we couldn't possibly . . ."

Sally and Janic tacitly explained that retirement was a time of reflection, of making priorities and putting your house in order. Which, for them, meant providing for their grandchildren. "We're able to do it financially," she said, "and as a self-interested benefit, we get to be near our grandchildren."

Now, at a random Hudson Bank branch in Poughkeepsie, Sally kept her mind focused on those grandchildren. That's why she was doing this. That's why she had entered this moral gray area. For little Jaq, whom everyone in the family called Monkey. She hoped there was no racist perception to the nickname.

It wasn't because he was Vietnamese. It was because he was always climbing things.

And poor little Lazlo. He'd been with Byron and Bianca the longest, but he still seemed the most disoriented. Perhaps he *had* been ripped from a loving Guatemalan family and was looking back over his shoulder toward another, happier life, which was Bianca's greatest fear.

There was no looking back for the sisters, who'd never had anything more than a terrible existence in separate Kazakh orphanages. They hadn't seen each other for more than three years, and each wasn't sure her sister was still alive or in-country.

Here was Harriet, bustling back toward her desk. The thrumming in Sally's chest returned.

Wait a minute. Harriet hadn't yet seen the cash. Sally could get out of this at any time.

Harriet didn't speak until she had shifted and settled her bottom into her executive office chair. "Okay," she said. "Here's what I learned."

Sally took a long blink, bracing herself.

"It depends on the amount of money we're talking," Harriet said. "Under twenty-five hundred dollars is fine, no questions asked. Twenty-five hundred to ten thousand, we'll need a federally issued form of ID, and there's a one percent deposit fee. Over ten thousand, you'll have to fill out a currency transaction report, which I can get for you. That goes to the government to guard against money laundering. Or terrorism." She shook her head. "Always with the terrorism these days." Harriet smiled apologetically at the notion of this particular transaction being money laundering or terrorism.

Twenty-five hundred dollars? Was Sally prepared to walk into nearly a hundred banks across the state and convert twenty-five hundred dollars at a time? It had been ridiculous to think such a thing would work. She was no less laundering money than anyone else laundering money.

Locked away in the trunk of her car, the money had done what she'd feared. It had turned her into a common criminal, someone who could no longer walk into a bank—forget her neighborhood bank; she had traveled thirty-five miles for cover—sit across from a woman much like herself and conduct the quotidian business of banking.

11

Keith's 911

This was a rare sight on Sylvan Street: a gathering crowd of men. Daniel was washing his car. Billy was coming back from a run. And Ash, eager for a little company, had stepped outside to check his mailbox, even though it was Sunday. Keith was lured by the scent of a car being washed. And was it . . . yes, a Porsche!

"How do you like it?" Keith asked Daniel.

"What, driving it or washing it?" Daniel said. "Because, frankly, I only really know about the latter. It's so damn impractical with kids. And with a wife who won't let the kids ride in it because they'd have to sit in the passenger's seat. Or, as she corrects me, the 'death seat.'"

"Wives," Billy said.

"You should talk," Keith said. Then, to Daniel: "The guy has a great wife, as everyone but him knows."

"Believe me," Billy said, "I know. I'm just being empathetic."

"How long have you had her?" Keith asked Daniel.

"My wife?" Daniel said.

Laughs all around, some real, some fake.

"I can't believe I didn't know there was a Porsche living on my street," Keith said.

"That's because it never goes anywhere," Daniel said. "Except the train station. Gets twelve minutes of road time a day, six minutes to the station at six forty-five a.m. and six minutes home at six forty-five p.m. Very exciting life we lead, my Porsche and I."

"How do you seal it?" Keith asked.

Daniel looked confused.

"True wax? Or that synthetic stuff? Elbow grease? What do you usually do?"

Daniel held the hose nozzle to his temple, as if to shoot himself in the head. "I'm a terrible Porsche owner. I don't know. I was going to wash it, leave it out in the sun for a while, for me and my neighbors to admire, then shamefully put it back in the garage."

"That is terrible," Keith said. "Animal cruelty. Maybe I can show you a thing or two, we can compare notes, when I get mine."

"Your what?" Daniel said.

"My Porsche." Keith smiled and rubbed his palms together.

"Whoa, wait," said Billy, taking his bandana off his head, as in, *This is serious.*

"Can't do that," Ash said. "We agreed not to live above our means, or people will start snooping around."

"So he can have a Porsche, but I can't?" Keith said. "Because I'm a cop?"

"Not because you're a cop," said Ash. "Because you didn't already have one, and he did."

"Frankly," Daniel said, "I'm living above my means with the damn thing, anyway. I was so midlife crisis when I got it. September eleventh had just happened, and—"

"Tell me about it," Keith said. "I spent time on the pile."

September thirteenth, Keith joined his comrades from the city, the state, the whole country, digging with picks and shovels, with their bare hands, calling ad hoc bucket brigades, calling for body bags, sometimes several in an hour, or, worse, sometimes none for an entire day.

"Live here longer," Billy said, "and you'll hear this more than once from Officer Margolis."

"Sorry for getting sentimental about the worst act of aggression on American soil," Keith said.

Daniel was looking off in the distance, a look Keith recognized.

"You were there?" Keith asked.

Daniel nodded. Keith wanted to hug him, clap him on the back, unfold a folding chair for him, get him a bottled water. How strange these small acts of humanity would be today, on Sylvan Street, all these years later.

"Where were you?" Keith said. "How'd you get out?"

"You know what?" Daniel said. "All due respect to all those guys, but I don't really want to talk about it."

"What?" Keith said. "Never forget. That's the bumper sticker, the one with the towers. Solidarity with New York's Finest and New York's Bravest."

"I will never forget," Daniel said. "Just that I'd rather not talk about it."

"Give the guy a break," Ash said.

"Yeah," Billy said, "go back to bugging him about his Porsche."

"This old thing," Daniel said, clearly eager for lighter turf. "Half the time I wish I didn't even have it."

Keith crossed himself and spit into his hand.

"Sell it to Margolis," Billy said.

"I don't want *his* Porsche," Keith said. "I want *my* Porsche. Black 911 Turbo. Sport Chrono package. Overboost. The whole thing."

"That's the way to do it if you're going to get a Porsche," Daniel said. "Know exactly what you want. You really have to be a connoisseur, or you can end up looking like a loser. Apparently, mine's an off year. Like it's a damn bottle of wine."

"Ninety-eight? That shade of gray was '98, I think."

"Look at this guy," Daniel said. "Yes, '98. You deserve a Porsche more than me."

"So *give* him your Porsche," Billy said.

"Even if you give it to me, I don't want it," Keith said. "I want mine. Black 911 Turbo. End of story."

"Speaking of . . . ," Daniel said to Billy. "My wife wants me to ask you how many miles a gallon you get in that enormous car of yours, that BMW SUV."

"I still can't believe you drive a BMW," Ash said, "and call yourself an artist."

"Who said I call myself an artist?" Billy said. And, to Daniel: "It's surprisingly good on that front. I have a wife, too. How many miles a gallon? Enough."

"Sorry," Daniel said. "She's on envirocop watch these days. 'Eight, nine miles to the gallon?' she keeps asking. First my fancy car is a pain in her ass, and now *your* fancy car is a pain in her ass. 'Men,' she says. 'There's a reason they call it *Mother Earth.*'"

"What's she bugging you for?" Billy said. "You want one?"

"It's really that she has no one to talk to day in and day out. So I'm the filter for everything that's on her mind. And what's on her mind these days is that someone on her street drives a BMW SUV—for some reason, BMW ticks her off especially—while the earth is going to hell in a handbasket."

"Tell her that I hardly ever use it. Only around town, or if I have some heavy lifting. In a way, I'm doing Al Gore and the enviro a favor, taking the thing out of the hands of someone who might drive it more."

"Maybe I should get a Beemer if I can't get a Porsche through this panel of judges," Keith said. "No, a Hummer."

"Oh, God, please," Daniel said. "My wife will kill me."

"A 911 gets good mileage," Keith said. "It's aerodynamic and gets where it's going *fast*. Before you even have a chance to use much gas."

"How did you get through high school math with that logic?" Janic had arrived on the scene with his chess set in hand.

"You don't even want to know, Teach," Keith said.

"Same way he's trying to tell us that buying a Porsche isn't conspicuous consumption," said Billy.

"In other words, denial," Daniel said.

"Takes one to know one," Keith said.

"No argument from me," Daniel said. "I'm the first to admit this is conspicuous consumption. Hell, that's why I bought it.

I was trying to prove something to the world through *stuff*. I knew I was doing it, yet I did it anyway."

"You're buying a Porsche, Keith?" Janic said. "I don't think that's a good idea."

"Go ahead," Keith said, in the singsong voice that sometimes took over when he was nervous. "Everyone feel free to judge me. Don't hold back."

"You know, maybe there's something to that," Billy said.

"Passing judgment on Keith?" Ash said.

"Get some kind of system going," Billy said. "Have people, I don't know, vote or something on what we plan to do with the money. I don't know—you're the systems guy." He addressed Daniel. "Maybe you guys could come up with a system. Or some kind of panel of judges."

"Judges?" Keith shook his head. "What is this, Russia?"

"How is that *Russia*?" Billy asked.

"You know, I'm the only one who stands to lose my job over this." Keith took a step forward, then two steps back. He wanted to change how he was standing in this group of men, but he wasn't sure which direction to go, closer or farther away. "Cop with ill-gotten gains? All I need is IAD sniffing around, and I'm hosed. The rest of you'd be fine. To Cane, it's all a damn pebble in the ocean. No one'd even notice his extra quarter mill, more or less."

"Less," Billy said. "But who's counting."

"And, hell, advertising," Keith said, turning to Daniel.

"Well, branding—"

"Christ, you get found doing something devious, you'd probably get a promotion."

"Yeah, we get paid by the lie," Daniel said.

"And you," Keith said to Ash, "you're a bachelor."

"I didn't know anyone still used that word," Ash said.

"Whatever word you want to use," Keith said. "Anyone comes sniffing around, you could just hightail it out of here. Go to Cabo San Lucas or something. Hey, if you do, would you please take my wife? She's always wanted to go."

"First of all—" Billy started.

"First of all nothing," Keith said. "We're already on, like, *fifth* of all."

"Okay, man, fifth of all," Billy said. "*N*th of all, for all I care. Whatever of all, it's not really a crime. It's not like we stole the money. It was on my property, for fuck's sake. That's nine-tenths of the law."

"You can fool yourself, if you want," Keith said. "But you don't have to be a cop to know that a briefcase with a million dollars in cash has 'illegal' written all over it. Reasonable-man standard, if you've ever heard of it. A reasonable person would report a briefcase full of money."

"Kidding me?" Billy said. "Any reasonable man finds money on his property, he does exactly what we did."

"Keith's right," Janic said. "You're right, Keith. That's why we're trying to figure out what to do. How to proceed with caution now that we've made the decision we've made."

"Why'd you go along with it if you're so against it?" Billy asked Keith.

"I'm as honest as the next guy," Keith said. "But look at the next guy." With his thumb, Keith gestured from neighbor to neighbor; they shuffled in something of a lineup. "Besides, I need the money. What's your excuse?"

"I already told you. It was on *my* property."

"Then why share it with us?" Keith said.

"Hush money," Ash said.

"Now you're on my case, too, for sharing a quarter million dollars with you?" Billy said.

"Less," Ash said. "A lot less. But who's counting? If I had a family, like the rest of you . . ."

"We have to figure something out," Janic said. "Some kind of vetting process. Otherwise we'll just implode like this, and we'll all get caught. Or die trying."

"Easy for you to say," Keith said. "You know everyone's going to nominate you as Chief Justice."

"In case you haven't guessed by now," Billy said to Daniel, "Janic is—what does Sally call you?—the voice of reason on Sylvan Street."

"Especially 14 Sylvan Street," Janic said. "But you know what? I'm through with that. This, right here"—he knocked on his chess set—"is the only place I want to arbitrate. You all carry on without me."

Billy tried to interject, but Janic held up a finger. "Uh-uh," Janic said. "If drafted, I will not run. If nominated, I will not accept. If elected, I will not serve."

12

Daniel's 9/11

For Daniel Hansen, September eleventh had been a continual emergence and reemergence into light, into affirmations that he was alive. He tunneled down the stairs, flight after flight, to emerge into the confusing and still fluorescent, as he remembered it, lobby of the North Tower. Then, he stood dumbly on the plaza with the masses until the thunder came and the sky caved in and rained down. Burrowing, pushing through the crowd, he was a mole, blind and literally thoughtless.

Finally, he emerged from the chaotic dusk of the ash storm into the severe clear of that Tuesday morning. Which didn't make things any clearer for him. He was still bound up in the crowd, a crowd that was at once milling and urgent. People were either keening or dazed and askew. *Why was no one in charge? Why was no one else trying to get away?* This felt vertiginous and bottomless, this desperate need to escape a crowd that moved at once with you, everywhere you went, and against you.

Somehow, he did escape. A block, two blocks, three blocks away from it, he emerged again. He was holding hands with someone he barely knew. Michelle something. Memory came back across the chasmic hour—couldn't have been more than an hour. He had just settled into the conference room for a kickoff meeting with the big new client. A tiny flicker of *before*: she was pretty, and he'd hoped she would be responsible for the account.

They'd grabbed one another—who knew who'd grabbed first?—and headed out the door, although the office was technically instructed to "remain in place." Then down the stairs, thirty-eight flights, a team of two moving more surely than a team of one. Couldn't hesitate. Couldn't stop to help someone else.

They didn't speak a word until they were several blocks away. "You okay?" he said. She nodded, for which he was grateful, although he could see tears right behind her set face. God, please don't let him have to take care of her, of anyone, right now. Just let him walk. Let him walk, and let him be.

They headed up West Broadway. Tribeca's crooked streets, a confusing mix of residential and commercial in the best of times, were now a confusing mix of before and after. Freshly washed and caffeinated people in business suits and sleepy people in pajamas were out among the ash-covered and shell-shocked.

At first, he'd been confused as to how people could have gone back to their lives already, slept, showered. How was it that he and Michelle—he looked over; *good*, she was still ash-covered and shaky—were traveling more slowly through time than everyone else in the city?

Soon, he realized. These people were not *after*, had not

returned to their lives, reunited with their loved ones, showered, changed, slept and had a fresh cup of coffee a day later. These people were still *before*.

Daniel and Michelle picked their way east, back south. City Hall's lawn was packed with refugees; the building itself looked like a relic from the days of civic order. East and east. The bridge loomed in front of them, and soon they were on it. Daniel was reminded—the first of this day's several disorientingly hopeful memories—of running the New York Marathon. Crowds of people, no cars, everyone moving the same direction and under their own steam.

When they got over the bridge, the stream of refugees thinned, dispersed. Spectators popped up everywhere, again like the marathon. Three times, greengrocers came out onto the street to offer him and Michelle bottles of water. Fruit, gum. *Come into our shop, get some food, get something for yourself.*

They squeezed each other's hand now and then but exchanged very few words. Several times, adrift in the Brooklyn streets, they noticed other refugees, joined them for a while on their march homeward, then drifted apart. No one spoke. They'd nod, fall into step for a while. But the slightest break in rhythm—stop and rub a toe, glance at your useless cell phone, slow down for a moment to get your bearings—and people would separate, peel off.

Each time, each encounter with the world, he thought of Shoshanna and baby Caleb. But there was nothing to be done. Phones didn't work. And he was heading home, wasn't he? He would walk Michelle to her Fort Greene apartment—how could he not?—then make his way to Brooklyn Heights.

He and Michelle were offered medical attention by an older

man who reminded Daniel of his father-in-law, trustworthy but a little pushy and self-righteous. He was a doctor, he said, and wanted to help. Daniel no longer recalled whether they answered him, the doctor, whether they even stopped or slowed down.

Many people, dozens perhaps, asked if they were all right, and, again, Daniel couldn't remember what or if he and Michelle had answered. They kept walking. He supposed, in retrospect, that that was answer enough. *We can walk, can't we?*

On Flatbush, a few people took pictures of them. Daniel vowed never again to snap pictures of the locals when he was in a foreign country.

Michelle had tried her cell phone several times, to no avail. She'd offered it to him, but after the first *circuits busy*, he declined. Yet another failed call on a stranger's phone was more disorientation than he could bear, the slender straw that just might break the camel's back. He had left his own phone, along with his reading glasses and wallet, on the conference room table. It hadn't sunk in yet that his triad of essentials had vaporized. As had the conference room where he'd been about to do business with his agency's newest, biggest client. As, quite possibly, had the client himself, as well as the very idea of the end of the day. Daniel wouldn't have an end of the day today. No one in New York would. The day had dropped off a precipice, and everyone would hang on the best they could. Just to keep from falling off. No one would move forward that day, not beyond Tuesday morning, not for the longest time.

On Dekalb and the park, right in front of the hospital—where a dozen doctors and nurses in uniform stood sentry, waiting, waiting—Michelle announced that they were coming to her apartment, around the corner on South Oxford. Only then did he realize how stunningly beautiful she was, despite ash in her hair and streaked on her cheeks and chin. He'd held hands over the span of two boroughs with the most stunning woman he had ever seen. He could not believe his fortune. *It had all been worth it.* This terrible bombing—that's what he still thought it was—had been orchestrated to bring together this man and this woman. Romeo and Juliet? Lightweights! What's a little family feud, a little poison to the lips? Daniel and Michelle would be lovers to end all lovers. They had been united by Fate to survive the end of the world together. No one in that world knew where they were, whether they were dead or alive, and here they were making out in front of her apartment building, tangled limb around limb, climbing the stairs. He reached around her and unbuttoned her shirt as she fumbled with her key in the lock, throwing her head back as he sucked on her neck. Her shirt was off before the door was closed behind them. And his shirt. They had sex on the floor. In the hallway of her railroad apartment. It was not even a room. Just the two of them naked on a hardwood floor.

Quick sex, lingering distance. The moment took him back to his college days, lying in bed next to girls who were and always would be strangers, knowing that they were both better than this but unable, nonetheless, to transcend it.

Her cell phone rang from somewhere in her cast-off clothes. She jumped up, fumbled for it, found it. "Oh, my God. Oh, my God. Oh, my God," she kept saying, breathlessly, crying now. "I love you, too."

It was her boyfriend calling from Boston, she told Daniel when she got off the phone.

"You didn't talk very long," he said.

"He had to go call a million people, apparently, and tell them I'm okay. He's even going to call my parents for me. He thinks I'll have trouble connecting." She paused. "Oh, I thought he meant with the phone. But maybe he meant with my emotions. He sometimes looks out for me too much."

"But you love him?" Daniel said, not sure what he was fishing for.

"I guess looking out for someone too much is better than the opposite." She tossed the phone back onto the pile of clothes.

In his marriage, he wondered, did he look out too much or too little? "I should try, too," he said. "If the phones are back."

She had to find the phone again, then handed it to him. "You get one call to your lawyer," she said, a little too loudly. He could tell she was going to attempt a joke. "Since that sex probably was illegal."

He nodded.

"Or anyone you want, of course," she said.

"My wife." He started dialing, but stopped. "What's your boyfriend's name?"

"David," she said. "How come you're asking?"

He shrugged.

"This whole thing *so* isn't about names, right?" she said.

"Michelle." He smiled sheepishly. "I don't remember your last name."

"Confession," she said, sheepish, too. "I don't know your name at all. I just know that you're the new branding guy."

"Ah, Daniel Hansen," he said, shaking her hand. "Nice to meet you."

"Michelle Dineen," she said. "I've never done such a thing in my life." She held her palm to her forehead. "Didn't even know your name! What's wrong with me?"

"I never have, either," he said, eager to get on record. "It's like we've been in a war, though, isn't it? And everything changes."

He pulled on his pants.

"Including you," she said, touching his naked waist in a way that now felt inappropriate. She pulled away like she'd touched a lit stove.

They both got fully dressed before he called home to his wife. Over the phone, he told Shoshanna only that he was fine, that everyone in the city was scrambling to call home, cell service was a mess, and he'd get home as soon as he could.

It wasn't until he had been sitting in his kitchen for the better part of an hour, had already showered and changed, that he told his wife he was in the towers for a meeting when the planes hit.

He never saw Michelle again. The client had not lost anyone in the attacks, he learned, but the offices were gone and, as with so much else at that time, a rebranding campaign slipped right off the list of priorities.

13

Toomer's 911

Barely off the ground, barely off the fucking ground, when Tasha turned into every other girl.

—I hardly ever see you anymore.

Five or six days gone by. A week at the most. He just needed a little space. Needed to lie by himself on the couch. Maybe ten days.

They were in line to order. He tried to talk her into getting the number 6, the platter, even though he couldn't afford it. He was getting his usual. Number 1, Plain Rice and Beans, $1.93.

—Can't buy me off with a stupid dinner.

Toomer stepped out of line, let another couple go next. Put a hand on Tasha's belly, one on her ass, pulled her to him. —Get some meat on you.

She yanked herself away.

—I haven't seen you for, like, two weeks. So no touching.

He grabbed the end of the pink silk scarf she was wearing.

Held it over his face, like some romantic mythical motherfucker. Sultan, or something. He hammed it up.—I *looooove* you.

The couple ahead of them turned around, chick smiled.

—That's what the guy always says right before he gets you pregnant and takes off.

—Shit, are you pregnant?

She slit her eyes. She looked like someone else, a grown woman, old.

—I haven't seen you in, like, a month. How could I be pregnant?

The couple in front of them turned around again. Guy smiled, chick frowned.

—I'm just saying, T. All of a sudden you're acting like every other guy that me or any of my friends have ever been with. Dr. Jekyll and Mr. Houdini. And you were supposed to be different.

—Supposed to? Says who?

—Says my stupid heart.

She turned away. He grabbed her scarf. She houdinied right out of it. Right out the plastic flap-door. *Slap* of the plastic. *Slap* of her hand.

He squeezed the scarf in his fist.

She peeled out of the parking lot.

Opened his fist and the scarf bloomed like a mutant rose. He put it over his head. World was fluorescent pink.

Fuck. Might as well get himself in line.

—Number one.

Shit-for-brains at the register didn't register his order.

—Deaf, sister? I said, Number one.

She turned into the truck and hollered.—*Kevin.*

Guy named Kevin, apparently, came out from the back of the truck, head ducked under the low ceiling. Huge fucker. Head took up the whole ordering window.

—The fuck you want? Harassing my girl?

Guy grabbed his belt buckle like it was a gun.

—A number one, man. The fuck's wrong with that?

—I seen you in here before. You a guy who shits where he eats?

The fuck? Toomer said to himself, backing off, shaking his head. Fingering the scarf. *Oh, shit.* He must have scared them, crazy guy with a pink scarf over his face. Like he was going to rob the place.

Toomer headed back to the window. To explain. But Kevin stuck out that huge head again. —Better get out of here before I fuck you up, skinny, crazy motherfucker.

The road home might as well be forever. Five lanes wide. Leading nowhere. No sidewalks, no people. Just strip mall after empty goddamn mall. Half of them boarded up. Car repair, home repair. Same thing, one after another. Dunkin' Donuts, Munchin' Donuts, Lucky Donuts. Wal-Mart, Kmart, Sav-Mart. Even some lazy-ass thing just called Mart.

Maybe Toomer *would* rob the Truck. Go right back there and get a little cash. Serve the guy right for thinking it.

When he was little, before he gave up on God, Toomer used to squeeze his eyes shut and beg to be invisible. Superpower. Not just for himself; for his mother and Aaliyah, his twin. But no. That was too much for God. He, God, wouldn't do it . . .

wouldn't do it . . . and again, wouldn't do it. God would let a woman and a small boy (his father never hit his sister) get pulped rather than alter His precious laws of the universe by making someone invisible.

Who did Toomer think he was? *Rey de la montaña?* Couldn't even rip off a stupid taqueria.

Maybe he should just get a regular job. Force his way into Nishal's quarry and ask that boss himself. Work like his *jai*. Every morning, every afternoon. No trouble. No questions. No balls. No escape.

Hell, apologize to that guy Kevin. Get a job at the Truck. He'd be better at it than that shit-for-brains. Make three dollars an hour. In about fifty years, he could get his own apartment, or bedroom, or mattress on the floor. In a hundred years, he could buy Natasha a diamond ring, take her to a fancy dinner, have a couple kids in clean, stiff clothes.

Or work it like Bats. Find some guys with their hand in the pot. Then steal the fucking pot.

Toomer would be walking for an hour. In the car, getting home from the Truck took no time. Two or three songs on the radio. One hot conversation with Natasha. Or one argument.

Damn. Rain. Back in his country, he'd hitchhike. But Nishal had warned him against doing it here. He pulled his hood over his *tope*. Hunched his shoulders against the rain. Settled in for the long walk home.

Did he hear a car slowing? He turned around. A car was definitely slowing on the shoulder. The horn honked. For him?

It wasn't Natasha's little red car. Or Nishal's piece of shit rust-colored car. He didn't know anyone else with a car.

Maybe, *maybe*, God was finally paying attention to Tasmin Toomer de Silva. How about that? Just when he was wishing someone would stop and pick him up, a car slows on the shoulder.

Look at it a certain way, and God was starting to prove. Gave Toomer a *jai* like Nishal, didn't He? Gave him a girl like Tasha. Next, maybe, God would give him an escape plan.

This car, white, crept along at walking speed. Right to Toomer's feet. Stopped right there, like someone showing off a miracle.

Toomer squinted to see who it was. Wasn't raining anymore. Just damp, foggy. The car was full. Four guys, or five. Lots of movement, hard to tell. He did not recognize anyone.

A window came down.

—Hi.

Driver, white guy, teenager, started things off.

Toomer set his chin. Stone. Slit his eyes like Tasha had done.—What do you want?

All the windows came down. Four white kids and the soaking smell of beer. Even from this distance.

—We want you to answer a bet we're having.

Guy in the backseat talking now.

Toomer started walking. Far to the side of the road as he could get. The car followed. One kid after another yelling out the windows.

—We took a bet.

—For a six-pack.

—Guess what kind of illegal alien this is.

—I say Nigger.

—Spic.

—Arab.

—No, Muslim.

—Same thing, dummy.

Toomer started jogging. Looked left, looked right. Looked for a place to land. Looked for another person, anywhere, on foot.

No one. And nothing. Across five lanes, down the road, neon sign said COFFEE. Might be open this time of night.

—Let's get a piece of that skin under the microscope.

—Spic skin comes right off, you know. They're snakes. That's how they sneak into the country.

Behind him, back in the other direction, another neon sign. Looked like a gas station. Looked open.

—If he's an Arab, he'll have extra skin on his pecker.

Toomer turned around, sprinted. He'd get to that gas station. Or back to the Truck. No friends there, but at least there were people. He'd explain everything to Kevin—huge mistake, my girl's scarf, she dumped me. I was just messing around.

The car screeched, hurtled in reverse, veering like crazy. Trying to hit him.

Motherfuckers! Too lazy to even come out of the car.

Toomer's abandoned God heard that. The car swerved and skidded to a stop. Bastards piled out, slamming doors, one after another. Slam. Slam. Slam. Slam. Four fucking doors.

What about *invisible*? It was his only hope.

He unzipped his hoodie just as one of the kids grabbed his back. The hoodie flew off, empty, in the motherfucker's hand.

Toomer was Superman. Drunken bastards couldn't run for shit. He kept running until he felt emptiness behind him. Then he turned around. They were miles back, *ha ha*, holding their knees and their sides. One of them was doubled over, throwing up.

Slammed to the ground. He'd missed a kid, lost track of him. The motherfucking driver. The kid was on top of him, trying to punch him in the face. Toomer slid his *tope* over his face. Softer. But still fists. Blind, by feel, he tried to hand-heel the kid under his nose. These faggots didn't know anything. Could jab at a guy all day. But one upper to that spot under the chin or nose, you cut off blood flow to the head.

Kid stripped off Toomer's *tope*. Now he could see. Two more guys coming. And another. All here now. Fat cowards. They were shouting at him. *Fucking Muslim—Nigger—Spic— Fights dirty like an Arab*. Punching him in the head, kicking him in the legs, stepping on his nuts. Until he came loose from his body.

His brain went dim. A shade, a curtain—like that. Eyes welded shut. Just as well. What was there to see? Blood, juice, brain. From his own body. He could feel dampness outside of himself. Inside: aches, shards, blur and brightness.

In a dying move, he lifted his head off the ground and managed to spit. Hell of a spitter, Toomer.

—The Spic got me on the pecker!

The other kids laughed.

—Fuck you. It's not funny. Diseases and shit.

The hornet's nest on top of Toomer began turning on itself.

—You got Arab spit on your choad!

The white kids were fighting each other.

—You're gonna grow a hood.

—Nah, I'm telling you, he's a Spic. You're gonna get a disease.

—A disease that makes you a migrant worker.

Toomer huddled into his dimmed brain. Which closed around him. Him into it, it into him. Darkness, his last resort, was where he'd wait for the light.

14

Industrial Revolution

When Ash Flemming was little, he made paint by soaking things in hot tap water until they leached color. Bark, berries. *My little Red Indian*, his mother called him. When he soaked her Hermès scarf, a gift from her first husband, Ash's father, she called him *my little Oedipus*.

She was glad to be rid of the damn thing, scarf *and* husband, she said, swirling her index finger dreamily in the bowl of blue-tinted water. *Hermès!* Who did the man think they were? He never acknowledged that she had a baby, that she might want to knock off the Hermès and high heels for a while and lie around on the couch with paste in her hair and peanut butter on her shirt. *Me and my boy*, she always said. When Ash went to college—not far enough, in retrospect; the School of Visual Arts was only a commute from Hoboken—she amended it to *me and my man*. Husbands #2 through #4 might well have agreed.

Ash still made his own paints. His current method was a

medieval Japanese one, mineral pigment in an animal glue base with malachite and gold or silver dust. He liked the holographic quality of the mixture. It could look contemporary and urban, or ancient and epic. It could capture darkness or light, depending on the balance of malachite and precious metal. The paintings could look pre-Industrial or post-, a tension that had been particularly resonant in Ash's old life. In Williamsburg, as in the Hoboken of his childhood, one was constantly confronted with the fruits of the Industrial Revolution, its successes and failures.

Here in Ashley, progress and decay ran along a different axis. It all seemed to be about a certain family wholeness, as far as Ash could tell. To friends in the city, he called Ashley his "near miss" at family. During their house hunting, he and Suki had made all kinds of plans and promises. When they had kids— that had been the first plan and promise—they would split their days, each working half-time on their art and half-time taking care of the baby. So went the plan.

At 9 Sylvan Street, the back windows had the better view, looking over town and the hills across the river. But the front windows had the better light, so the world outside Ash Flemming's studio was his neighbors passing by. Billy on a run, Maggie walking the chocolate Lab, the oldest Margolis walking up or down the street on her way to or from the Canes' and, lately, Janic Levlovic doing this as well. The other Margolis kids were out now and then, too, calling for that little one, Kelli, or chasing after the boy. Now, as Ash glanced out the window, he saw his new neighbor at the top of the street, straining under more bags than his chivalric side would have liked.

Ash decanted the animal-hide glue. As usual, he was long

on pigment and short on gold and silver. Next trip to Hudson Hardware & Fine Art, he would buy all the gold dust and silver he wanted, rather than his usual rationing. There was another malachite, too, a pricey one that ran more toward a precious metal, that he had been dying to use. He'd buy a tub of it, a vat. A hundred seventy thousand dollars? Christ, he would buy all the materials he wanted.

Commotion drew him to the window. His new neighbor had dropped bags in the street. Groceries scattered around her. She picked up a few things, then joined the whole mess on the ground, sitting with her face in her hands.

He would have rushed outside, definitely would have, but she looked like she might rather be alone. Besides, there was an optimal timing to getting the dry ingredients into the animal glue. Blue, silver, and enough malachite to capture impending nightfall. That's where this round of paintings was set, the bittersweet end of day, waning light, waxing regret.

He glanced back at the window. Shoshanna was gathering her things from the ground. He gave the paint a final mix and headed up the street.

"Ah, just in time to not help," he said, arriving as she put the last item, a box of pasta, in her reusable bag.

"Thank you very much," she said with a chagrined smile.

"Are you all right? What happened?"

"Fine," she said, putting the bags back down to brush at her knees. "I don't know what happened. Something was slipping, and I made some kind of smooth move and . . ." She pantomimed a tumbling out of her arms, although it looked more like a cradled baby than groceries.

"What's the matter with your car?" Ash asked.

"My car?"

Maybe he was going down the wrong road, so to speak. "Uh, just wondering why you're walking."

"The ancient art of walking," she said. "I guess I don't know why more people on Sylvan Street don't walk to town. It's only a half mile, although it is all hill."

"You're right. We should."

"I'm not saying *should*," she said. "I just honestly wonder why more people don't."

"Lazy," he said. "That's my excuse. Simple as that."

A car turning onto the street turned both their heads. "Oh, shit," Ash said. A black Porsche.

"Hit man?" Shoshanna widened her eyes in mock fear.

It did look the part, tinted windows, low to the ground and fast. The car could barely contain its propulsion as it slowed to "Caution: Children" speed.

"No, Margolis," Ash said. "We told him not to get a Porsche."

"Gas guzzler?"

"Conspicuous consumption. It's like he's trying to get us caught. Some kind of *I told you so*."

Keith stopped beside them and rolled down his window. "Need a ride?" he asked Shoshanna.

"Turn back time about ten minutes, and I'll take you up on it," she said, "avoid the whole embarrassing mess."

"Keith," Ash started.

"Midlife crisis," Keith said. "You guys can't arrest me for that." He shifted into neutral. "Not fair to make her run so slowly."

He let the car roll down the street. "Even in neutral, she handles beautifully," he called behind him.

"Maybe I'm just jealous," Ash said to Shoshanna.

"Are you?" Shoshanna asked.

"I don't think so. A cool car is pretty low down on my list." He drove a 2000 Saturn, which he bought used, for next to nothing, before moving to Ashley, figuring he and Suki would get a more appropriate car once they settled in.

"What is on your list?" she said, turning conspiratorial. "What are you going to do with the money?"

"There's a new malachite I want to try," he said. "It's rare, mined in some tiny corner of Brazil or something. It's really expensive, but it's supposed to look gorgeous with precious metals, gold and silver."

"Metals?" she said. "I thought you painted."

"I make my paints, and I mix in some metals. Silver, gold dust. Medieval Japanese method with a little post-Industrial thrown in. It lets you play with the scale of ancient to modern."

"What a fascinating way to look at the world," she said. She looked around. "Where would you put Sylvan Street on that scale?"

"Still trying to figure it out."

He did not elaborate, to her obvious disappointment. But he needed to figure such a thing out on canvas, not in conversation.

"Just the two-hundred-thousand-dollar malachite?" she said.

"Hundred seventy thousand," he amended. "Remember—no kids, not even a girlfriend. But at least I have enough for materials."

"Should just about cover it," she said, smiling at the exaggeration.

"Unless I'm Cane," he said.

She looked at him blankly.

"Don't get me started on Billy Cane," he said.

"I didn't know I was," she said. "Wow, you're actually grinding your teeth."

"It just makes me furious. Because he has a rich wife, he spends thousands of dollars on rocks. Then he chisels away with some superexpensive copper thing for an afternoon. *A whole afternoon, Billy? My hero.*" He wasn't sure who he was after with the falsetto. Certainly not Maggie Cane. "Don't get me wrong, the rocks are beautiful—he has good taste in rocks. But if that's what it means to be an artist in the suburbs, it's a pretty sad state of affairs."

"Why is *that* what it means?" she said. "Why isn't it what *you're* doing? You're an artist in the suburbs, too, aren't you?"

"You're right," he said. "But I certainly don't think of myself that way."

"I'm sure Billy Cane doesn't either," she said.

And here he was, right on cue, turning onto the street, back from a run.

"Have a good run?" Shoshanna said.

"It's all part of my process," Billy said, with mock *haute grandeur*. "Avoidance is a very important part of art."

"Not necessarily," Ash said.

"That's why you're the successful artist, and I'm just a guy with a bunch of rocks in his yard and a well-traveled six-mile running loop."

Ash caught how Shoshanna was looking at Billy Cane as he went into his house. What was it about the guy?

"I'm afraid he heard us," she said when the Canes' front door closed.

"Nah," Ash said. "He doesn't listen to anyone but himself."

"Oh, I think you're wrong about that," she said. "I don't know him from Adam, but I get the sense that if there's one thing he *does* do it's listen. He sort of quivers with it, if you ask me."

Come to think of it, Cane did sort of quiver. He had an odd nervous cool that Ash had always read as fraudulence. And the whole time it was because the guy was *listening*? To women, maybe. Women were Billy Cane's thing, something Ash also attributed to fraudulence.

"Anyway," Shoshanna said, "this malachite, this rare, expensive malachite from heart-of-darkness Brazil—you're not denuding any Amazon rain forests, are you?"

He shook his head, and they shared a smile. He couldn't read her tone. Her husband's disclaimers preceded her, but Ash thought she might be making fun of herself, exaggerating the "envirocop" for comic effect. If she was, he liked her quite a bit.

After a few rounds of protest, she let him help her carry the bags up her driveway. "I'm really not as helpless as I looked, sitting in the middle of the road," she said. "I'm a pretty capable person."

"I can see that," Ash said.

"So you can go back to your painting with a clear conscience," she said.

"If only it were that easy," he said with a laugh.

He'd meant this lightly—in fact, had not meant it at all—but, as was becoming increasingly common for him, he spent the rest of the afternoon sitting in front of his canvas without painting a stroke.

15

Changing Guard at Buckingham Palace

Rather than "May I sit on your bench?" Shoshanna heard herself ask Sally Levlovic, "Can I ask you something about this money?"

Sally opened the screen door, motioned her inside as though she'd been expecting her.

"Honestly, I came to sit on your bench," Shoshanna said as they walked through the kitchen to the living room. "Husband at work. Kids at camp. But I don't think I need any more 'getting in touch with myself.' Getting in touch with others—I could stand to do a little more of that."

"I know just what you mean," Sally said. "Sit, sit."

The chair was surprisingly uncomfortable. She would have imagined lived-in comfort for the Levlovices. The room was beautiful. Spare, neutral, architecty. Well suited to the house. Only, not comfortable.

"So . . . ," Sally started. "All this money got you down?"

Shoshanna exhaled with relief. "Thank you!" she said. "Daniel keeps saying, It's all good—"

"Janic, too. Or his generation's version of it," Sally said. "Which is basically silence."

"But it's not all good, is it?" Shoshanna said. "You were right. You didn't want to take the money. Why did you give in?"

"Why didn't you speak up?"

"We're new," Shoshanna said. "I don't know. I'm not quite sure how things work here."

"Heavens, we're not all that strange, are we?" Sally said. "I think we're as normal a neighborhood as you're ever going to find."

Back and forth, they enumerated could-have-would-have-should-haves, each emphatically agreeing with the other. They could have walked away from the whole thing, let the neighbors divvy it up or left it the Canes' problem. They should have gone to the police, the moral thing to do. Maybe there would have been a small reward in it, and they could have gotten a vacation or a new outfit out of it—worry free.

"Actually," Shoshanna said, "I'm trying to look on the bright side of this."

"Oh, my, look at us." Sally shook her head. "Almost half a million dollars between us, and we have to talk ourselves on to the bright side. Okay, riddle me the bright side."

"Philanthropy," Shoshanna said. "I'm going to get it out of our house and into a good cause."

"What a good idea. Who's the lucky cause?" Sally picked up a magazine from the coffee table and fanned herself.

"That's the pathetic thing," Shoshanna said. "I don't know.

Can't even decide on a good cause. Peace on earth? Save the planet?"

"Well, why not start at the top?" Sally raised her hands wide, acting out *the sky's the limit*.

She backed into the bookshelf and knocked down a few books. She picked up the top one, checked it as if it were animate, then stayed with it for a moment, balancing it corner to corner in her palms.

"My favorite. *When We Were Very Young.*" She opened it. "Signed by the author. Very valuable." She laughed ruefully. "Although now I have a trash bag in my basement worth much more."

Shoshanna nodded in sympathy.

Sally opened the book and read, "*Down the corner of the street, / Where the three roads meet, / And the feet / Of the people as they pass go 'Tweet-tweet-tweet—'*" She looked up. "Oh, I love that."

"Sweet," Shoshanna said. "Very sweet."

Sally turned the page. "*They're changing guard at Buckingham Palace—*"

"*Christopher Robin went down with Alice,*" Shoshanna cut in.

"*Alice is marrying one of the guard—*" Sally paused expectantly.

"*'A soldier's life is terribly hard,'*" Shoshanna exclaimed. "I have no idea where that came from. I would never have told you that I'd committed A. A. Milne, a Brit, to memory."

"Memory, I hardly knew ye." Sally's smile was so warm that Shoshanna wondered for a moment if her hostess wasn't mistaking her for someone else. An old friend, perhaps, or one of her adult children.

"One more," Sally said, thumbing the pages. "*What shall I call / My dear little dormouse?*" She looked at Shoshanna expectantly again. But the moment had passed.

"I'm afraid that's all I know," Shoshanna said.

"*His eyes are small . . .*" Sally went on, nodding with an English-teacher mix of encouragement and pending disappointment.

Shoshanna shook her head.

"Ah, well," Sally said. "*His eyes are small, / But his tail is e-nor-mouse.*" She waved her hand to change the subject. "I'm suddenly stifling in all this heat. Parched. Let me get us a lemonade."

"That sounds lovely."

From the kitchen, Sally called, "Do you want some vodka in it?"

Shoshanna blinked in surprise. "Are you?"

"I will if you will," Sally called.

"Well, I will if you will."

When Sally handed her a glass, Shoshanna wasn't sure which side of the tautology they'd landed on.

"To mutually assured destruction," Sally toasted.

"Hear, hear." Shoshanna couldn't remember the last time she had hard liquor. And when, if ever, she'd had it in the middle of the day. A few sips, and the bracing, erasing sensation of the vodka at once released her from and connected her to herself. *This*, a good stiff drink, was what she should be doing when she didn't know what else to do.

"Why can't we fuel cars on vodka?" Shoshanna said, feeling fueled. "It's a renewable resource."

"Maybe that's your good cause right there." Sally made an aerial study of her drink. "Fill the tank, hold the olive."

"What are you doing with your money, if I may ask?" Shoshanna said, feeling drunk already, marinating in summer heat.

"Ask away," Sally said. "No one else really does." She had a perfectly good cause—her family. When Keith Margolis had used the word "cause" to describe the Levs, she said, Janic had read him the riot act. But indeed they were. "Everyone's family," she said, "should be their own best good cause."

Shoshanna put her chin in her hand. Daniel had once accused her of making Caleb into a cause. She was working with the school, doing thirty-minute lessons with him three times a day, participating in the health department study, reading up on post-9/11 airborne toxins, interviewing tutors and specialists. She was trying to make his life easier. How on earth could Daniel have a problem with that?

"We're buying a house; shhhh, don't tell," Sally was saying. She and Janic were putting a down payment on a house in Ashley for their son and daughter-in-law, moving them up from a cramped apartment in Queens so the grandkids could flourish. Queens, Sally said, was crippling them, or at least aiding and abetting crippling ailments that they already had.

"That's why we left the city," Shoshanna said. "Cripples all but the strongest. I used to think we were the strongest, but then I started to doubt it."

She told Sally about Caleb and the study. How she, his mother, had put his developing brain in jeopardy day after day.

Caleb was born July 11, 2001. Just about every day, in the same postpregnancy white nightgown, fearing she would lose her mind if she stayed in their small apartment another minute, Shoshanna carried a sleeping or feeding or squawking infant and his developing brain up to their roof garden overlooking the Brooklyn waterfront, taking in the whole of—then the remainder of—the Manhattan skyline. She watched the smoke mass and hover like an occupying enemy. Over months, she watched it thin to a plume, a thread, then a smoldering haze visible only in shifting winds.

"How do you know the best way to keep your kids safe?" she asked.

Sally gave her a *sixty-four-thousand-dollar question* shake of the head.

Before she started her philanthropic foundation, Shoshanna would spend the money on two things: a tutor for Caleb and a weapons cache–worthy lock for her front door.

Maybe taking the money *was* a moral act, Sally and Shoshanna agreed, drinking to the possibility.

16

The Brothers Grim

Chapter 1: The Anniversary

You're the first one here, which is surprising. Your brother is usually the first to arrive and the last to leave. He is the older and the dutiful son.

You agitate the handful of pebbles you've collected from your travels these last few months. This is a particularly sooth-ing ritual of Jews, placing pebbles on a headstone to honor the memory of the dead.

Here comes your brother.

Is he alone, or is his wife with him? . . . Wait for it . . .

He's alone.

That means he's going to talk to you about your father.

"Robert," he says before he's halfway to the gravesite.

That, too, means he's going to talk to you about your father. Normally he, like everyone else, calls you Robbie.

You quickly place the pebbles atop the tombstone. You notice a little chip in the serif of your mother's *R*. You feel impossibly sorry for her, that someone, her husband, her sons, was not able to protect her entire ROSE WILLS from damage.

"Let me talk to you about Dad," you say. You'll head your brother off at the pass.

"First things first," he says, unwilling as ever to give you an inch. "Let's pay our respects."

You look at the pebbles. *There.* Those are your respect. Symbols of it, anyway. With all the love, honor and millennia-old tradition they convey. You've come to appreciate Jewish participatory funereal traditions. You've come to appreciate Judaism—Jews—in general. You're in love with a fellow Jew for the first time ever. Perhaps you're finally ready to be part of a tradition.

What you're sure Charles is about to pay is not respects. It's lip service. That's Charles's job. He's a deputy press secretary for the mayor, and every day for him seems to be a busman's holiday. He's always speaking for somebody or another. Has been ever since you were kids.

"Do you want to say anything?" he says.

"To her, or on her behalf?" you ask.

"Whichever," he murmurs.

He murmurs something else, but it's windy out here in the open cemetery, and his words get swept away.

Neither of you says anything else out loud. You both keep your eyes on your mother's headstone. You wonder if he sees it, too, the chip in the *R*. Probably not. If he saw it, he'd say. Charles keeps very little to himself. As opposed to you. You see more than you say.

You're here for your mother, the first anniversary of her death, but still it is your father who dominates. Both you and

Charles are brimming to tell something about Dad. You're not
sure what Charles wants to tell, but you know it's something.
Yours is that you went to see Dad for the first time since you've
been back, and he had no idea who you were.

"How long has he been that bad?" you ask.

The irony of your father's Alzheimer's is inescapable. He has
held on to a secret his whole adult life. Now he couldn't tell
anyone even if he wanted to.

You have wondered if the secret would slip out, in some
form, at the home. His memory, long-term anyway, is not
erased. Just that everything is misfiled. One doctor explained:
The brain is essentially an extravagant filing system. Now here
comes Alzheimer's, and it's like a tornado, a cyclone. Just tosses
everything up in the air. Try finding your keys . . . That piece
of information is up a tree. Which way is home? That data is
under an I-beam in the basement. Try remembering the name of
a loved one. That closely held information is over there, in the
neighbor's yard, just beyond reach.

Another doctor debunked the tornado analogy, encouraged
you to think of it instead as a series of worn-out connections
rather than a tempest-tossing wind. This seemed a distinction
without a difference. Let the aggrieved sons hold on to whatever
metaphor helps them understand.

Even if Dad does confess, it would sound so unlikely that
his attendants would certainly find it as nonsensical as a perfectly shod man desperately searching for his shoes, which
you've heard has happened a number of times. Or an elderly
man insisting that he can't leave his room because he's waiting for his own father to pick him up from school. Or his telling anyone who'll listen that you, whoever you are, have been

sneaking into his room every day to poison him a little at a time, even though—hardly in your defense—this is your first visit in three months.

A giant crow, the biggest damn one you've ever seen, flaps down onto Mom's tombstone. How rude!

You can't help wonder if it's, somehow, Dad. Charles wonders, too, because he looks at you the same way you're looking at him. You are, after all, brothers.

Charles shoos it away—if he didn't, you would have—and goes to his car. He returns bearing a dozen roses.

"I love you more, Mom," you whisper quickly, as your brother makes his long-legged way back to the grave.

"I'm the better son," you whisper. "I forgave you right away."

Charles lays down the roses, which will die immediately. It's January.

"It's been a year," he says. "But not a day goes by, Mom, when we don't all think of you."

He sounds as if he's speaking for the mayor's office.

I love you more, Mom. I forgave you. You say it to yourself this time. She's dead. She can perfectly well hear inside your head.

"Now that Mom's been properly honored," Charles says, "can we talk about Dad?"

You look up at the sky, trying to avoid Charles's holier-than-thou (thou, *Robbie,* in particular) eye contact. Then you nod and shake your head in quick succession. You know an answer to Charles's question is not required of you. Charles will do what Charles will do.

He tells you that Dad wants to give his money to you and Charles now, before he dies.

"How could Dad have said this?" you ask. "I just went to see him, and he didn't even know who I was. How is he all of a sudden sound-mind enough to make financial decisions?"

"Not all of a sudden," Charles says. "He told me while you were away—for, what was it, six months?"

"It hasn't been six months," you say. "It's been three."

It's not that you simply lost track of time. You were *staying* away, and a person who's staying away knows exactly how much time has gone by. You've been avoiding a girl, someone you could fall in love with. You left a couple weeks after September eleventh.

Right after the attacks—for a few days, anyway—you were seized by the same sentiment everyone else was. Life is short, love the one you're with. You *would*. You loved her. You would make the commitment.

You tried.

You couldn't.

So you left.

"Whenever it was that I talked to Dad," Charles is saying, "he was better then. In November or so, when we had this conversation, he was fine. Well, not fine, but he had his moments. The doctor told us—the lawyer and I, since my brother was AWOL, as per usual—to take advantage of any *compes mentes* we could get. It wouldn't last. This Alzheimer's is a one-way street."

"Convenient," you say.

You immediately want to take that back.

Charles responds by not responding. He reaches down to the grave and takes back one rose.

Then he responds by responding.

"There's nothing in it for me to have that conversation without you," he says. "I would have appreciated it if you were sharing this burden, frankly. You still get the same amount of his money as I do."

"Same amount?" you say. "I don't even know what to do with that. I've never in my life thought of Dad as an *amount*."

"Well, you should start," he says. "Because it's a pretty big number, even after we settle his long-term care."

"Big number?" you say. "Dad?"

Your father ran a small, independent publishing company. Hardly made any money from one year to the next, as far as you could tell. Mom worked for him and could not retire when she wanted to. Or so the story came to you. They always needed the money.

You tried publishing, too, because it was an easy job to find after college. Go work in the industry with the idea of taking over the business one day. Back when people still thought you might be good for something. But you hated it, passing the entire sunlit day at a windowless cubicle. Without a window, you had to take it on faith that the sun rose and set every day. A terrible position for a skeptic.

Turns out that that wasn't unique to the publishing industry. You quickly came to realize that the nine-to-five work life was indeed nine to five (at least, often to seven or eight). You wanted no part of it. So you, as you used to write in letters and post-cards when you were young and full of yourself, "set to wandering." You would never say that now—you're only admitting it here because it is just that, an admission.

Charles tells you that your father's estate is worth $1.8 million. Apparently, the whole time he was living as a miser, he was investing uncannily well in the stock market, wanting only to leave something to his sons.

"Guilt must perform brilliantly in the market," Charles says.

You can't quite read his tone, whether he's angry or feeling sorry for Dad, or whether he's simply as baffled as you are about the whole thing. The stock market? One point eight million dollars? Nothing is more incongruous to the family you knew.

You wish you could tell him: Don't feel guilty on our account, Dad. What did we miss out on? The chance to be saddled with the name Snodgrass, his actual surname? Instead, you got the name Robbie Wills. Elegant and easy. Plain and simple. When you found out, when he revealed the truth to you and Charles after your mother died, you could see in hindsight many clues to the fraudulence of the family name. You never met any Wills relatives—both your parents, the story went, were only children whose parents had died before the grandchildren were born. You never had any sense of the name's heritage, its provenance, not even what country your parents were from. The question was asked plenty in grade school, and your parents always changed the subject. Again, it's only in hindsight that you realize they changed the subject. At the time, the subject always seemed to change *itself*. The first time the question arose, during studies of immigration in second or third grade, you just went ahead and said England. You had no idea, and England was the only other country you could name. For your fourth-grade report "What My Heritage Means to Me," you still remember copying sentences about England out of the encyclopedia. The north of England is covered in moorland. The Queen is guarded by the Yeomen of the Guard, also known as Beefeaters. The Union

Jack is a combination of the flags of England, Scotland and Ireland. Great Britain has been an island for about eight thousand years. Apparently, that was what your heritage meant to you.

Okay, what else? What else did you deny us, Dad? Not a sense of right and wrong. Despite the fact that your father questioned his own moral authority, you and Charles learned an abiding sense of right and wrong. You don't always do right, but you always *know* it. Certain people, certain women, could probably read your knowledge of right and wrong in tire tracks on the road.

Charles, as far as you can tell, has a by-the-book sense of right and wrong. For himself and others. You could call it judgmental (indeed you have, several times). And, although it drives you crazy, you would have to say that it is something a father, especially your father, could be proud of.

All these things to tell your father, but you've missed your chance. You're the wanderer, and you've missed your chance. You wonder if Charles had a reconciling, an emotional one, a spiritual one, beyond settling the estate. You wonder if he even cares about such things. Your mother used to joke that Charles was made of wood, meaning that he could miss obvious emotional cues. Talk about a self-fulfilling prophecy; Charles grew up to be a real stiff.

That crow shouts, screeches, Poe-like, from a single tree at the edge of the cemetery. *You did what you had to do, Dad*, you say to yourself.

You look back to the grave. You're standing about three feet from the headstone, which puts you about on her abdomen. You step lightly to the side. *Sorry, Mom.*

She was part of it, too. She waited in the car, apparently. She didn't know there would be shooting, your father told you, or she would never have gotten in that car. "I'm guilty for that," he said. "If anything, I'm guilty for that." She waited in the car; he waited at the door. Dad as lookout is a dispiriting image, as is Dad running away once shots started firing.

"Are we ready?" Charles says. He nods; this isn't a question. He starts back to the cars, and you follow. As you weave among graves, you hope you're not stepping on anyone. You think of all ground as sacred because you can't be sure exactly how much room each casket takes up.

One point eight, divided by two? Nine hundred thousand dollars. You don't even really know what that means. Probably not as much as one would hope, with estate taxes and whatever else eats away at a fortune (you wouldn't know), but whatever it is, it's a lot more than you've ever had before.

This woman you've been dating—well, *running from*—you'll ask her to marry you. With a ridiculously showy diamond ring (do women still like that?), you'll buy her away from the perfectly satisfying future she could have had with another, more stable man but one who would never be as full of surprises as you. You'll get a job, a good job . . . Wait, that's one thing you don't have to do anymore. But you'll get a purpose. Maybe you'll buy a small-town newspaper. That's something you've always wanted to do. You'll hire smart young journalists, you'll give them leadership, encouragement and freedom. And a good salary. All the things you would have loved when you were starting out in your career.

You've done it. You've gone ahead and bypassed the need for a career. At least you won't be running from one anymore.

The crow flies off, flapping loudly to call attention to itself one last time—*Evermore*—then out of sight.

"What are you going to do with that one rose?" you ask your brother. "Give it to someone else? Are you two-timing Mom?" Or maybe he's trying to save it from the certain black winter death of the others.

"They threw in an extra, baker's dozen, at the flower shop," he says. "I don't want to leave thirteen. Bad luck."

Charles has parked off the road, on the grounds of the cemetery. From the grave, you wondered how he could have parked next to you and not behind you, since the road is only one lane. You hope his car is not pressing on the head or feet of someone's loved one. *Made of wood*, damn brother of yours.

As you get into your Honda Civic you say, "Bad luck? She's already dead, Charles."

"All the more reason." He gets into the Lexus leased for him by the mayor's office.

On your passenger's seat are flowers, too, a greengrocer bouquet, which you were going to leave upon leaving. But now it seems puny, leaving eight or ten daisies and carnations, and one proud lily, whose scent has filled your car, pervasive, smelling to you like false hope. That's the cynic in you. Someone else might read it as actual hope. Even in the greengrocer's, it gave you a headache, but you thought your mother would like it. You can imagine her in the kitchen, turning her head to the light-filled front window and saying *Pretty*, thinking no one was listening.

Robbie, a wanderer with a dream and now a million dollars. Daniel had written that before he himself had come into his own portion of a million dollars. He was sure no one would believe the coincidence, should there ever be someone who both read his novel and knew of Sylvan Street's secret. He had trouble believing it himself.

As on every weekday for the last three and a half months, he spent his Cheever commute in another world. He began writing a novel years ago but never found the time and space to work on it. Now, with fifty minutes until the train approached the small railroad bridge at the river's bend into Ashley-on-Hudson, he could clock almost two hours a day.

His stop was next. He shut down his computer, put it in the bag, slung the bag over his shoulder and walked to the train's doors, knowing exactly how many steps it would be. He always sat in the same seat in the same car. Habit—the commuter's code of conduct.

He stepped onto the platform and stopped in his tracks, his fellow travelers crowding past him. "Oh, my God," he said. How on earth had it taken him so long, more than a week since he unpacked the money, to realize this? "I'm quitting my job." He said this out loud, to no one but himself.

He would write full-time. Not much more than one year's salary, but tax free. A tax-free, year-long gamble.

Now that he'd realized, he couldn't believe he hadn't pictured this as soon as he put pencil to paper and written a sum: *Hansen/Yaniv, $210,525*. If only he'd realized earlier. If only he'd made his claim on the money before his wife made hers—giving it to a good cause, a cause to which, he was sure, she was now absolutely committed.

Mightn't he talk her into investing in him instead, his potential talent as a novelist? *There's your good cause right there, honey*. He knew she found advertising morally ambiguous. (Call it "branding" if you want, but she knew, as he did, that the two were essentially the same thing.) Let him liberate the family from the specious world of advertising by writing the Great American Novel.

He would tell her right when he got home. Or as soon as he figured out how to state his case. His marriage had grown increasingly tactical, a constant staking out of territory. Shoshanna had already staked hers.

17

Painkillers

—Guy says he's your brother. Or cousin. He's hurt.

Took Nishal a couple minutes. *Paramedic? Brother?* Phone call at two in the morning.

—Gotta get him. Or we'll have to leave him. Don't have a name, and he's refusing hospital. Wait, my partner's saying . . . apparently he's saying 'Tumor.' That mean anything to you?"

Paramedics. Toomer. Swirling picture of a military hospital back in their country. Little Toomer. Three, four. His father, Toomer's, swore it was a mistake.

In a blur, Nishal got dressed and drove to the address he was told. Out by the Truck. Luckily, Nishal could drive these particular roads in his sleep.

A jumble again. Middle of the night knocking loose past and present. Nishal, in the backseat, holding Toomer's head in his lap. In the front seat, Toomer's mother, crying, and Nishal's mother cursing and yelling, *I'm going to kill him. If you don't, Mami, I swear I will. I don't care if he is your husband.*

Fourth or fifth time Toomer went to the hospital, his father went to jail. Both boys off at once, said the ladies in town. Not blaming his father. That had been Toomer's mother's greatest worry, that people would blame his father. To side against the father was to side against the family.

Now, not a hospital at all. An ambulance on the side of the road. Lit up. Guiding him in from the dark fog.

He got out of his car. Stepped lightly. Felt strange. A setup? He peeked into the ambulance. A woman, back to him, tending to tubes and a body. She whipped around when she heard him.

—You him?

—Yes, ma'am.

She let him in. The light hurt his eyes. *Titi.* Eyes swollen shut, cheek bloodied and bruised, tube in his nose and hand. Chest bloomed bruises.

—Your cousin—or brother, we weren't clear—apparently was walking home from a date—girl apparently took the car, they had a fight—and some kids, white kids, attacked him, called him names, racial slurs, beat him up.

Nishal sat down. The woman kept talking.

—First, we thought gang. Found a pink scarf, bloodied, near the victim. Found no match, though, in the PD's gang symbols handbook. Which doesn't mean it couldn't be local. You know, some freelance activity.

—He's not in a gang.

She nodded, took him at his word.

—We got a 911 call from a passing motorist, saw what

he thought was garbage on the side of the road, but then he thought he might have seen a head and an arm. Someone *in* a garbage bag? Hit-and-run? By the time we arrived, your cousin, or is it brother—?

Nishal set her straight on his country's concept of cousin brother.

—Conscious and breathing, but low and low, on both counts. Multiple lacerations and contusions. He accepted treatment up to a point. Then he refused. Refused to go to a hospital. AMA. Against medical advice.

—We figure he's undocumented.

This, from a guy sitting on the curb. He startled Nishal, who thought it was just the woman. (Although it had been a man who'd called him.)

She explained:—My partner. He's doing some paperwork while we waited for you.

The partner stood up, joined them. Took over the talking.

—We don't usually do this, even if they're undocumented. Supposed to take them to the hospital, let the hospital make the call.

Bless the girl. She jumped right in:—But poor guy, your cousin brother, he's been through enough. So we just said to each other, This kid's been through enough. Let's call the contact number. Let's patch him up, and let's let him be.

—So here he be. And he be your problem now.

The girl smiled to Nishal, apologizing for her partner.

—If you want us to take him to the hospital, that's okay with us. He's on some pretty serious painkillers, so he won't exactly know the difference.

Guy piped up:—He'll be okay. He'll hurt like hell for a while, and I'd check up on him for the next couple nights, make sure his breathing doesn't get clogged by his healing, if you know what I mean.

Nishal didn't know what he meant. But he knew enough to know he should not take Toomer home with him. Look at him. Clipped to a pulp. But at least here in this ambulance, he was halfway to decent care. Tended and clean, laid out on a fresh white sheet. Had bandages where he should. Tiny, taped stitches at his eye.

Nishal couldn't do any of this in the apartment. Didn't even have an extra bed for his *titi*.

The male paramedic was sliding tubes out of Toomer, taping him closed.

—Just so as you know, fella, this means we wash our hands of your brother. Anyone asks us, we say, RT. Refused treatment. We'll overinventory to make this dose of painkillers go away. Get your own, though. The kid will hurt, capital *H-u-r-t*.

The girl was shaking her head.

—Whoever did this to him should be arrested. I hate to just—

—That's not on us, sweetheart.

The guy opened Nishal's car door to lay his burden of a little cousin brother on the backseat.

—He probably won't bleed much, if you're worried about your car.

Nishal waited until a decent hour to call Natasha. Took him a few tries. First time, she hung up. Next time, she was already cursing when she picked up the phone. A running start, Toomer would call it, when Natasha got going like that.

—I know that bastard put you up to it. Don't call any-more.

Third try, Nishal snuck in the news right away:—He's hurt.

—Fuck him, hurt.

Click.

One more try. Nishal tried for that running start himself:—Attacked, beaten, bleeding. Almost dead.

—You better not be telling me no stories, Nishal, or God help you, I can give as good as I can get.

She didn't know Nishal well enough to know that he didn't tell stories.

—Where is he?

Tasha still didn't trust Nishal. She looked around the living room for Toomer.

—The bed.

Nishal was surprised to learn that she didn't know where the bedroom was. In this one-bedroom apartment. Least it put to rest Nishal's suspicion that Toomer and Natasha had sex in his bed when he was at work.

Nishal led her to the bedroom.

—Shit. T?

She sat on the edge of the bed. Jumped up when it *crunched*.

—That his bones? Am I hurting him?

Newspaper. Nishal didn't know what to do, didn't have much to work with. He took newspaper from his neighbors' recycling bin, put it under the bedsheet.

—Like a puppy.

Natasha seemed to cheer herself up with this.

A puppy? Wouldn't that be nice, instead of a grown man who couldn't take care of himself?

Natasha's sister was studying to be a nurse. Charysse. Had a break in classes this afternoon, came to the apartment with her kit. Nishal wondered how far along she was in her training. She named everything as she took it out of her bag. Like she was reminding herself.

—Sprague stethoscope. Aneroid sphygmomanometer. Rigid-tip digital thermometer. Lister bandage scissors.

Nishal was entranced. Other than the reciting, she was silent. Working patiently and diligently. Natasha kept sitting down next to her, crunching the newspaper, until Charysse finally sent her to the store for gauze pads.

Once Natasha was gone, Charysse, who hadn't said a word to Nishal, asked, Is he a drug dealer?

—No, ma'am.

—Why'd he get so beat up?

She had to ask? Had to ask why a skinny undocumented brown kid with no job and no money, a wool hat and a hoodie, jeans hanging off his ass . . . why that kid got beaten up?

Was she stupid, or did she live in a better world than he did?

—White kids.

Charysse nodded at this and went on with her work. Fingered around one of the bandages on his chest. Took out a roll of tape and big box of gauze pads.

—Didn't you just send Natasha to the store for those?

—Had to get her out of here. She was blocking my light and making me nervous.

She smiled. He smiled back.

—I'll need that other box at some point, anyway, looks of this. Want to learn how to change a dressing?

Sorry you got clipped, titi. *But this girl!*

And, not to be selfish: *Look, you finally got the bed.*

TWO

18

The Sushi Lesson

It was April's sixteenth birthday, and she was headed to the Manor House for a sushi lesson—her present from Maggie.

"Don't sixteen-year-olds want pizza anymore?" Jen said.

April had made the mistake of stopping in the kitchen to tell her mother what she was doing. Jen sat at the wraparound counter paying bills, with Tiger at her feet, untying her sneakers and tugging the laces. Jen was in the kitchen not because she ever cooked—that was Keith's job—but because it was the center of the house.

"Mom," April said, "this isn't the same world it was when you were sixteen."

"A hundred years ago," Jen said.

"Sixteen years ago," April corrected.

"Big difference," Keith said, coming in from the garage. Every door in this house seemed to lead into the kitchen. "Although I have no idea what you girls are talking about."

"I'm going to the Manor House to learn sushi," April said. "That's what I want for my birthday dinner tonight."

"I could grill," Keith offered. "Put your old dad to work—burgers, dogs. I could do steak for you, baby, if you want. You only turn sixteen once."

"If you're lucky," Jen said, then burst out laughing.

April shook her head, held her tongue and went out the door.

It had been years since April thought of this as a hill, the short road to the Manor House. Not since she was five, learning to ride a two-wheeler. Then, Sylvan Street was all hill. Heading up, she would zig and zag, trying to stay upright. Going down, she raced like the wind. Often, she was able to stop only by crashing up onto her lawn. As she walked up the hill now, she remembered the feeling of downhill, steadily gaining speed, the mounting sense of both terror and release because she knew what was going to happen, *crash*, and knew that she could not prevent it.

She squinted until the Manor House looked tiny, as if it were far away, looming on a different plane. A changeable-weather mist had gathered in the boxwoods in front of the house, and she imagined a Disney castle floating over clouds. Why did Maggie and Billy live in such a big house by themselves, when five kids and two parents were squished into the Margolises' house? She didn't mind sleeping in the basement—a whole floor, even a bathroom, of her own, although it had no shower so it was kind of useless. The twins didn't mind sharing a bedroom *with each other*, but they didn't want Kelli there. So half the time she'd wander off, to the foot of her parents' bed, the racetrack rug next to Tiger's race car bed or, more and more, to the beanbag in April's basement.

Maybe April should move into the Manor House. Her parents could pay rent or something, or she would help Maggie cook or do things around the house, or keep her company, which was what Maggie once said was all she wanted. Then Kelli could move into the basement bedroom, and everyone would be happy.

Including Maggie, to judge from how she greeted April at the side door. A big hug and a genuine excitement in her voice about the fish she'd bought and the sushi tools she had unearthed, a wedding present that they'd never once used.

Maggie took the tuna from the refrigerator and slapped it down on the center-island butcher block. "Our lesson is going to be a little incomplete," she said. "Learning sushi should really start at the fish market. Or even the sea—it should be that fresh. But, as you can see, I've already caught us some fish at Dave's-on-Hudson. So we'll start with step two—the knife." Maggie pulled the nine-inch knife from the rack. "This should do."

"This is so nice of you," April said.

"It's a birthday present," Maggie said. "You only turn sixteen once."

"If you're lucky," April said, and giggled nervously.

"True enough."

April's face changed.

"What, April? What's the matter?"

"I just made the same joke as my mother," April said.

"And I didn't even get the joke, or whatever it was, when she said it."

"A girl turning into her mother?" Maggie said. "Stop the presses." She pulled the sharpening rod off the knife rack. "This is when it starts. Sixteen's right about when it starts."

"Aaach," April said.

"Daughters unite." Maggie raised the knife and sharpener overhead.

April looked confused. "Oh," she said after a minute. "That's funny. I forgot that you're a daughter, too. I was thinking of you only as a mother."

"Although I'm not," Maggie said.

April scrunched her dark, downy eyebrows.

"No kids," Maggie clarified.

"Oh, duh," April said, touching her forehead. "I didn't really think of that. Makes you wonder if you really need kids to be a mother."

Maggie swiped knife against steel. *Swish, swish, swish.* The harmonic undertones of productivity took her back to Maine, to the giant old, cold kitchen where she had learned to cook from Glacia the Scandinavian, as Maggie's father called her. Glacia was the only one in that house who seemed to know what to do with a child. She always gave little Maggie a kitchen chore, no matter how meaningless. When Maggie was a toddler, Glacia would set down two bowls, one empty, one filled with new potatoes, and have Maggie transfer them back and forth.

After what was called "the loss in the house," Maggie graduated to dumping premeasured ingredients—flour, sugar, water, oil, whiskey, rum—into mixtures. Glacia's specialty was something called whiskey pie (Maggie could no longer remember whether it was sweet or savory), which, while it was cooking, made the whole kitchen smell like her mother.

Soon Maggie was a full-fledged sous chef, slicing and dicing and chopping. Potatoes, always potatoes, garlic, herbs, tomatoes, lots of hard-boiled eggs.

"I should pay that Glacia less if Maggie's doing all the work," Mother once said.

"Or pay her more," Father said, "for doing double duty as a babysitter."

Mother the sinner and Father the saint, as Maggie had it.

"Okay, my dear," Maggie said to April. "You should learn to sharpen a kitchen knife. We can work out a little of this mother-daughter aggression. Watch and learn." She held the edge of the knife against honing steel. "The key is twenty degrees. Once you get the feel of twenty degrees, you're a cook for life."

She swiped back and forth a couple of times, then handed the weaponry to April. "Now you."

April took the knife and sharpener tentatively, with a screwed-up face.

Was this all right, Maggie wondered, giving a sixteen-year-old a knife? She wrapped her arms around April from behind, to guide the sharpening.

"You know how you said about my mom?" April said. "About girls turning into their mothers?"

"Mmm-hmm." Maggie set April's knife hand at twenty degrees and guided her through a few gentle swipes.

"You know what my mom was doing when she was sixteen?"

Drugs or drinking, Maggie imagined. Like any other sixteen-year-old back in the day. Pretty, social, suburban kid like Jenny,

with little drive and seemingly simple notions of what consti-
tuted a good time.

"Having me," April said.

"Wow," Maggie said, with genuine surprise, although a little publicly accessible math could have already told her that.
"Good for her."

April shook her head. "Not really." She stiffened her arms.
"I don't think I should do this," she said. "I feel like I'm ruining
your knife."

"No, you're right." Maggie took the knife back quickly,
swiped a few more unnecessary times for the subject-changing
energy of it.

"What?"

April was blinking back tears. "I'm a bad daughter," she said.

"Impossible."

"Uh-huh. I'm wishing *you* were my mother."

"Hoh, no," Maggie said. "You'd turn into me, and then
where would you be? Now, let's slice some fish."

Maggie motioned April back into an apprentice's embrace.
"Twenty degrees. Like I say, twenty degrees and you're a cook.
Start like this, at a right angle." She set April's knife hand
again. She would be a terrible mother, wouldn't she, always
taking over, even if it *was* a $140 knife and a $50 piece of toro?

"Good," Maggie continued. "Then cut it in half, to forty-
five. Cut that in half again, and it's twenty."

"Twenty-two and a half, to be exact." Janic was in the
kitchen doorway.

"Hey, neighbor," Maggie said, overloud, feeling *caught*.
"Looking for my husband?"

"Unless one of you beautiful women wants to take me on in chess."

"We're making sushi," April said, with a trill of pride.

"Ah, the life of the upper classes," Janic said.

"It's a special occasion," Maggie said. "Today, April is sweet sixteen."

"You are sweet," Janic said to April. "But sixteen already? My goodness."

"I'd say, '*Only* sixteen?'" Maggie said. "I think April's an old soul."

"Is that a good thing or a bad thing?" April said.

"Good," Maggie said. "Perfect."

"You stick with me, kid," Janic said, winking. "Us old souls have to stick together. But first—" He held up his chess set in inquiry.

"TV room," Maggie said. "Or studio."

"Of course," Janic said and went off to search.

Back to it. Sushi rice, tuna, nori. The first maki came out like a kid's art project, thick and lumpy. But each one got better. At April's surprisingly fierce insistence, Maggie held on to some of the finished sushi, and April took the rest home on a bamboo tray.

"My family's going to hate it," she said.

"Impossible," Maggie said. "You made it, so they will love it."

They did hate it. Keith was the only one who was the least bit game, making a big show out of how raw fish was good for a man's masculinity. "It puts hair on your chest, boy," he said to Tiger, in a vaguely John Wayne accent.

"I want Farmer John cheese," Tiger said.

"It's not pasta, Tige," April said. "It's sushi."

Kelli was under the table, having none of it, and the twins were staring at the sushi, poking it, waiting for something.

"It's not alive," April said.

"Mom said it was," Brittany said.

"No, she didn't," April said.

Jen was nodding.

"God, Mom," April said. "It's not *alive*. It's raw. There's a difference."

"Excuse me, Julia Child," Jen said.

"Don't be fresh to your mother," Keith said.

"I'm not being fresh. She's being dumb."

"Enough," Keith said.

A scolding tension fell over the family.

Keith became oversolicitious. He ate his maki in exaggerated delight, closing his eyes sumptuously with each bite.

"Really good, Ape," he said. "Why don't we have this more often?"

"Because it costs, like, a hundred dollars," April said.

Keith punched his daughter lightly on the arm. "Chump change, chump."

"To be exact, it's not the money," Jen said. "It's just not *us*. Sushi? Come on, Keith. Last time I checked, we all preferred our food cooked."

"Stop," April said. She stood and stacked everyone's plates, dumping uneaten sushi after uneaten sushi into a mound on the top plate.

"Hey, I was eating that," Keith said.

"It's not that big of a deal," April said from the sink. "It's just for me. Not everybody else in this family. For me and Maggie. You never have to eat it again."

Billy and Maggie, on the other hand, loved it. Maggie raised a toast to April.

"A toast should never be done in absentia," Billy said, repeating something he'd heard. "Unless the toastee is dead."

"Don't say that."

"So sensitive," he said, raising his glass. "To April, alive and well. Although I'm sure this is all Maggie. Maybe not this one"—he chopsticked a particularly lumpy maki—"but the rest of them. The perfect ones."

"I wouldn't have done any of it without the excuse of a sweet sixteen," Maggie said.

"Glad the kid had a birthday," Billy said.

Oh, no. Here came the tears. Whether it was the mention of a kid or a birthday, it didn't take much these days, with Maggie on the brink of her fortieth birthday.

Fortunately, Billy had a grand gesture up his sleeve. Paris for her birthday. He excused himself, went to the computer and printed out the e-tickets, along with a few other pieces of the itinerary—nine-course tasting menu at Guy Savoy, early Sunday dinner at L'Ami Louis, tour of Poilâne. He'd meant for it to be a surprise, a wind-up-at-the-airport thing. But she needed the grand gesture now. Offer it too late and the moment's gone. The grand gesture can only do so much. It cannot revive the dead.

"I got you your present," he said, returning to the kitchen with his piece of paper.

"Oy vey." Her terrible Maine Yiddish. "Slippers?"

Their first Christmas together, they both confessed to gift anxiety. They had been dating for only three months. How big a gift should they get one another, how intimate? What if one gave a bigger gift than the other, or a more revealing one? They found their answer while window-shopping—actually, just walking down the street, but in New York City, walking down the street in December *is* window-shopping. Looking in a pharmacy's window entirely full of slippers, Maggie remarked that slippers were the fruitcake of presents. They agreed on the spot to each get the other the most awful, *giftiest* slippers they could find.

Periodically, when one of the them was feeling unusually nostalgic, intimate or apologetic, a pair of gift-wrapped slippers would show up in the house. The tally, as Billy had it, was about even.

"Not slippers," he said. "But a place to wear them."

She picked up the paper. He wished he had an old-fashioned cardboard airplane ticket in an envelope.

"Good," she said. "Let's go to Paris. Start over, meet again. Do the whole thing over."

"Is it really so bad?" he said. "I mean, bracketing out—"

She shook her head fiercely. "How can you do that? Bracket it out?"

"Maybe we have a four-chambered heart for a reason, Mag," he said. "I can't do this anymore. Not right now. You've won for tonight, if that's what you want."

"That's *not* what I want."

"What do you want? Do you want to try again? You want to go through the whole damn thing again, only to end in a bloody mess?"

She shuddered. He hadn't meant it literally. But it was too late. She was gone, quicksilver Maggie, head down on crossed arms like a kindergartner. She wasn't sobbing, heaving, like she used to. Nothing. Just gone.

He put a hand on her head. "Mag. This beautiful head of yours. Give yourself a break."

She tensed up, pulled away.

He'd read an article—more accurately, he had been given an article to read—called "The Infertility Minefield." He agreed with the title, even if he hadn't read a word of the article.

"We'll drink that wine at that place," he said, sitting back down. "We'll go on that walk. We'll have that thing we have for breakfast at that café, the one with the killer espresso."

He slid an elbow over to hers. She pulled her arm in. He continued to go after her with his elbow until she poked back. Just a little, but something.

"What are you, in fifth grade?" she said, peeking her head back up.

He smiled. "I don't think you want to be talking about, ahem, *maturity*."

She swatted at his arm; he ducked and bobbed.

"Want me to tell you more about our trip?" he said.

"I just hope you used all the money," she said.

"Two-hundred-thousand-dollar trip?"

"I'm sure there are."

"Sorry, Mag. A lame nine grand, which until a minute ago I thought was pretty extravagant."

19

281 River Rise

"*A poem begins as a lump in the throat, a sense of wrong, a homesickness, a lovesickness. It finds the thought and the thought finds the words*," said Janic, paterfamilias, quoting Robert Frost. "Well, a child's place in the family begins in much the same way. As a lump in the throat or a lovesickness. Then the child finds the parents, or the parents find the child, and the whole lot of them finds this thing called family.

"So, to the newest members of the Levlovic family." Janic gestured to Renata and Ulaht and looked around for the boys, who had apparently left the room. The granddaughters remained expressionless, possibly overwhelmed, possibly underwhelmed.

"Welcome to Ashley-on-Hudson," Sally said. "Welcome home."

Raised glasses all around.

Bianca looked concerned. She leaned in to whisper to Byron.

"Pop," Byron said.

"Something wrong?" Janic said.

"I think it was a perfectly lovely toast," Sally said.

"It was, it was," Bianca said. "More than lovely. It's just that we have something to tell you."

"More kids?" Sally asked.

Bianca laughed. "No, I think we're done for now. But we're no longer Levlovices."

"What does that mean?" Sally said.

"Tell them, Byron," Bianca said. "Tell your parents."

"Oh," he said, as if it just occurred to him now. "We've changed our name."

"What name?" Janic said.

"Levlovic," Byron said.

"Our name?" Janic said. "My name?"

"Yes, Pop, that's what I'm trying to tell you," Byron said.

"We're Byron and Bianca Love," Bianca announced. The Levlovices of Astoria, Queens, were now the Loves of Ashley-on-Hudson. She put down her champagne glass and explained. "People are always mispronouncing Levlovic," she said. "You must get this all the time."

"Seventy years," Janic said, "and I hadn't given it a thought."

"I always say," Bianca went on, " 'It's pronounced Lev-*love*-ich, emphasis on *love*.' "

"That's a nice way to do it, Bianca," Sally said. Of course people were mispronouncing their last name. *Lev*-luh-vick, people wanted to say. But Sally hadn't given it much thought, either. Leave it to Bianca. Janic always said that her antennae were too sensitive for this mortal coil.

"Now," Bianca said, "as we try to explain to people how we're making this far-flung collection of people into a family, the same explanation came to me: 'Emphasis on *love*.' As you can imagine, once I heard that come out of my mouth, I knew we had to change our family name. Corny as it may seem, it's honest and hard-won."

"No one's saying that it's not," Sally said. "That's not it at all."

"Plus, it'll help the kids out," Byron chimed in, "free them at least a little from these names worthy of a U.N. translator. Lazlo Levlovic, the Hispanic Pole. Ulaht Levlovic, and a lifetime of *What, what, that's your name? How on earth do you spell that?*"

"I don't think a new last name will help much," Liz, Blake's wife, whispered to Sally. For some reason, Liz kept thinking her mother-in-law was on her side.

Then Liz asked, in her social voice, "How *do* you spell that? Ulaht. It's a beautiful name. Does it have an English translation?"

"It means Pride of the Nation in one of the local dialects." Bianca put her arm around her daughter's shoulder, pulled her close. "Now Pride of this Nation. This Family."

Ulaht still betrayed no emotion, just shifted foot to foot in her red watch plaid pinafore. Renata wore a similar one in green. Ulaht's blouse was busy with Scottie dogs, Renata's with evergreen trees. Had they gotten the blouses on this side of the ocean or that? Liz wondered, sotto voce, to Sally. "In either case," Liz went on in her whisper, "you're supposed to launder new clothes before wearing them. Sizing isn't good for the skin. And it's terrible for the drape."

"Hang *sizing*," Sally whispered back. "Look how proud they look."

There was a holographic quality to the girls, who seemed at once well older than their years—imagine, just a year or two away from a life as sex slaves—and younger, like little six- or seven-year-olds in stiff new dresses. Sally wasn't exactly sure what the girls' essence was right now, but pride seemed as good an invocation as any.

After the formal toasting, Sally stood in the corner of the dining room, pretending to be lost in thought but really eavesdropping on her sons. Ever since they were little, she delighted in catching them at being brothers, falling into easy conversation, sharing identical gestures, even fighting in that binary way that brothers fight.

Blake was complimenting his brother on the house. They were both looking around the barely furnished place, belongings from a two-bedroom apartment spread awfully thin. They'd moved in in record time; Byron jokingly called it a "shotgun mortgage." The owners had long ago left town and were desperate to close. Meanwhile, Byron and Bianca didn't want to pay another month's rent in Queens if they didn't have to.

"It hasn't really sunk in," Byron said. "I keep thinking, This is a nice place for a party, but we better get going soon, beat the Sunday traffic back to Queens."

"Welcome to the surreality of the American dream," Blake said.

"Sad," Byron said, "that I need Mom and Pop's help for the American dream. If that's what it is, our dream. I don't even know."

She leaned half a degree closer to see if either brother would probe further. *How can Mom and Pop afford it?*

Certainly, the boys were not picturing Mom and Pop living off cash from a trash bag in the basement. Or, more accurately, *not* living off it. Sally couldn't bring herself to get on bended knee and reach behind the washer for the cash. What would that make her, a beggar? A felon? Or simply part of a modern, transactional world? These days, Mom and Pop were living off what was in their wallets and pockets, in the quilted jelly jar by the coffee and in the rapidly dwindling checking account, $183 as of Friday, and retirement payments limping along, under fire from the plunging stock market.

Janic and the two girls sat on the only three chairs in the living room, marooned dining room chairs lined up on a diagonal. Jaq weaved in and out of and under the chairs, braiding grandfather and granddaughters together. Sally could have sworn the little boy's arms were longer than his legs, that he did look like a monkey.

He stopped, looked at his grandmother looking at him, bared his teeth with a hiss and ran off.

"Jaq," she called after him, "Grandma loves you."

Janic and the girls were silent, heads slightly bowed, with hands in their laps, as if in church. Janic looked like he'd just joined the family, too. Or like he was a minder, here to chaperone the girls from one heritage to another.

Sally read moral rectitude in Janic's straight back, head held high, although that might have been due to the stiff, formal dining chair he was sitting in. Janic had agreed that they should buy the house, but beyond that, he didn't want to talk about it. *No more Voice of Reason on this subject*, Sally thought.

Do you take this man, Janic Levlovic, to be your lawfully wedded husband, till death do you part? Over the course of forty-four years, Sally regularly caught sight of Janic and asked herself this question anew. So far, so good. She mouthed *I do*, feeling it between her tongue and the roof of her mouth, sealing her conviction.

20

Opportunity Knocks

With a graying mustache just this side of handlebar, and a fedora and trench coat, the man looked to Billy like someone who knocked on doors by occupation. Salesman, evangelist, pollster.

But Christian Gray was not salesman, evangelist nor pollster. He was a gallery owner who saw Billy's rocks from Deveau Hill and wanted to know where he showed. Christian Gray had a gallery in Chelsea and another one up the river, in Hudson. He had a patron who would *love* this sort of thing. These materials were usually too expensive for young artists, and the older, more established artists wouldn't work on commission for this particular patron he had in mind, who had a hundred-plus acres upstate and was establishing quite a collection. This man, a German who did nothing to give Germans a better name, wanted to "partner" on his commissions. It was a fantastic opportunity, Christian said. Was Billy interested in continuing the conversation?

"The paint-by-number patron," said Ash. "I'd run."

"Just did," Billy said, tapping his running shoe on the pavement.

He had stretched and stretched after his six-mile run, did a few sprints up and down the street, stretched some more. He had been baiting Ash, willing him out to the street so he could ask his advice in an incidental way.

"Tell me why," Billy said. "Why would you run away?"

"I wouldn't run away," Ash corrected. "I'd stay right where I was, but I would turn down this so-called offer. It depends what you want. I wouldn't do it because I want to be the only one who decides what I'm painting. Doesn't make sense to me otherwise."

"What kind of sense does it make in the first place?"

Ash looked disgusted. Billy did his just-kidding shrug.

"It would remind me too much of being a carpenter or a handyman," Ash said. "People ordering things from you. This dimension by that, to fit the wall next to the TV, over the desk, in the breakfast nook."

"But it would still be my work," Billy said. "So what if the guy says basalt or granite or white marble, square or round, big or small. The process is still mine. Presumably, that's why he's coming to me in the first place."

"Why *would* you do it?" Ash said. "Not for the money, I assume."

"May I remind you that money no longer divides us," Billy said.

"Oh, I think it still does."

Ash Flemming struck Billy as someone who passed up opportunity. He was pretty talented, from what Billy'd seen and heard, but he didn't seem to be going anywhere.

"Okay, man," Billy said, balancing on the curb, bouncing out a nascent cramp. "*Why would I take this deal?* For the purpose, I think. For the discipline."

"Go ahead, then," Ash said, "if that's what you need. But money doesn't mean purpose. Since I've gotten a basement full of cash, I'm finding it pretty hard to paint."

If Billy were being entirely honest, he'd say he was doing it for the chance to be discovered as better than he thought he was.

They met at the Christian Gray Lower Gallery in Chelsea, then walked across town for lunch at a new restaurant called Local. On this hot, but not too hot, summer afternoon, strolling through Madison Square Park, Billy felt young; anything was possible. He wondered why he'd ever left the city. The restaurant was full of handsome, confident, interesting-looking people. He'd never before been taken out to lunch as an artist. Studying the bookmark-size menu for the three-course prix fixe lunch, Billy thought that the commission was worth *this*, if nothing else: a moment at that rare confluence of youth and success.

Over lunch, Christian described the patron and his collection. Joachim Akeman had Noguchi, Serra, Calder, di Suvero. He'd been instrumental in discovering a young artist heralded as the next Calder, a Brooklynite named Paget Williams. But things had gone terribly wrong after the German and Paget Williams got involved romantically.

"I'm happily married," Billy said to Christian's inquiring look. "To a woman."

The waiter set down the first course, cilantro-infused sweet pea bisque with grass-scented chiffon. "Sorry to interrupt," the waiter said and recited the provenance of the soup's ingredients, which, according to this restaurant's conceit, were all locally grown on Tri-State farms.

When the waiter left, Christian reached over and all but touched Billy's cheek. "I'm afraid Joachim's going to love this face," he said.

"Flattering," Billy said, "but futile."

"I like to know things in advance," Christian said, "especially if it's going to affect my commission down the line."

"That's one thing that won't."

"Anything else?"

"I'm sure," Billy said, "but I couldn't begin to tell you what it is. Lack of talent, perhaps."

"No," Christian said. "That's never it. I've seen it all, and that's never what stands in the way. For my male artists, it's usually the sex that derails the art. Sex or drugs. For my women artists, it's the arrival of the Baby." He ballooned his hands to indicate a giant looming presence. "And for my old-timers, it's debilitating disease. Long and drawn out. For some reason, death never comes swiftly to my artists."

"Good to know," Billy said. "I'll make sure my health insurance is in order."

"Always a good idea." Christian ran a finger inside his empty soup cup. "My goodness, that's delicious. Grass! Something our bovine friends have known since prehistoric times."

He wiped his hands, then bent down to his bag for a notepad. "So," he said, tapping pen on paper, "tell me your secrets."

"I'm an open book," Billy said.

Christian waved a hand. "No, no, no. Never admit that," he said, "unless, of course, you're hiding something."

"Sorry to disappoint," Billy said, "but I've got nothing to hide."

"We'll find something," Christian said. "Or we'll make something up. Let's dig in. Tell me about Billy Cane. William, I presume?"

"R. William, technically."

"See," Christian said. "Hiding something already. What's the mysterious *R* for?"

"River." Billy had to dust it off. It had been so long since he'd uttered his given name.

Christian clapped his hands together like a Wallace Shawn character and gathered his sky blue ascot closer around his neck. "I love it. I hadn't dared hope for anything more exotic than Rafael. *River.* Really? Where did that come from, and why on earth don't you use it?"

Billy's parents were full-blown hippies, taking their inspiration for names, as they took most everything else, from the land around their cabin in the Oregon woods, where Billy grew up. It was between River and Birdsong for their firstborn, so he could be thankful for small favors. Mercifully, his kindergarten teacher, Mrs. Osgood, mixed up the order of his names and called him by the middle name, William (for his capitalist grandfather, whom his mother loved anyway), which stuck.

His sister, too, had jettisoned her hippie name, but much later in life. Married to a commodities trader in Chicago and president of her children's Lake Forest private day school, Willow Cane was now Pepper. Pepper Windsor. Last time he saw his sister, she was emaciated and papery, all bone structure and expensive clothes. Gone in name and spirit was the breezy Willow of old, the Willow whom Billy doted on and explored the world with, growing up.

Christian began his litany of questions:

Training, shows, awards?

Not much to speak of.

Prison?

"Not yet."

Childhood abuse?

"Spin again."

Substance abuse?

"Waiter, another martini."

"Not to worry," said Christian. "You're an undiscovered gem, rare in your purity. Joachim will love that."

Joachim Akeman was coming to town in a few weeks to round up his latest commissions, and Christian would arrange the meeting, first at 44 Deveau Hill Road, then at Joachim's Hilltop Farm, outside Hudson, where artist and patron would site the piece. Or pieces. One could always hope.

"This is his last trip to the States for a while, before open-heart surgery. That debilitating disease I mentioned goes for my patrons, too. He has quite a full schedule." Christian opened his BlackBerry. "The week of . . . August twenty-sixth."

"No, no," Billy said. "That's the one time I can't. I'm taking my wife to Paris for her fortieth birthday. Really, any other time

I'm just lying around the house waiting for paint to dry and the phone to ring."

Christian scrolled with his stylus, shaking his head. "He's here from the twenty-sixth to the thirty-first, and that's it. Then, back to Germany for the bypass."

"It'll have to be another time, then, I'm afraid," Billy said. If the German had a house in Hudson, less than an hour from Ashley, surely they could do this later.

"I'll tell you something, my undiscovered gem," Christian said. "Never put off meeting a big patron. Especially before he undergoes open-heart surgery, if you know what I mean. And always ask for the check up front."

21

Going Places

"Apparently, it's the only place in the world to really learn about food," Jenny reported as she got into bed. There was about a ten-minute window before Keith would be snoring to wake the dead.

"Paris?" Keith scowled. "How about 18 Sylvan Street? Someone could stand to learn about food in this house."

"How can we say no?" Jen said.

"What about school?" Keith said. "Isn't school starting soon?"

"They come back right before school."

"Convenient," Keith said. "Tell her we can't afford it."

"First of all, apparently she would pay," Jen said.

"Absolutely not—"

"And second of all, we *can* afford it," Jen said. "That's the hell of it all. More madness over this money."

"Tell her we can't afford to make it—what does your accountant call it?—a 'financial priority.' "

"Why do you always call him *my* accountant?" Jen whacked her pillow. How did the damn thing get so matted down? "Like I have a whole separate trust fund that needs managing or something. He's *our* accountant. He does our family's taxes. Why is that so hard for you to understand?"

"I just don't love him as much as you do. *He's so smart—he's Jewish.*" He did a high-pitched imitation that sounded nothing like Jenny.

She took two earplugs out of her bedside drawer, her nightly ritual to guard against her husband's snoring. "Two separate thoughts," she said. "Those were two very different conversations. He is so smart, and he happens to be Jewish. I only mentioned the Jewish part when you wanted him to do our taxes on Passover."

"I'd be happy with TurboTax on the Christian sabbath," Keith said.

"He saves us money in the long run. It wouldn't kill us to aspire up." She put in one earplug. "That's what my accountant means to me."

"That's all I'm saying," Keith said. "*Your* accountant."

"Fine," Jen said dismissively. "Settle for less." She moved to put the other earplug in, but Keith took her arm.

"Listen," he said. "A Porsche. A pool. I'd hardly say that's settling for less."

"Maybe it's a different kind of *less*," she said, removing the first earplug, rebalancing herself. Shouldn't they be going after something bigger? Travel the world, open up their children's eyes. Forget the Porsche. Forget the pool—even though she hated to give in to Maggie Cane on that front.

The other day, under the guise of looking for April, Jen went to ask Maggie about a pool, woman to woman. Keith had it all planned out. But Jen wanted their pool to be classy. For that, she was sorry but she trusted Maggie Cane over Keith Margolis.

To Jen's surprise, Maggie begged her not to do it. Please, Maggie said, if the whole streets decks itself out in bells and whistles, someone's bound to get suspicious. She told Jen that the Margolises may use the Canes' pool anytime they wanted.

"What do you mean by anytime?" Jen had pressed. "Can we go skinny-dipping in the middle of the night, Keith and I, when the kids are sleeping? Can we take Tige in there, even though he's not potty trained? Can the kids invite their friends?"

"We can work something out," Maggie said.

"You only say that because the answer's no. That's why we want our own pool."

"What about a schedule or something, splitting it fifty-fifty? You and Keith can come over whenever and for whatever you want."

"But it would always be *your* pool," Jen said. "I'm not trying to be difficult. I'm really not. But we want to enjoy a few things of our own. It's human nature."

"Human nature plus fifty thousand dollars—which, I have to say, *we* have some say over since it was on our property."

Maggie may have thought she'd gotten the last word. But the Margolises were breaking ground next week.

"Let's let her go," Jen said to Keith. "Let's let the poor kid go to Paris. Let her learn about food as God intended food to be, or whatever it was Maggie said. Let her see the world. Lord knows, she deserves it. She's been essentially tied down all her life, and she's only sixteen."

"*We* should take her," Keith said. "Forget Mrs. Cane. We'll take our own daughter to Paris."

"Why do you call her Mrs. Cane, Keith? We're practically the same age. She's only, like, five years older than me."

"She's *older* than you?"

"Shut up," Jen said, pushing in both earplugs.

He pretended to mouth something direly sentimental, which he often did right after she put her earplugs in.

"Good night, you big dope," she said. "And don't snore tonight or I'll leave you."

"Promises, promises," he said.

She could hear perfectly well, even with earplugs in.

They gave April their okay the next morning over breakfast. Saturday, and Keith was making pancakes.

"You have to go to Paris," Bethany taunted. "You have to learn French."

"With Mrs. Cane!" Brittany said.

And to think, Keith and Jen had been worried that the twins would be jealous.

"Mom," April complained.

"Why does everyone call her Mrs. Cane?" Jen said.

"That's not my point, Mom," April said.

"I know, but I can't help wondering why everyone calls her Mrs. Cane. Do her kids call me Mrs. Margolis? I don't think so."

The twins laughed. *She doesn't have kids!*

"Why doesn't she?" Keith said. "What's a woman like that doing with no kids? How old is she, anyway?"

"Forty, Dad," April said. "Paris is for her fortieth birthday."

"Maybe she's waiting for her husband to grow up," Keith said. "Hah. Have a nice wait."

April explained that Billy had bought the tickets for her birthday, and now he had this art thing to do.

"Cane? Really?" Keith said. "I didn't know he had it in him."

"We know, we know," Jen said. "You don't think Billy Cane has *anything* in him."

Maggie said he had been waiting all his life for a big break, April explained, so she was really happy for him to stay home and do that. But neither of them, Billy or Maggie, could see why she should have to stay home, too.

"She's taking *April* to Paris for her fortieth birthday?" Jen said.

"I'm right here, Mom," April said, waving her arms in front of her mother's eyes. "You don't have to talk about me like I'm not here."

"I'm just saying, baby, that that's strange," Jen said. "I hate to break it to you, but you're not coming on that romantic trip to Cabo with *me* on *my* fortieth birthday. Adults only, all the way."

Keith gave her a big, suggestive smile.

"Only if you play your cards right, buster," Jen said, laughing.

22

Kill or Be Killed

In days, just days, Toomer was up and around. Hurried every-thing. Sitting. Standing. Walking six steps to the living room. Walking the hallways. The dingy-ass streets around the apartment.

Had a feeling if he could get around, he could make some-thing happen. Had a feeling Bats might not be as batshit as everyone thought. How smart were runners? How smart did you have to be to outrun them? Have to be crazy, Nishal had said. But he never said you have to be a genius.

Tasha followed Toomer everywhere. Even to the bathroom. Stood outside the door, saying, In case he needed anything. Said she was scared he'd get jumped again. Or that one of his cuts would open and bleed him to death.

Come on. She was scared he was with someone else. Meeting another woman in the bathroom!

Truth: he was falling for someone else. Charysse. But not how

Tasha feared. Not a sex thing. Nothing like that. The *opposite*. Like a mother. Sacred. Beyond sex.

She wasn't even hot, Charysse. She was not for him. She was for his *jai*. It was about time Nishal got some.

Sometimes, when Charysse was teaching Nishal nursing— *Fold the end under itself . . . Swab in only one direction*—Toomer pretended to be asleep. Close his eyes and vacate. Leave the two of them alone. *Some date, brother, ha ha.* Besides, pretend to be asleep long enough, and Tasha would leave him alone.

Rumor was, Toomer'd gone crazy. Snapped. Killed a guy for looking at him wrong. For saying the wrong thing. Got jumped by the guy's friends, I hear. Five, six, eight. Ten guys. Football players. Cops. Gang fuckers. And he killed another one in *that* fight. And saved his own skinny ass. From death *and* from prison.

Pure Batista. Story might as well have a tag.

First day back to the parking lot. Couple of the older guys told him to go home.

—No one's going to hire you, beat and broken like that.

—Makes us all look bad.

—No one hires him anyway.

The *foráneos* laughed. Guys could have been talking about any of them.

Toomer squinted against the summer sun, barely feeling his now-closed butterfly stitches. Didn't know what he was doing there, but didn't know where else to go. Bandages were hot under his T-shirt. He wondered where time went. Just the other day, wasn't it, they were standing around in giant green down hunting jackets. Stamping boots in gathering snow. Clapping gloved hands to keep the blood flowing.

Day already this hot meant the time for getting hired was gone. *Foráneos* were just kicking around now. Nothing to do, nowhere to go.

Batista started talking again. Going on about the guys he knew, the runners. How something was going down.

—How long you been saying that, Bats?

—It was supposed to happen months ago. But, you know, shit happens. And now this shit's happening for real.

Noon. One. High, hot sun in the mean upstate sky. Everyone gone but the Haitian, used to heat, and Toomer, too fucked up to move. Truth was, they all came from this kind of heat, every last one of them, but some had left it farther behind than others.

Bats, turned out, had told his friends the runners about this guy Toomer. Crazy motherfucker who'd kill or be killed. Might want him with you. In case something goes down.

Toomer took a little bow for his friend. As in, *At your service*. If he didn't move too fast, nothing hurt. He had a good nurse. But Christ, he was weak.

Did they believe he was a crazy motherfucker who'd kill or be killed? Good to have around if you back into something heavy. Or was this a lightning-doesn't-strike-twice principle—keep a guy near you who's already been pulped, and you'll be spared?

Whatever it was, Toomer found himself in the backseat of a car heading up to the Canadian border to buy an impressive amount of pharma.

There were three other guys with him, two in the front, one in the back. No introductions, of course. But Toomer caught names. These *bakas*, supposed to keep everything DL, kept chawing. Nonstop talk. Guy in the backseat with him was Bibi, or Vivi. Driver was Alex, other guy was called Weevil.

Bibi, Vivi, was constantly at the edge of his seat. On his heels and toes to be part of the front seat conversation. Toomer felt sorry for the guy. Loser that they wouldn't let in the front seat. As for himself, backseat was exactly where he wanted to be.

—Hey, how's your guy back there?

Bibi looked at him. Nodded.

In a disoriented moment, Toomer wondered if these guys had been responsible for fucking him up. If they had sent the white frat boys in the red car. But no. *No.* He got hold of time again. That wasn't how it went.

—He's good. Our good-luck charm is good.

They all laughed. Nervous as shit.

So, they had him for luck. And if luck turned, maybe they'd use him for bait or barter. Who the hell knew what they were getting into? Use him as a hostage. Something to hold or give away, no big deal. In any case, less than human.

Or else they wouldn't have all three gotten out of the car together to go piss by the side of the road. Leaving Toomer, crazy motherfucker who'd kill or be killed, alone in the backseat.

23

April in Paris

"How long have you been up?" Maggie asked. She had a dim memory of April restless all night.

April stood at the window, holding back the gossamer curtain and pressing her nose to the glass. "Everything's pink," she marveled. "Pink and really pretty."

Maggie went to the window. The buildings and the sidewalks below were pearly with sunrise. No one was out except a thin woman in a long sweater pushing a baby carriage and two similarly dressed businessmen hurrying in opposite directions.

This was no time to be in Paris, August, with the rest of the tourists, with the heat. But this morning, still cool, still quiet, Maggie felt hopeful. About Paris. About travel. About herself. Maybe it was because she was with someone through whose eyes she would see this city for the first time. Maybe it was because she was away from her house. Not Billy, in particular, but the house. Sylvan Street. And the new secret. That was how she was thinking of it, as a secret rather than as money. A fleeting thought: when she got home, they'd turn theirs in to the police. No need to mention anyone else on the street. *Here it is, Officer. The briefcase from our pool shed. Just about a quarter full of cash. Couple hundred thousand dollars.* She'd ask for protection, surveillance, what have you, to be on the safe side.

April told Maggie she'd been up all night. She loved the hotel so much that she didn't want to miss a minute of it by going to sleep. "Plus," she said, raising her T-shirt to reveal a flesh-colored money belt, "this makes me nervous."

Maggie smiled. "Sweetie, you don't have to sleep with it. This is a pretty safe hotel. That's one thing five-star usually means."

April kept her hand on it, a dueler minding a holstered revolver. "It's kind of a lot," she said.

"We'll put it in the hotel safe, and you'll feel better," Maggie said. "Now, how much do you have?"

"Twelve thousand."

"Twelve thousand *what*?"

"Dollars," April said in a tiny voice.

"Oh, fuck," Maggie said, knocked a little dizzy. "What the hell—what on earth are you doing carrying twelve thousand dollars in cash across international borders?"

"I want to pay my share."

"Twelve thousand? Jesus." Maggie shook her head. "Don't you have parents? Where were your parents when you were packing all that cash?"

"They . . ."

"They gave it to you, didn't they?"

"They want me to pay my way," April said haltingly.

"First, it's nowhere near twelve thousand. But in any case,

a check at the end is what people do. What you've done, what your parents have done, puts us at risk in so many ways." Maggie's anger was visibly shrinking April. "With the cops *and* the robbers. We didn't declare it to customs, for starters. Nor would I have had you do that. But you know what happens if you're caught?"

April shook her head.

"They detain you and take the money," Maggie said. "I half wish they would. I don't know what we're going to do with it. You're certainly not walking around town with twelve thousand dollars. And I don't know if it's even legal to leave that much in a hotel safe. Jesus, they probably add you to some sort of terrorist watch list."

When she looked up, April was frozen in place, tears streaming down reddened cheeks.

"Oh, God. Come." Maggie motioned April to her. "Sometimes I forget how young you are."

April broke down in sobs, dampening Maggie's shoulder. Maggie felt a thrill of desire. Let April transfer the weight of the world to her, child to mother. April was no smaller than Maggie, but the pliable little thing seemed to disappear into Maggie's embrace.

Jen and Keith wouldn't miss *one* child. All the things Maggie could teach her. Starting with: don't smuggle twelve thousand dollars into a foreign country.

Maggie put her lips to April's hair, messy with sleeplessness. "Sixteen," Maggie whispered. "Just how old is sixteen?"

"Old enough to know better," April said dutifully.

"No, no," Maggie said. "I'm not fishing for that. I'm honestly just trying to remember. The older you get without having children, the less you can remember about them. So, at forty . . ." She drifted off.

"Happy birthday," April said, wiping her eyes.

"I'm trying to forget about my birthday."

"I thought Paris was a birthday present," April said.

Maggie smiled at the idea of the city of Paris itself as a birthday present. "When you get to be a certain age," she said, "you'll see. Birthday presents are so you can forget for a moment that you're another year older."

April nodded, although she couldn't have had any idea what Maggie was talking about.

"So my husband wisely thought, *Paris*," Maggie went on. "Where I can drown my sorrows in wine by the unmarked bottle at La Something or Other in Montparnasse. Or an *apéro* at that little place on the Left Bank that we called Apéro. I forget the real name, but it's at a spot where the Seine opens and catches a perfect reflection of sunset over the city."

Billy had a habit of forgetting place-names and directions. Whenever he tried to take them back somewhere—*That place with that fabulous* grande crème *is around this corner*—they more often than not rounded the corner to find . . . another part of the city entirely. But they'd always discover something else. That was something she loved about Billy. He didn't hold on to things, so he was free to discover again and again. Another great *grande crème, apéro*, langoustine, keyhole view of the city, tiny courtyard Rodin museum. Maggie, who had never been lost a day in her life, learned to love the liberty of this.

She should call Billy. What time was it at home? Midnight— he'd probably still be up, maybe out in his studio with a cup of coffee and a verboten cigarette. Or lying on the couch, legs kicked up over the arm, watching an old sci-fi movie. The Billy of old. When they first met, she'd described Billy to a friend as a blank slate. She'd meant it in a good way, although she wasn't deaf to the disparaging undertone. She'd meant that he was open to everything she wanted to do, to everywhere she wanted to go (despite all their travels, poor guy had still not been to Machu Picchu, the place he most wanted to go in the world). He was open to everywhere she wanted to live. He moved into her Upper West Side apartment even though he loved, for some reason, his scary Red Hook loft.

Then he moved with her to Ashley-on-Hudson, even though he loved the city. He'd agreed to have a child when she wanted, even though she knew that he was not yet through with being unencumbered. Maybe he'd been holding something back. Maybe that was the problem. She was thirty-five when they started trying—her window was closing—but he was only thirty, and a young thirty. Now he was a young thirty-five. He still wore a ski hat around the house half the time, for God's sake, like a college kid.

April was wilting. Sitting cross-legged on the daybed that was also to be her bed by night, she tipped over in slow motion, head finding pillow, legs still crossed.

"Pretzel." Maggie straightened April out and draped the blanket over her, even though Maggie knew that jet lag preyed on those who slept at the wrong time. April looked so sweet, so blissful, so childlike, drifting off on the five-star linen pillow. Maggie kissed her forehead, then kissed her warm, impossibly smooth cheek, letting her lips linger and the tension—and age— drain out of her until she, Maggie, felt like a blank slate.

*   *   *

Billy was indeed in his studio with a cup of coffee and a verboten cigarette. One verboten cigarette after another, as he tried
to figure out how he'd live up to the image he feared Christian
Gray was cultivating of him.

An artist? He was just a guy who chipped away at rocks, as
Ash Flemming had told the new neighbor. A rock chiseler, this
guy Cane. Who does he think he is, meeting with a patron who
collects Serra, Noguchi, Calder?

Christian Gray wanted him to go by the name River Cane.
Sounded like something from Exodus, or Revelation. *And lo,
when the Israelites crossed the River Cane, the soothsayers and
tale-tellers among them were smote by the hand of God. The
frauds and the quacks were sacrificed by the people for perpe-
trating untruths upon them.*

He faced his rock. Working title, *Coupling*. He'd found a
nice piece of basalt with a deep split. Human couples in mind,
he planned to treat the two almost-separated parts as differently
as he could, see how far he could push it and still have them
hold as a couple. He would pit and score one while finishing the
other to a high polish.

*And one among them took tool to rock, refusing to be sac-
rificed, despite his lamb's-blood marking as a fraud. He would
prove the marking wrong. He would battle Goliath, his demons
and doubts, and finally the critics. He would emerge victorious,
the next Serra, a new-generation Calder. How, the people asked,
did it take us so long to realize?*

He ran his hands over the rock, gauging its shape, its fullness, its hardness, where it might give, where it better wanted to be left alone. He stepped away to take in the whole of it.

What could he add to this? *Here, Joachim Akeman. Here's a brilliant piece of rock straight from the quarry. I can't do any better.*

Flemming was right. Billy did have good taste in rocks. This one, ruddy with flecks of black and umber and the deep split that refused to be entire, was art enough. He could pit and score the hell out of it, or burnish it until you could see your reflection, and what would he have? Nothing more meaningful or beautiful than what he had right now.

Why the hell not start over as River Cane? What did he have to lose?

Janic said something recently, during one of their chess sessions, about expectations and how to live with them. He'd been giving Billy some sound advice on the game, and Billy remarked on how Janic was always expected to say something judicious and wise.

"That must be quite a burden," Billy had said. "To live with other people's expectation that you will always tell them the right thing."

"Here's one thing I've realized," Janic said. "Living up to people's expectations has more to do with them than you." He couldn't tell you how often he was right or wrong these days, but because people expected him to be wise, in their eyes he was. Live with expectations long enough and other people make them come true.

"Resting on your laurels?" Billy'd said.

"I guess you could say that," Janic said. "And at age seventy, good for me."

Billy had let down his guard the rest of that game, let go of his edge. Janic won—not unusual; they were evenly matched—but Billy knew he had let the old man win. Unintended consequence of Janic's confession.

Now, Billy poured himself another cup of coffee even though it was the middle of the night, and lit himself another cigarette. He should have gone to Paris just for the ease of smoking, the lust of it, the joy. Maggie hated the linger of indoor smoke and banned it from the house and even the studio, which was his alone. The fact that he would have to endeavor to erase the smell before she got home sucked the fun out of smoking.

He circled his rock again, warily, daring it to reveal itself. Wait! The half-split rock was not a mismatched couple trying to hold together. That was all wrong. That was why it wasn't working. It was parent and child trying to split apart. *Parenting*. Rather than treating this as two different entities brought together, he'd treat the two pieces as one, then adjudge how different they would become upon splitting apart.

Pitted or polished? If this was a child striking out and a parent holding on, there'd be turbulence. That called for pitted. But there was a certain Madonna-and-child idyll he was after, a certain romance, more than the three a.m. feedings, the tantrums, the teenage insolence, the things that he and Maggie had enumerated as consolation each time they decided to stop trying. Let art make order out of chaos, presence out of absence.

He hit on it. He'd polish the outside edges: the unblemished surface of infant child coming into the world; the smooth isolation of parent aging out of the world. The closer you got to the split, the rougher the surfaces would be. Maybe the title would be *Letting Go*. Or *Holding On*.

The phone rang, jarring him back to the reality of his studio in the middle of the night. *What's wrong?*

"Hello?"

"Hey."

"You okay?"

"Yeah. You up?"

"Yeah," he said. "You sure you're okay?"

"Yeah."

They went on, tentatively making themselves present to one another, until they established each was awake, all right, missing the other but happy to be in this place at this time. Maggie explained that she'd gotten up early, April was still asleep and she was gambling that Billy, relishing his time alone, was up late in his studio.

"You know what I was thinking about?" he said, feeling reckless. "Kids."

"What about them?" Maggie said.

"Having them, having kids. Being parents."

"Who, us?"

It was impossible to discern her tone with all the space and time between them.

"Not exactly," he said, feeling a little less reckless. "More abstractly, I guess. My rocks, really."

"Your rocks?" she said. "Thanks a lot."

"Life imitates art?" he tried.

Nothing from her end.

He should have gone to Paris.

"Okay," she said after a minute. "I'll stay tuned." Her tone remained inscrutable. "Thanks for my trip. It's beautiful here. Hotel's great."

Then again, maybe he was right not to have gone. Perhaps, as with chiseling rocks, the better part of valor lay in leaving the subject alone. Maggie had leapt at the chance to invite April Margolis to take his place in the City of Lights. "How about someone your own age?" he'd said. "One of your friends from Manhattan who you haven't seen in so long. Or, Christ, even Jen Margolis, if you have to take a Margolis. What the hell are you doing, Mag?"

Now, on the phone, he asked, "How's your substitute husband?"

Maggie laughed. "What an odd image," she said. "She's sweet. She's so young!"

"That's what I've been trying to tell you," Billy said. "Looking for love in all the wrong places."

"I wish you were here," Maggie said.

"That bad?"

"No," she said. "It's good. I wish you were here, too, with me and April."

"One big happy family," he said.

"Are you smoking a cigarette right now?"

"Yup," he said.

"Not inside, I hope," she said.

"Nope," he said.

They lingered together for a moment, then said good-bye.

24

April in Paris *Encore*

As Maggie'd predicted, she had trouble getting April on Paris time once she'd let her sleep most of the first day away in the hotel. That night, April was up until the wee hours and was nearly impossible to awaken the next morning. But Maggie persisted. She sat her up on the daybed, made her eat a few bites of bright, buttery croissant and drink a few sips of fresh orange juice. She waved her tiny, potent espresso under April's nose. April finally got out of bed to avoid smelling the coffee.

What was Maggie doing in Paris with a teenager, someone who didn't even appreciate French coffee? Her husband had paid thousands of dollars for a five-star trip, and she was essentially babysitting. Maybe she should leave April in bed and power through Paris herself, like the days of old.

* * *

First stop, Eiffel Tower. Maggie capitulated to tourism for the sake of her young charge. Even though she'd been in Paris more than a dozen times and had lived here for a year during college, Maggie had never waited in the wraparound line to ride to the top of the tower. Just as, living in New York for all those years, she'd never been to the top of the Statue of Liberty, Empire State Building or World Trade Center. After 9/11, Maggie was one of the many cynical-turned-sentimental New Yorkers and ex–New Yorkers who lamented never having been to the observation deck and now, tragically, it was too late.

Shoulder to shoulder, hip to hip, she and April walked the Champ de Mars. They were about the same size, a height Maggie had been since fifth grade and April had been for a matter of minutes. She was changing so fast, as Maggie was surely not the first person to notice. Maggie wondered if they looked anything like mother and daughter. She could see green in April's hazel eyes, but it wasn't her, Maggie's, deep grass green. Green as the hills of Ireland, her father used to say. To *sing*, actually.

The age difference was right. If Maggie had had a child when she was supposed to, in her midtwenties, that child would be about sixteen. Maggie could not imagine having had a child sixteen years ago—or *for* sixteen years. Sixteen years ago she had just moved to New York after kicking around Providence for a couple of post-Brown years, Europe for another. She was dabbling in catering, in triathlons, in inappropriate men (depressives, brilliant, older, married). She had a clutch of girlfriends, mostly from college, who were fiercely devoted to one another and to their Sunday brunches in Soho, very *Sex and the City* before its time.

She could not imagine Jen Margolis's life, having been tied to April, and April to her, since Jen herself was sixteen.

Maggie recalled a story she'd read recently in the miasma of TTC and infertility chat rooms (always her first stop when she was getting back in the game): a couple was using a surrogate who, they'd just discovered, was only sixteen. She'd lied on all her paperwork, saying she was twenty-one. The prospective parents were horrified when they found out, in month five. They were on the horns of a moral dilemma, but the only course, they and the other chat room posters agreed, was to move forward. The teenager was already, as one poster wrote, "more than a little pregnant."

Maggie shifted her hand, which found April's hip. How impossibly skin-and-bones she was—and this from Maggie, who herself weighed all of 108 pounds. Maggie imagined what a body like April's, rosy and downright elastic, would do with a pregnancy. Expand buoyantly, then snap right back into shape.

As for Maggie, her knees hurt on long bike rides; her lower back, that complainatory mark of age, had started to make itself known. Every morning and night, she confronted the sagging skin around her eyes with increasingly expensive potions. She was sleeping less and less thoroughly, and it took more and more out of her to do just about anything out of the ordinary— throw a party, clean the house from top to bottom, travel. Had she missed her window, even if she could miraculously conceive?

To Maggie, hiring a surrogate had always smacked of exploitation. But now she could see that it smacked of something more understandable—desperation in the face of mortality.

The Eiffel Tower, which had been in view for some time,

suddenly struck Maggie as something to behold. "Voilà," she exclaimed. "*La Tour Eiffel.*"

April blinked herself out of sleepiness. "That's the Eiffel Tower? It's so . . . so . . . so *real*. I sometimes forget that we're really here, really in Paris. And not just watching a video. We can actually touch it, right, and go inside?"

April looked at Maggie so expectantly that Maggie couldn't help what she did next. She kissed April on the lips. To seal something between them, a promise to show April the world. Maggie ran a finger over April's lips and felt the miraculousness that she imagined motherhood would be—beholding a child so nascent and yet so perfectly formed. She tried to believe that the touch was maternal, all bond without barrier. The two of them were one, mother and child, cleaved together, cleaved apart.

Maggie kissed her again. April closed her eyes. Maggie cupped April's cheek, kissed with a hunger that startled both of them. Maggie touched her tongue to April's parted lips, to her tongue. April moaned a little.

Maggie pulled away, horrified. April blinked herself back to the here and now. Poor thing, poor April, world so blurred between sleep and waking, dream and reality. And now this.

Maggie squinted down the sunny *champ*. "Look at the line," she said, overloud. "Do you still want to go up?"

Wide-eyed, April scanned Maggie's face for the right answer. "If you do."

Maggie touched April's cheek again. Maggie could make everything all right with the right touch, a touch to show April that she, Maggie, would protect her from just this sort of thing, from the adult world coming at her too soon. Maggie traced April's features. April looked up at her, then quickly down.

"You're beautiful," Maggie whispered.

"I'm just me," April whispered. Or something like that. Maggie could barely hear her.

"Are you dating anyone?" Maggie said. "Any lucky boy I should know about?"

April shook her head.

"A lot of boys must have crushes on you."

April shook her head again, fitfully. "I don't want to end up like my stupid parents, having to stop their lives at sixteen to have a kid. Well, my dad was eighteen. He should have known better by two years."

Oh, God. Jen Margolis. And Keith. Maggie had thought of them as impediments before, but not to *this*. Maggie conjured a terribly real image of Keith Margolis undercover, prowling the madding crowd at the base of the tower. He wouldn't stand out one bit among the tourists until he fired his service revolver.

Maggie brushed at her knees as if she'd just gotten up from a fall. "So, *shall we*, to the tower?" She spoke with forced jocularity to cover up the embarrassing, if phantom, fall.

April nodded tentatively.

"You only turn forty once," Maggie said.

"If you're lucky," April said, in an odd, saucy tone. "As my mother would say."

Maggie started walking fast toward the tower, toward Keith Margolis and his service revolver. Let her face her punishment.

She heard April's footsteps behind her and walked faster. A skateboarder slalomed past, and another one, two . . . and three, a little one. April's girlish steps dissolved into life along the Champ de Mars. The quotidian, peaceable Field of War.

Maggie would stay here. She would never go home. She

would send April back by herself. Maggie had flown to Paris *par elle-même* when she was sixteen. Her parents sent her on a summer language-immersion trip to the Lycée Louis-le-Grand, but her mother had missed some paperwork and Maggie couldn't travel over with the group. She flew by herself and had all kinds of stories to tell when the plane was detoured by a bomb threat and made an unscheduled stop in Dublin.

April didn't know the first thing about the world. Maggie could just see her at JFK, with her twelve thousand dollars cash, unable to even get herself a taxi. There were about twelve thousand ways April could be taken advantage of. Why wasn't she smarter, savvier, better able to protect herself? She was sixteen. She was not a child.

Maggie heard running behind her. She took a steeling breath and turned around. A burly man jogged by. Maggie's dread had added a hundred pounds to April's feather weight.

The *champ* was bustling, constantly changing. Just because she could still clearly see the spot on the path where they had stopped a moment ago didn't mean April was still tethered there. Just because Maggie had heard April's heeling footsteps when she, Maggie, first started to speed-walk away didn't mean April was still connected to Maggie's trajectory. April could just as easily be the one running away. She was, after all, the teenager.

Maggie floated out of the moment and into a children's picture book, one of any number in which you, the reader, search Paris for someone or something—Adèle's brother Simon; Spaught, the visiting English bulldog; Madame Laville's heirloom chapeau—on a bright blue day against emerald grass amid a crowd much like this one, both touristic and native, filled with every sweet one-, two- or three-person narrative you could imagine. The lovers, vendors, families, schoolgirls. The prams, bicycles (one unicycle), skateboards. There was even an organ-grinder and his monkey.

But no April.

Maggie searched faces of people passing by. No one looked visibly stricken, which at least meant there hadn't been some grisly scene of murder and mayhem involving April, while she, Maggie, who was in charge, had been too self-absorbed to notice.

Had anyone else seen them kiss like that, anyone who'd been thinking of the pair of them as mother and daughter? Had some civic authority been summoned and taken April away for her protection, having also learned that, furthermore, Maggie lured the teenager to her house day after day with the promise of cooking lessons and expensive food, of quiet time and plenty of space to do homework or write in a journal, of all the time she wanted on the computer rather than sharing it with a houseful of kids, even the three-year-old brother shouting *Thomas the Tank Engine game! Thomas the Tank Engine game!*?

Maggie pressed onward to the tower and its shuffling line of tourists. Why had she brought April here? Why not to the out-of-the-way Saint Something or Other, whose tower had a fabulous, unscripted view of the city? They'd discovered the view from an everyday neighborhood church when Billy was, of all things, talking to a nun about two rocks embedded in the façade. Why hadn't Maggie taken April to her favorite balcony, a tucked-in third-floor spot on La Mouffe, at the home of an old college friend who'd lived here for years and whom Maggie had not even contacted to say she was coming to Paris?

Maybe she had come to the well-trodden base of the Eiffel

Tower to do exactly this, give April back. April was not Maggie's and never would be. This was Maggie's version of delivering an infant to church steps. A safe haven for the unwanted. Or, worse, for the much-wanted but impossible-to-keep. Ringed with guards, the place was teeming with harmless American families, probably scores of them from the Tri-State area, who could chaperone April to JFK and put her in a cab to Ashley-on-Hudson.

How had April gotten ahead of Maggie? There she was, April, pacing the line, scanning faces. Who was she looking for? She had her eye trained on the tallest heads in the line, although Maggie was no taller than she was.

"Where'd you go?" Maggie said.

"I was following you," April said, catching her breath. "But then I lost you."

Maggie'd hoped to come upon an April who looked clearly younger, or older, pure child or pure adult, something edifying. But no. Still a holographic teenager. Once again Maggie felt the confusing *eye of the beholder*.

"I lost *you*," Maggie said.

"Why were you walking so fast?" April said. "It was like you were running. Because of the line?"

"That's it," Maggie said. "I hate lines."

"Me, too," April said. "I was going to cut. I was looking for somewhere to cut. But I couldn't find anywhere. Couldn't find, I don't know, anyone that I knew or anything—"

She was talking fast, a nervous, inane teenager, someone Maggie'd never heard from before.

"Are you okay with what just happened?" Maggie said, nervous, too, and quite possibly inane.

"I love Paris," April said. "I love you." She blinked hard and winced visibly. Because what she was saying was true, Maggie wondered, or because it was false?

Maggie held April's face, kissed her on the crown of her head. "Me, too," she said.

They didn't talk for the rest of the afternoon, moving silently through the city. Now if an onlooker gave the pair a second thought, surely they would seem like mother and daughter, not sparing a word to each other, not needing to.

April did not sleep in the daybed that was also to be her bed by night. At Maggie's insistence, April slept on the high king bed with sheets so crisp and soft they felt like daybreak itself. Maggie took the daybed. She would have taken a bed of nails if it were available in a five-star hotel.

25

The Hole

Keith sat on the back steps, awaiting today's work crew for one of the last days of excavation. Even with a mini Bob rather than a full-scale tractor, which wouldn't fit the narrow passage to the yard, the digging was going swiftly, fingers crossed. Funny construction project, a pool—addition by subtraction.

There was no evidence elsewhere in the neighborhood of any construction, by addition or subtraction. Keith kept waiting for the construction and delivery trucks lumbering down Sylvan Street to stop at a house other than his. No one else was getting a sixty-four-inch plasma or that new supersilent dishwasher their wife had always wanted? No one else was putting in a pool or getting a new car, not even Ash Flemming, whose car you'd think would be embarrassing for a single guy?

True, probably no one else had Keith's cop-access to the gray market, not quite legal but not quite illegal, where he could spend his cash, no questions asked. Cash for a television, cash for a pool, cash for a car. He'd bought the two-year-old Porsche off a guy he knew from a case, a guy who would not question fifty-eight thousand dollars if Sergeant Margolis did not question the car.

Keith was getting less joy than he'd envisioned out of his 911. Inside the car, he was indeed a person transformed. Zero to sixty in four seconds. One, *one thousand*, two, *one thousand*, three, *one thousand*, four, *one thousand*. In those four seconds, he was one of the most powerful people on earth. His skin tingled from sheer horsepower, and his body stood at attention. Not *that* part of his body, although at a different time in his life there could have been something sexual about it.

The instant he got out of the car, however, the joy of Porsche ownership ceased, as thoroughly as if it had never existed. In the end, it was just a car. And, for the most part, a secret car. After that initial drive home, when he encountered Ash Flemming and Shoshanna Yaniv on the street, he drove it only before work or after the kids went to bed. Mostly what he did with the car was the valet ballet, moving Jen's minivan and his Honda down the narrow driveway and out onto the street, slipping the Porsche into the one-car garage, then putting everything back the way it was. Vice versa on the way out.

So he had a Porsche squirreled away in the garage, a hole in his backyard and a few grand appliances. Almost half their fortune down, and they had yet to put anything away for April's college, a bigger house or Jen's overall happiness. *Great job, Margolis.*

The way he was spending, he couldn't exactly quit his job.

That was okay; he liked his job. Cruising and, for a few years in the '90s, bicycling the zones of his town. Checking schools, inside, outside, behind and, in the case of HHC Middle School, under. Poking around parks and playgrounds, behind the movie theater, under the highway overpass. Checking doors, windows and locks on the few businesses in town, Upper and Lower Villages. He didn't know what he'd do without his daily beat. Guys like Flemming and Cane—what do they *do* all day? No job, no kids.

Kids. Don't mention one in particular in the Margolis house right now.

April had called from Paris about a half hour ago. She told her mother how much she was loving it, everything, all the sites, the art museums, the people, with everybody speaking French . . . the wine.

"Wine?" Jen said. "Did you turn twenty-one while you were in Paris?"

"Kids are allowed to drink in France," April said. "Kids as little as, like, eight or ten have wine. It's like juice for them."

"Tell your parents that it's good wine and that it's only with dinner," Jen heard Maggie say in the background. "No one can complain about a good Bordeaux with a steak au poivre."

"I don't care what French kids do," Jen said. "You're an American kid, and I don't want you drinking wine when you're only sixteen."

"Maggie says that you're supposed to drink wine with French food, that it makes the food—"

"I don't care what Maggie says," Jen said. "Unless she's the one who's going to put a roof over your head and buy you back-to-school clothes and struggle to get you the computer stuff you need for school."

"She would," April said. "And she wouldn't even call it a 'struggle.'"

Jen told Keith afterward that it had taken every muscle in her body to keep herself from hanging up the phone right then and there. Instead, she took three deep breaths, as she always encouraged the kids to do when they were mad, and was surprised to find that it worked. She composed herself, thought of the right thing to say and, miraculously, still had the opportunity to say it.

"There's nothing wrong with a little struggle," Jen said. "It's part of being a parent. Which your friend Maggie would know if she had kids of her own. Which she does not. It's a struggle of one kind or another, even if you have all the money in the world."

"Not with Maggie it's not."

"The only reason there's no struggle is because she's not actually your mother," Jen said, "and you're not actually her child."

"She doesn't even treat me like a child," April said.

Jen told Keith that she knew she'd won the argument because April sounded so childish in protesting that she was not a child.

"Maggie could stand to treat you more like a child," Jen said, "since technically you are one. She's not always right, you know. Sometimes your own dumb mother really does know best."

"You're right about one part of that," April said, and hung up the phone.

"Who does Maggie Cane think she is?" Jen said afterward, recounting the conversation to Keith. "*Tell them it's good wine, not that cheap stuff they probably drink.*"

"You mean, Who does she think *we* are?" Keith clarified.

"She thinks we're people who wouldn't know a good Bordeaux from a cheap whiskey if it hit us on the head," Jen said.

"Would we?"

"Goddamn it, Keith. I would. I don't know who *you* think we are, but my favorite drink happens to be a kir royale. I bet you didn't know that."

He shook his head.

"I bet you don't even know what a kir royale is," she said.

"I'll see that bet," he said, "and raise you an I-don't-care."

"It happens to be champagne with a drop of Chambord," she said.

He slapped his forehead. "I could have had a V8."

"I have kir royale all the time with my accountant," she said, "over steak au poivre in Paris. All the things you don't think we Margolises are capable of."

She doubted everything they were doing with the money. He knew full well he couldn't keep the Porsche out on the street, or even drive it in broad daylight, but she kept reminding him. She never touched the new plasma and kept sending the kids down to April's basement to watch the old TV. Last night before coming to bed, Jen peered out the window at the pool construction and said, "It looks like a mass grave."

Now Keith stood at the edge of the hole, facing the mound of excavated dirt. The gathering morning drew the scent of earth from the open ground. The pile held nothing more than roots and small chipped rocks. For the pool permit, the town had inspected and certified the dirt. He could sift through forever and never find a trace of human life.

There was no dusty orange haze rising from the rubble. It exhaled no ash for you to inhale, making you feel like you were in a room full of cheap bastards smoking cheap cigarettes. There was no need here, at 18 Sylvan Street, to keep your mouth shut and breathe through your nose to protect your teeth from slime and grit, until you worked your way over to a particularly putrid part of the pile and had to open your mouth and pinch shut your nose. No waves of urgency—*something's burning, someone's buried!*—followed by dread: the worst had already happened.

He'd spent a week on the pile, then he was asked to walk the perimeter, helping NYPD guard the hot zone from too many people who wanted to help. There were already people bringing food, water, clothing, supplies to each and every volunteer. There were people serving the people serving the volunteers, and people serving those people. There was a waiting list a mile long, he had heard, people milling around the Javits Center for a chance to help, even if help, at that point, meant basically folding and unfolding folding chairs, or carrying toilet paper into Porta-Johns—jobs that no one would want, would refuse to do, in everyday life. But it was not everyday life. It was some prehistoric, postfuturistic time, when everyone was united in a visceral mission to dig through the pile before them and find . . . and find . . . what, exactly? All he found, all anyone found, were ruins of a civilization. No one found the rescuer's holy grail: someone to lift an I-beam off of, pull free, deliver CPR to and visit in the hospital several days later, marveling at the resiliency of human life and the evidence of God on earth.

"You're still out here?" Jenny was at the back door.

"I'm just waiting on the pool guys. They're getting close to the end of excavation." He kicked dirt from the bottom of his sneakers.

"April just called again," Jen said.

"Everything okay?"

"Damn that kid. She called to say she was sorry. I can't even stay mad at her. She's too *good*."

The seismic rumbling of construction vehicles turned onto the street.

"Have you noticed," he said, "that every truck coming down this street is always headed to our house? Construction. Delivery. No one else seems to be building or buying anything."

"Maybe our neighbors are buying smaller things," Jen said. "Maybe they're more discreet than we are. Maybe they're buying expensive wine—French, of course, which we wouldn't know anything about. Or Picasso paintings. Diamond jewelry."

The convoy pulled up the driveway, and Keith rose to meet them. Behind the trucks, he spotted a car parking on the side of the road between the Canes' and Flemming's. He might have seen it on the street before, a rusted-out tan car, notably broken down for this neighborhood (although Flemming's old maroon Saturn was not much better, but at least Keith knew who that one belonged to). A lawn guy? A carpenter? Maybe one of his neighbors *was* doing something.

The golden rule of law enforcement: look for breaks in pattern. Keith quickly committed the clunker's license plate to memory.

Tiger, from out of nowhere, ran up the driveway shouting, "Pool truck, pool truck."

Jen put a hand over her eyes.

"Christ, Jen," Keith said. "Tiger," he yelled, "get away from those trucks. Come onto the grass."

"I'm going inside," Jen said.

"Take Tiger with you, would you?" Keith said. "I'm going to

head to the office soon. Do a little paperwork before my shift."
Run a license plate.

"Keep him out here," she said. "All he wants to do is watch construction. Like father, like son."

The pool was Jen's idea in the first place. Why did she ask for a pool if she wanted Picasso and diamonds? From the beginning, Keith had never been able to figure Jen out. When she told him over the phone sixteen and a half years ago that she was pregnant, he assumed she was calling him off his none-too-subtle attempt at courtship. But it turned out she was essentially giving herself to him. He'd reached for what was at hand, an invitation to the prom, and was shocked when she said yes.

Let people think Keith Margolis didn't know a good Bordeaux from a kir royale. He knew something more important—how to get what he wanted, even if it seemed out of his reach. First, Jen Hotten. Now, a Porsche and a pool. In his rare mystical moments, he felt that he was responsible for the money showing up in the Canes' pool shed, that his fruitful will had somehow put into play the chain of events, whatever they were, that catapulted the money from bad hands to good.

26

Deliverance

The three guys stood off the thruway down a sloping grade of grass. Faced the woods like a firing squad. One shoved another. *Bakas*. They'd probably start pissing on each other in a minute.

Hurt like hell to jump over the seat. Glass pain through his bruised ribs. *Sorry, Nurse Charysse*. All her hard work!

Driver must have been high. Guy left the keys in the ignition.

In the rearview mirror, Toomer watched their heads whip around. One after the other. Like levers on a machine.

Toomer pulled off the shoulder. Thought of the first set of motherfuckers, those white kids, as this car kicked up gravel and squealed onto the thruway. And Kevin. That huge, floating head. Toomer's father, too. Fist like a rock. Open palm like a sheet of burning metal.

Shit—*finally*. God had been listening all this time.

Toomer witnessed the arc of day turning into night. Golden light, the whole bit, a last gasp of daylight, then the sky darkened.

A "No U-Turn" sign showed him where to turn around. Get him off the road to Canada. And on the road to his proper Life's Journey. Heading south to his people. With a shitload of money in the trunk. Didn't know how much. Didn't care. It was more than he had when he woke up this morning. More than he had ten minutes ago.

Jesus. Moses. Mohammad. Fuck, Toomer didn't know much, but he knew that they were his forefathers on a mission to fulfill God's promise. Sacrificial but divine. Jesus got beaten to a pulp. Died with nails in his hands and thorns in his head. Moses wandered and wandered. Like he was stoned. And Mohammad. Everyone thought he was a crazy motherfucker.

Toomer was exhausted. Which was worse—upstate darkness or the random, piercing light of oncoming cars? A martyr's mission is not meant to be easy. Hours to go before he slept.

He would never sleep. Could never again pull up in front of the rat's-ass cinder-block apartment, throw open the door to see his *jai*, Tasha, Nurse Charysse. Couldn't just park this tin-can car around the side, take the bag out of the trunk, go up to the third floor and live out the rest of his life with his people.

He could deliver. He could provide salvation. But he himself could not stay. Like Moses.

He was following signs now. Like other martyrs before him. Burning bushes, stone elephants, loaves and fishes. Glowing white and green highway signs.

Light started to come up. Just a seam in the horizon, but enough to make him realize he was a vampire. Dead man driving. Stole money from drug runners? The balls of it knocked the breath out of him. Light in the head.

Daylight! He ran his tongue, his finger, over his teeth. Check for fangs.

He had to stash the money. Then come back when he figured out a plan. Or stash it for his *jai*, who had more to live for.

He cut off the main road. Turned left. Then right. Left again. Checkerboarding through what was clearly a better life than his. Sweet, neat houses, each one different from the next, sitting on plots of land big enough for you to feel ownership. Not too big, but big enough. Neighbor upon neighbor, with a little extra space.

He slowed. Turned onto a street whose sign he'd remember to read on the way out. He let his eyes linger on the big white house at the corner. Who lived in such a thing? Rich-ass, law-abiding family. No doubt. Kids in stiff, button-collar shirts.

Stopped the car. House was dark. Barely dawn. On the lawn stood three, four big rocks. Polished, pretty things. All quarried and fussed over. Not land-robbing things that kept people poor and crowded along the coast.

Across the lawn, a pool. A pool! Growing up, he dreamed about this. Having the escape of the sea in your very own yard.

He turned off the car. Opened the trunk, got the case. Wouldn't look now. No time, no time.

Hurried across the lawn, straining his ribs brutally. Pool gate was easy to open. Pool shed, too. Inside, it was clean and neat. He moved a couple of big pails, put the case behind, under. Time was short. But God was on his side. For the hour or two it would take Nishal to come, the case would be safe.

*   *   *

Toomer was halfway into morning when he felt the heat. Chest was a mass of flame. Heat spreading like water, slithering like snakes. Who knew what time it was? The clock, like the speedometer, was shit. Whole dashboard flickered when he sped up. Or slowed down.

White and green signs said PHILADELPHIA, PITTSBURGH. Kept these signs to himself when he called his *jai*.

—Doesn't matter where I am. Tell you where I *was*. Where you got to be.

He told Nishal he did it. Finally did it. Outran the runners. Stashed the money in a pool shed. Pretty little street called S-y-l-v-a-n Street. (He did remember to look at the sign.)

What town? Let him think. He remembered a bridge, a highway running by the river. Little streets. Big houses. Jewel blue swimming pool. Loaves, fishes. Stone elephants. Glow of sunrise. Wasn't that enough?

27

The Brothers Grim

Chapter 2: The Telling

"Tell me again," you say.

"Don't ever tell me again," Charles says.

As though he could stuff the genie back in the bottle.

"I want to understand," you say.

"I don't," Charles says. "I know too much already, enough to know what this does to me."

"To us all," your father says with a sad smile.

"There goes my career in politics," Charles says. "Kaput. Thanks, Dad."

"I gave you life," your father says. "So I guess a life in politics wouldn't have been in the cards *without* me, either."

He speaks more tenderly than the words might suggest, but Charles storms out of the room anyway.

You're not sure why you're feeling so big-hearted toward them. But you are. You don't begrudge your father his life-altering secret, and you don't begrudge your brother what might look to an outsider like selfishness. Okay, *is* selfishness. But it's perfectly justifiable. Having parents who've been wanted by the FBI for forty-some years pretty much disqualifies one from public office—for which Charles has spent his whole life preparing. And now, through no fault of his own, that life has vanished.

You say, "Tell me again, Dad. I'm really trying to understand."

Perhaps liberated by the absence of his elder son, your father speaks less like he's confessing a shameful secret and more like he's telling a damn good story. "*Imagine*," he says. "Imagine what it was like in those heady days, when two young Jewish kids thought we could change the world. We were full of potential, your mother and I. Young, handsome enough, smart. Overeducated, really, her with a degree in social work, mine in journalism—"

"I didn't know that." You thought your father was a scrapper who maybe iron-willed his way into publishing. You didn't think he was actually educated for the trade. And your mother? You'd been told—then again, maybe you assumed—that she didn't go to college, that she did what other women did in those days, left the outside world, the world of school and work, to have her children.

"Life is full of surprises, kid," your father says. "One being that your parents were maybe more interesting than this dull life."

He gestures around him. He still lives in the apartment where you grew up (although that will soon change, with the swift onset of Alzheimer's and the move to residential care, followed quickly by advanced residential care). Two pocket-sized bedrooms in Flatbush. You always wondered why they didn't complain about the place. "We're on top of each other," you and Charles said. "We can't get away from each other." And worse, only one bathroom.

"At least we're together as a family," your father would say. "Some people don't have that luxury."

You and Charles complained ad nauseam about the stairs. Fifth-floor walk-up. "Keeps us young," your mother would say. Until she died of an aneurysm at age sixty-three.

Come to think of it, which you are—coming to think of everything, now that nothing is as you've known it—just how old *was* your mother? She'd had, it turned out, a whole life before you and Charles were born. College, graduate school, maybe some years at a job, a career. Then, of course, you have to allow some time for a bank robbery gone deadly and life on the lam. And you thought the excitement in your mother's life was the sterling achievements of her two sons.

How you wish she were alive so you could give her face a good once-over and see what you've missed. Her age. Her edge. Something that would help you understand. You try to conjure her face, but it is already smudged unreliable by memory.

When you return to the here and now, your father is looking at your face as you were just thinking you'd like to look at your mother's.

"What are you thinking?" he asks.

You laugh.

"Quite a bit, huh?" he ventures.

"To say the least," you say. "Just go on with your story. That's what I'm thinking. I'm thinking, Just go on with your story, Dad."

"Hmmm, where'd I leave off?" he says.

For a moment, he seems to have utterly forgotten his story.

Later, you will come to wonder if this is a sign of the Alzheimer's—which will reveal itself in a matter of weeks—or is the natural consequence of unburdening a forty-year-old secret to one's unsuspecting and surprisingly fragile sons.

He tells it: "We were young communists then. I've never understood why communism was the enemy, morally speaking. Politically, patriotically, I'll grant you. The Soviets were the enemy. But communism itself? How can you argue that any fellow American deserves less than any other fellow American?"

He looks across the room—not at you—for the answer.

"I'll tell you how," he says. "Racism. Insidious business, thinking one race is worth less than another, thinking one *man* is worth less than another. Once you start to justify man's inhumanity to man . . ."

Not on purpose, you are circling your hands, as in, *Get on with it.*

"There's a lot of backstory, son," says your father, who never calls you son. But he is someone else now. Someone he used to be. Someone he meant to be?

"Well," he goes on, "there is and there isn't. A lot of backstory, that is. There's always backstory, and yet what changed our lives was very much a singular incident. We had just joined this local group, like the Weather Underground but not. Ours was trying to advance the cause of civil rights through communism, or vice versa—in any case, fight for equality everywhere, across class, across race, across countries of the world.

"Not bad, right?" he asks, his mouth quivering.

"As everyone knows," he goes on, fortifying himself, "money is the root of all evil. If the System could be starved of its life-blood, money, the System would weaken, and man's better nature—man's humanity to man—would take over."

He closes his eyes and laughs a little, a helpless laughter that feeds on itself until he is laughing uncontrollably.

"What's so funny, Dad?" you venture.

"Man's humanity to man," he says. "*That's* what we thought human nature was back then. In any case, long story a little less long, our group organized a robbery of one of the biggest banks in Boston. We were a small group, so everyone had a role, even your mother, who I wanted to keep out of the whole thing. Not that she would have. Back then, boy, back then . . ."

He drifts off for a moment.

"She changed afterward," he says. "I don't think I did. Not essentially. But she . . . she was a force back then. Afterward, it was like she was afraid to make a move. Without me, anyway, when I'm the one who probably got her into trouble in the first place.

"If there's one thing I'm sorry for," he goes on, "it's that you never knew that side of your mother."

"The side I knew was fine." She was your *mother*. You took her exactly as she was, loved her and never for a moment thought to lament a missing side of her. And you don't want to start now.

"Wrap it up, Dad," you say. "I can't take much more of this."

You wonder where Charles has gone. Has he left the

apartment? You didn't see him go out the front door, but you can't imagine him still being in the apartment. Unless he's somehow locked himself in the back bedroom, the boys' room, and is blasting the stereo—like the old days, only in this case, it would be something with headphones. No throbbing through the walls, just in his head.

"In short," your father says, "things went terribly wrong. One security guard was shot and killed; a bank teller was shot and wounded, became a vegetable. One of our people, my friend Bobby Wright, was killed. And three of us got away. Macky Fine, your mother and I. Don't know what happened to Macky. He always dreamed of going out west, Wyoming, California, so maybe that's what he did. Your mother and I didn't go too far. We were living in Medford, Massachusetts, then, and we were essentially homebodies. We wanted a northeastern city like the one we had to flee, and Brooklyn was the farthest we could bring ourselves to go. Your mother wanted Philadelphia. She had a cousin there—forgetting that this was not about moving to family. Another reason for Brooklyn was that we knew no one. Of all the millions of people in New York, we didn't know a one. That, of course, was the hardest thing, leaving family. Changing our name and never looking back."

"What was the name?" you ask.

"Snodgrass," he says. "You and your brother can thank us for that. 'Wills' was your mother's choice. Liked the sound of it. 'Mellifluous,' she said."

"Parents?" you ask. "Brothers and sisters?"

"Yes, yes and yes," he says. "Your mother had a brother, around whom life revolved in her family. That, she might have said, was her biggest sacrifice. I had a younger sister. We weren't all that close, but still. Our parents, too. We've had to live with the wondering. Their wondering, are we alive or dead? Our wondering."

"Why are you telling us, *me*, this now?" you ask.

"I don't know," he says. "With your mother gone . . . I don't know. I guess I don't want us both to die with this secret."

After an uncomfortably long silence, one in which you both know the transition is being made from story told to story received, you finally ask a question. "How old are you?"

"That's it?" he says. "That's all you want to know?"

"What if it is?"

You have to start somewhere, and what you are starting with is the comprehensible. The incomprehensible will come. You are sure of that.

"How old was Mom?" you ask.

You don't really care how old your father is. He's always seemed ageless, an indeterminate age immaterial to his character. But your mother more visibly marched through ages and stages. A young, bright-eyed mother, with a strong Roman nose, freckles and a quick smile. Then, as her boys got older, and she did, she regularly changed hairstyles, changed wardrobes, went on and off diets, perhaps trying to hold on to, or recapture, that easy young-mother beauty. Once you and Charles went to college, moved out of the house, had children of your own (Charles, anyway), she seemed to relax back into herself, a little stout, a little crooked, defiantly gray haired and always bright eyed. She died while still in the prime of that stage, a vibrant woman with a long, gray braid, who walked wherever she went. The mile and a half to the public library. The sixteen blocks to the farmers' market. Even over the Brooklyn Bridge into Manhattan, for some protest or another, or, on the rare occasion, shopping for clothes, the great love-hate relationship of her life.

"She was sixty-six when she died," your father tells you. "And I'm almost seventy."

"How about me?" you say.

"You what?" your father wonders.

"Me, how the hell old am I?"

The sand is shifting under your feet rapidly now. He senses this, puts a hand on your forearm.

"You are still *you*," he says. "Born October 9, 1967. Brooklyn, New York. Your brother, too, is as he's always been, born April 18, 1966. However old that makes him, who can keep track?"

"Thirty-five next month," you say. "Going on fifty."

He smiles, then grows serious. He tightens his grip on your forearm. "Listen to me," he says.

You damn well have to. He's speaking louder than you've ever heard him speak.

"Everything about you and your brother, your birthdays, your personalities, your relationships with us, with each other, with your friends and lovers—all that is *real*. There is nothing about your identity that is anything other than how you've always known it.

"We changed *our* name, your mother and I, and our ages," he continues. "But you were born into the next life, the quiet life. Life as the Wills family, where we all did quite well, thank you very much. We loved each other, Abbe and Rose Wills, and their smart, stalwart sons, Charles and Robert."

"But Dad," you say, "it was a lie."

"A *true* lie. A true lie." He is starting to tear up. "Call it getting away with murder, if you will, but I won't. One makes certain choices in certain climates that cannot be graded on an ordinary moral curve."

He is sobbing. You've never seen him cry like this, even when your mother died.

But you won't let him get away with it, calling an end to the conversation when *he's* ready.

"What's your real first name?" you ask.

"Howard," he says, a distant look returning. "Never liked it. I took my father's name, Abraham. Abe, Abbe. Had to sacrifice his last name, so it was only fair that I took his first."

Howard Snodgrass? Abraham Snodgrass? You've never known people like that. So *old country*.

"How about Mom?"

As soon as you ask, you close your eyes and put your hands to your ears. You can still hear, but you're poised for heartbreak, for a mother you never knew.

"Rose," he says. "My Rose. She couldn't bring herself to change it."

You let out a giant sigh and a few of the tears you've been holding back.

"And she was right," your father says. "Holding on to that flower of a name hasn't tripped us up yet, and I don't suppose it will."

* * *

Daniel's parents hadn't changed their name. His father had served his time—and not very long, either. Eighteen months for embezzlement. The act was clear enough. His father had admitted to appropriating some three hundred thousand dollars from his business partner. But the degree of criminality was less clear. His father maintained that he was owed the sum by the structure of the business, contractual obligations, promises made and the volume of business generated by him versus by his partner. As far as his father was concerned, what he took was legally his, although he agreed that his methods might have crossed a line.

His father's aggrieved business partner stayed in Greenfield, Massachusetts, so Daniel's family had to leave. They didn't go far. For all his adventures in white-collar crime, his father was not very adventurous. His mother apparently wanted the ocean, and his father felt they had to at least leave New England. Next oceanside stop, Long Island, New York.

Daniel was in second grade then, and that was when his life began. To this day, he could tell you the name of every boy in his Boy Scout troop and the street address of his first piano teacher. He could describe in detail the layout of each of his Long Island schools, could name every teacher and teacher's assistant since second grade. But he could not remember a thing about his life in Massachusetts. He knew that while his father was in prison, he and his mother lived on their own in what must have felt like solitary confinement. Daniel must have continued to go to school, which must have been awful. But he could not even imagine any of that, let alone remember it.

Daniel had always wished for a brother. Someone, anyone, to share his childhood. Not a brother like Charles, although if he'd had a brother like Charles, maybe he could have been a brother like Robbie. Free, really free, to run away.

Ah, but that's what he was doing now. Every morning for the last six weeks, Daniel had driven to the train station, like always, where his car, like always, spent the day, tagged with its monthly parking permit in case anyone was wondering. But he did not ride the train south with the other sardines, or lemmings, as he used to think of his fellow commuters, depending on whether he felt trapped physically or spiritually. He headed north, and on Amtrak rather than his Metro-North commuter train. The Amtrak train was three times more expensive and stopped at many fewer places, but he was after the promise of *last stop, Montreal* rather than *last stop, Poughkeepsie*. So far, he was still disembarking fairly close to home—Rhinecliff, Hudson, Saratoga Springs. Laptop over his shoulder, he'd take a cab or, on especially nice days, walk into town, whichever town it was, and look for a place to sit and write.

He marveled at how easy it was to fill his day writing, something he suspected would not be nearly so easy if he had announced his plans to his wife. If anything had actually been expected of him. He called home now and then, and fielded the very occasional call from Shoshanna, his cell phone his preferred office number anyway, as if he'd been preparing for this all along.

His favorite spot came to be the RiverSwept, a beautiful nineteenth-century mansion, with a 240-degree river view, former home of a well-known Hudson River School painter that was now part restaurant, part museum, part inn. Daniel spent most of the day tucked into one of the nooks, or unabashedly out on one of the verandas. He'd order from the restaurant to earn his place, breakfast, lunch, a limeade or an ice tea. Now and then, he'd complete the escape with a house-special mojito. Lime, mint, rum, a little sugar and the high that came with no one knowing where he was, something he'd been craving since 9/11.

28

IM

How's David?

   Who?

   Your husband—is that not David?

   David Pace? How do you know David?

   Don't know him. Didn't know "Pace." He was your boyfriend then.

From his productive perch on the RiverSwept's side veranda, Daniel had Googlocated Michelle Dineen, e-mailed her and established that she was on maternity leave with a five-month-old. Over the last few days, they had exchanged several informational e-mails before shifting to instant messaging.

Michelle and David—one of the many casualties of 9/11, she wrote.

If you can't stand the heat, Daniel wrote, *get out of the tower.*

   That's terrible.

Daniel's decorum—casualty of 9/11. Now, what happened with the boyfriend?

He smothered me.

Daniel's mind ran to a lustier kind of smother, the two of them on her hardwood floor, his imagination now leading her to a bed, a generous mattress laden with pillows.

Who's the lucky guy now?

Tomas.

That's it? Tomas? Not even an "h"?

What more do you want?

If you only knew . . .

Who says I don't?

Togga go, he typed, or mistyped (*Gotta go*). *Fone call.*

It was so easy to lie in IM—the form almost beckoned it. No second thoughts, no permanent record. No context, no accountability.

TBC, he wrote.

He started it; he'd suggested this venue. But it was a mistake. IM was the Krispy Kreme doughnut of communication, so unsatisfying in moderation that the only reasonable thing to do was to go too far.

So how could he hold himself back a couple hours later, near the end of the commuter's day, sitting deep in an Adirondack chair on the back lawn, not even feigning work?

You there? he pecked.

Always. Baby's napping, I'm here. Baby's not napping, I'm here. You have no idea how many hours there are in a day.

I think I have some idea.

My husband doesn't. Doesn't understand anything.

There went the gauntlet.

I'm sure you'll work it out, he typed.

Let's get together, he typed.

He separated the two sentences with the space bar, so he could better see the angel on his shoulder, and the devil.

He sent neither.

You still there? she wrote after a minute.

IM, he was reminded, was no place for reflection.

I remember kissing you, he wrote.

Extenuating circumstances.

Her response came so fast, instantly, that she must have had it at the ready.

Very. He typed slowly, to catch his breath. V-e-r-y.

I have a baby.

I have two.

I have a husband.

And I have a wife.

Now the pause was on her end.

He waited her out.

He looked around at where he was, a pastoral scene that had become thoroughly familiar. The burnish of high-hill early autumn crept over Storm King Mountain, across the river. He was in it now, his secret life; seasons were turning.

Damn. Baby's crying. Togga go (says you).

Wait—, he typed, but didn't send. Delete delete delete delete. *Bye,* he wrote. *For now.*

29

Running Plates

Nineteen ninety-one Dodge Colt. Color: bronze (actual color: rust). Owner: Nishal Tamobour, 7047 Palisades Boulevard #313, Rippeskill, New York. *Awfully far for a yard guy or a pool guy to travel*, Keith thought, as he drove up and up and up Route 9W.

He had nothing more. No record. Not even a moving violation. Nothing but name, age and address.

Seven oh four seven Palisades Boulevard. Fly-by-night apartment building, fake yellow brick, chipped here and there down to the cinder block. Sergeant Margolis, way off duty, walked right in through the building's jimmied front door, up the stairs to apartment 313. Knocked and knocked, although he recognized the familiar echo of an empty apartment.

"Guy's long gone." A woman poked her head outside a neighboring apartment door.

"Guy, two guys, who can tell with these people." A man—her husband?—joined her at the door.

"These people?" said the woman. "We're all *these people*."

"Speak for yourself," he said. "I ain't."

"Know where he went?" Keith asked.

"Who wants to know?" The husband stepped out the door, stood square as a superhero.

Keith's badge sat in his back pocket. *Think fast.* "He stiffed me on a poker bet."

"Good one," the woman said.

"Nah, we don't know nothing," said the husband, letting down his guard. "You're lucky we knew his name."

"Which means what, exactly, I don't know," said the wife. "Nice guy, fine. Polite, quiet, held a door for you as soon as look at you. But kept to himself. Real island in this wastewater, if you know what I mean."

"Now *that's* something that means what, exactly, *I* don't know," the husband said.

Keith could spot this pattern from a mile away—tightening marital noose—and excused himself with a quick flurry of *Thanks, thanks anyway.*

Nishal Tamobour—polite, quiet, kept to himself. Isn't that what the neighbors on the television news always say about the serial killer?

30

Running. Waiting.

Before Nishal left his place for good, he ransacked what little was left. Made it look like someone had already been there. In case his *titi* was telling the truth.

In case.

Toomer, in that final phone call, had told him to get there right away. —Those runners, *bakas*, idiots, will never find the money. But someone else will, *jai*. Some rich family, fat, happy kids. Just more money to add to their piles.

Nishal thought different. *Bakas* may be too stupid to find the money. If there was money to find. But they would not be too stupid to find the sucker who lives at that motherfucker Toomer's address. Nishal Tamobour, soft spot right behind the ear, under the skull. Bullet right there ought to do it.

Nishal packed everything he needed, left the bed and the couch and headed to Charysse's. Two towns over. Just in case.

Didn't even know who to be on the lookout for. Didn't know enough about his *jai-titi* to know.

That Haitian, maybe. Toomer had said, Oh, Bats? Doesn't care shit about shit. Wouldn't raise a hand. Besides, fucker moves too slow to catch a snail in the sun.

—*You*, titi. *It's you who doesn't care shit about shit.*

'Course, if Toomer was still on this planet, he wouldn't be able to hear Nishal. Be hundreds of miles away by now, phone ditched or dead.

—*It's you*, titi, *who's making me move from my apartment. Crappy but mine. Packing one lousy box, one, so I can see with my very eyes how much I have in this world.*

Nishal knew Toomer could hear him.

—*Bullshit if I'm going to run for my life for some hot-wired money. I got a plan, too,* titi.

One day at a time. One dollar at a time. That was Nishal's plan. He didn't want to spend *his* life running from runners.

—You expecting something?

Charysse had his number. They were sitting there watching TV at her place (now his place, too). But she could tell something was up.

—You're not watching the TV. Not looking anywhere. Just inside your own head. Like you're waiting for something.

—Nah. Just getting used to a new place.

She asked about Toomer. It had been more than a week since they saw him.

—Stole a car. Boy's on the run.

—At best, Nishal. No one looking after those wounds? Still pretty serious stuff. If no one changes those bandages . . . if he's too weak or stupid to notice red lines of infection . . . if he's off those antibiotics . . .

Toomer had been so alive in his head these days. Nishal argued with him, with Toomer, all the time.

—*Thanks,* titi. *Gone and made me a runner, too.*

—Infection, "the snakes," is some pretty terrible stuff. Boils your blood, then cooks your brain. Can't think straight, can't act right. Which makes everything worse. Vicious circle to die in.

Nishal made her stop.

He should have let her continue. Let her be a nurse. Once she stopped, she cried.

31

S-y-l-v-a-n Street

Library was good for something. Nishal got online there and found three different Sylvan Streets near enough to drive to. Two to the west, one to the south.

First, he drove west.

—S-y-l-v-a-n. A street? That's all you got?

—I snap a giant case of money for you. And you complain about directions? Fuck you.

—Fuck you. Going and dying on me. If that's where you went.

—Nah, man, listen. You thank your girl for me, saving my life.

—So you could die of the snakes? That's what Charysse calls it.

—Die rich. Something to pass on to my blood. You, mi carnal. Mami, Aaliyah.

Poor kid, whose first wish in this world—and his last—was

to save his mother and his sister. From the very first, from the father. That coward, who took on a woman, a little boy.

Nishal remembered his own mother huddling with Toomer's mother. First, because she was beat up. Next, because her boy was. Before he was three, Toomer became the one who "found the fist," as Nishal's mother put it. From then on, his father stopped beating his mother. Didn't have to. Had his boy to beat. Only now did Nishal see: Titi, *you did it! You already saved your* mami. *Years ago.*

It was a bright Sunday morning. Nishal was glad to be away from Charysse. Her church. Her simpleminded notions of truth. Believed what Nishal told her.

Nishal was driving south now. Across a bridge. Looking for signs.

What if Toomer had made the whole thing up? Lost his mind. Those delusions that Charysse was talking about. Couldn't think straight. A *jai* was supposed to look after his *jai-titi*. And Nishal had gone and let the little one lose his mind.

Nishal's first two trips, S-y-l-v-a-n Streets to the west, had been a bust. Couple busted towns that looked a lot like Rippeskill. Big blue swimming pool? *Ha ha, very funny.*

Now he could feel it. Houses and yards got bigger. Money. Sky expanded, river widened.

—*Right onto Deveau Hill Road.*

—*Point seven miles, left onto Sylvan Street.*

Slow. Round the corner. Fate takes its own time.

Nishal smelled the pool before he saw it.

Pulled past the house, to a spot between houses. No doubt his *titi* had been here, had seen this place. Nishal felt like a beggar. Or a junkie. Following a whiff of the good life—someone else's good life. He was as crazy as his *jai-titi*.

Now what? How would he make his way across the lawn, through the pool gate and into the shed? How had Toomer done it? He was no smarter than Nishal. And no more criminal, really.

A car slowed at the corner. Pulled to the side of the road. Stopped.

He touched the scrap of paper in his pocket. He had thought of everything. If anyone asked what he was doing here, he would speak no English—*look at my dark skin*—and show an address written on a piece of paper, *11 Hill Road*. Stupid handyman who'd gone to the wrong house. The wrong street.

The other car cut its engine. A girl around Natasha's age got out. Laughing with her friends. Good-byes all around. Engine started up again, overcranked.

The girl looked over at the big house, gave it a shy little wave. She walked a wide path around his car. Headed down the street. A couple times, she looked back at him—him or the house? Then disappeared up a driveway at the end of the road.

Had she noticed him? Would she care? What did a kid know, anyway? Well, Tasha—she knew plenty. But all of it wrong.

Nishal didn't move. The teenagers' car lurched forward, backward, forward, backward. An overlapping, thousand-pointed star, before it finally screeched out onto Deveau Hill Road.

Probably the girl would not give him another thought. Brown guy staring—was he staring?—at the big house and pool. Like he wanted something.

He pulled back out onto Deveau Hill Road, much more quietly than the teenagers had.

Night. He'd gone home, to Charysse's, only to sneak back out. While she was asleep. Yes, he'd have some explaining to do. But that would be easy enough with a bag full of money.

He parked on a gravel shoulder on Deveau Hill Road, about a quarter mile down the hill from Sylvan Street. Once he started walking up the hill, he realized: if he really found anything, this would be a long way to run. Or would it? How heavy is money?

It was dark, no question. A weak half-moon.

Where Nishal lived, first his crappy apartment and now Charysse's triplex, floodlights blared all night. Kept an eye on—or lit the way for—all the crazy motherfuckers who came and went. All hours of the night.

No streetlights on this Sylvan Street. No floodlights. No need. Everyone was tucked inside for the night.

His eyes adjusted to the dark. Eyes and body working together. He clicked the pool gate's hammer-latch. Swung right open. He picked silently across the deck, through the chairs. Clicked the shed's latch. Again, no resistance. He was welcome here. Expected, even.

He closed the door behind him, shone his small, bright flashlight on the floor. Neat shed, quick inventory. He swung the light: plastic tubs of chemicals, coiled rope, couple poles with net baskets. No case. Nishal felt around the filter. Tipped a half dozen green-and-yellow folding chairs. Shuffled pink and green chair cushions. Four, five, six. He unstacked floats. Red, yellow, blue. And quickly restacked them.

He dared turn on the light. With an overhead light, rather than the beam-by-beam of his flashlight, Nishal could tell there was no case of money in here. Everything was colorful, buoyant, plastic. See-through, blow-up.

He spent about ten minutes moving things around. Now and then touching the paper scrap in his pocket. On a middle shelf, he did see a toolbox, which stood out from all the colored plastic. But the case was full of only tools. A full set and each in its place. Nothing out of place in this place.

Nishal turned off his flashlight. Waited for a sign. For Toomer's ghost.

But he scared himself. Hurried outside. The night looked much brighter, now that he'd been in true darkness.

A rustling over by the fence split him in two—

Quick, run.

Quiet, stay.

Only a deer. Two deer. Large and small. Flickering white tails and glass deer eyes catching glints of moon.

The big deer suddenly ran off, out the open gate. The smaller one ran the other way, toward the back fence.

Nishal made himself walk, though he wanted to run. Out the gate. Shut it behind him, quiet but firm. He wondered whether the deer, that little one, could jump the fence, or if it was trapped.

How long had it been since Toomer had called him? Two weeks? Whoever came and went from this shed already came and went a dozen times. If there was a case full of money—*ha ha*—whoever lived there could have, would have taken it.

Finally. Nishal had waited long enough to never know whether his *jai-titi* was telling the truth.

32

Janic's Brain

Sally couldn't have been gone too long—two hours? three?—although it could have been the longest she'd been away from Janic in months. Perhaps since they retired. One errand had led to another, and, with three hundred dollars in her wallet, she began losing herself in domestic flights of fancy.

First she'd driven the extra twenty-five minutes to Trader Joe's, raising the bar on the Levlovices' mealtime possibilities. Spicy masala, bright lemongrass, decadent mole. Breads and pies, a rack of lamb—when had she last made rack of lamb? Her usual daily routine had diminished these days to roast chicken (which would last three nights), poached salmon or, because she and Janic really ate very little, a hard-boiled egg apiece with a tossed salad. But today she was mapping whole new culinary adventures.

On the wings of the rich, hopeful feeling that Trader Joe's had given her, she stopped at Panorama Gardens, an epic, rolling nursery she and Janic used to visit each spring. They hadn't been in years. These days, they just went to the small, local plant store if they needed an addition to their mature garden.

So much of her life felt this way, *mature*. But Panorama had her feeling expansive again, acquisitive. A whole section of grasses! Hearty big bluestem, delicate sideoats grama . . . She started imagining. Feathery Indian steel, beautiful pink cleome. Or even a simple variegated ribbon grass, which would probably take over the whole lawn, and Janic would kill her (in his way: with silence).

She meandered over to Panorama's arbor section, and her imagination really took root. Maybe they'd buy a cherry tree. Or a Japanese maple, nature's lacy architecture, at once minimal and lush. There was a beautiful Japanese maple in town, near the high school, which she'd noticed every day on her way to work. Why had she never thought to buy one? She turned over the price tag: $195. That was why. Lifelong habits die hard.

She had two one-hundred-dollar bills left in her wallet. She could take this tree home right now. And she could walk down to her basement and get 1,897 more hundred-dollar bills.

She came home to collect more money and to dream a little. She didn't go inside right away, didn't even take the groceries in. Instead, she paced the property to see where she would put the new Japanese maples she was going to get, the new cherry trees.

She felt full of quotidian life-changing energy. The day began with it, energy, excitement and a physical challenge—making no sound while ripping yards of packing tape off a garbage bag.

Although Janic knew full well where the money was and that his wife was presumably drawing off of it, she had kept the basement dark as she reached the full length of her arm behind the washer and worked long and hard to muffle the sound as she unsealed the bag.

Now, well above ground, Sally spotted the perfect place for a Japanese maple—the far corner of the front yard. The eye would be drawn across the expanse of peaceful stones to the burst of deep red. Wouldn't that make the other corner, and a spot right here against the house, look stark by comparison? Janic had designed and balanced this yard so precisely that the addition of one glorious maple would make the negative spaces, once in perfect balance, seem empty. Instead of adding a single maple, she'd have to add two or three. Instead of pulling three bills from the contractor bags, as she'd done this morning, she'd pull six or eight. Easy enough. She had folded a tiny corner of the packing tape under itself for a starting point next time she opened the bag. *Six, eight, ten.* If three bills had liberated her, just think what she had in store. A thousand dollars in her pocket, two thousand. By the fistful.

She had even formulated an alibi should anyone come to ask why and how a woman such as herself was paying cash for everything. Sally Levlovic, age sixty-seven and counting but still very much of sound mind and sound body, had taken a post-retirement job waiting tables. What better security for herself and her family than cash in hand? Maybe she'd even help the kids with the River Rise mortgage, if she made enough in tips. Who wouldn't believe such a mundane alibi? She would keep up the story—to herself and others—until the kids' thirty-year mortgage was paid off, she was caught or she was dead. If she was lucky, it would be a horse race to the finish when she was ninety-seven.

A few red leaves from the sugar maple across the street fluttered to the ground—a glimpse of fall—returning her to her arboreal flights of fancy. She pictured the play of jeweled sun and lacy shade and couldn't imagine how they'd lived this long without a stand of Japanese maple trees.

She had traveled her whole life down Janic's path. Closer than most couples, they had created a small, tidy life that was comfortable but, if you chafed at it for a moment, a little stultifying. No Japanese maples, no trees *at all*, in the front yard?

She stared into the twin faces of Benjamin Franklin. She wondered, of all things, how old he was in his hundred-dollar-bill portrait. He had lived to a ripe old age of eighty-something. She ran a finger over his broad forehead. This was nothing more than printed paper, nothing more than a finely inked portrait of Benjamin Franklin.

Sally rubbed the bills together between her finger and thumb, as though their purpose was combustion. Indeed, she felt fueled, ready to make a great break. With life as she knew it. Change! *Sally Love.* She could see Bianca's point.

Maybe it was old age—and not life with Janic—that was stultifying. How about a grand vacation to slap away this deadening paw of retirement? *Live a little.*

Sally's first impulse was to calculate backward from airfare. *Was Europe cheap these days? Or the West Coast?*

She pinched her mouth and willed herself to think big. The effort was like reintroducing a forgotten muscle to use. She could feel her brain trying to shuck its usual impulses: *too expensive, too much of a hassle, too unnecessary.*

Florence came to the fore. She and Janic had honeymooned in Florence, and Sally had fallen in love. Oh, the view from the duomo! Why had civilization ever developed any other way? They were schoolteachers; they could come back every summer, she'd thought with delight. For a few summers, they did. They had no money, but Sally did her research, found which budget hotels were clean and convenient, which days which museums were reduced or free, which out-of-the-way trattorie were cheap and good. They walked everywhere. The whole city was open to them.

Then they had babies. Travel was impossible. Summers were filled with the earthbound stuff of life, which thankfully she had come to love. They were making a world, weren't they, on their comfortable cul-de-sac?

It had taken them a long time to get back to traveling. The children were teenagers, Blake off to Harvard already, before they left the country again. More often than not, they went places of compromise, good deals that offered practical advantages. Quebec, a taste of old Europe but only eight hours by car. Mérida, Mexico, a tiny gem of a colonial city, affordable and barely fifteen hundred miles away. Portugal, which she had heard was a wonderful way to see Europe on the cheap. The country was indeed beautiful, but Sally couldn't shake the feeling that it *reminded her* of Europe.

Dream places came to her. Kyoto. The temples, the carved stone, the humble, majestic maples and the exuberant, dignified cherry blossoms. The spare materials of existence, just enough to hold light and air and an onrush of beauty every spring. Kyoto would remind her of home, then her home would come to remind her of Kyoto. The Amalfi coast, the south of France. Or Paris, where she'd never been.

Could you believe it, an otherwise cultured sixty-seven-year-old woman who'd never been to Paris? Surely half of Sally's students, which over the course of her forty years amounted to thousands of teenagers, had been to Paris. Little know-nothing April Margolis was in Paris right now.

The blame fell squarely on Janic. He'd traveled to Paris after graduating from college and had a terrible experience. He stayed at a crumbling hotel full of mold and rust. He'd found everything in the city either crowded or closed, it rained every day and there was one civil-service strike after another. No trolleys one day, no electricity the next; he left the day of a garbage collection strike. To top it off, he'd gotten food poisoning. Felled by a villainous snail, he concluded that Paris had it out for him. One wayward bivalve had forever changed the course of Sally's life, rendered her an old woman who had never been to Paris.

Retirement was as good a time as any to right life's wrongs. Sally's foremost wrong right now was never having been to Paris.

She laughed at a ridiculous image that came to her: Janic confronted by a giant snail. Janic standing his ground while the huge thing lumbered inexorably toward him, like a steamroller. Janic was mounting an oral argument, trying to talk the evil snail down. *Look, you don't want to have this on your conscience.* Under the rules of dream-logic, the man could not simply walk away from the oncoming snail. He could only feint side to side and moralize.

The comic confrontation brought Sally a surprising degree

of girlish glee. With the conviction of a woman renewed, she marched inside to tell Janic the plan. *Steel your stomach, gird your loins, we're going to Paris.*

"Dear," she called from the kitchen, even though she knew this would tip him off that she was up to something. She couldn't remember when either of them had last used a term of endearment.

"Janic, dear?" she called from the living room.

Maybe he'd gone up to the Canes', although he'd been doing that less frequently these days. Apparently Billy was busy in his art studio, something Sally'd always assumed was more for ego than for actual work. She'd check upstairs for her husband, then head to the Canes' if she had to. She didn't want to lose her head of steam, which might well happen if she waited for him to come home.

"Janic," she called down the hallway, her voice casting out before her like a fishing line. No Janic in the bedroom. Only a bed that surprisingly needed making. She ducked her head into the guest room on the way back down the hallway on the very off chance that Janic was on the computer, which he wasn't.

Idly, she tapped the half-closed bathroom door on her way down. It creaked open a bit, then stopped. Blocked. Strange.

"Janic?" she whispered.

Janic lay on the floor, splayed on his back, razor in his hand. He must have fainted while shaving. Half his face was clean shaven, half lathered in shaving cream. A thin line of blood ran down the clean cheek. His mouth was twisted, as though he were trying to smile with the blood-threaded, clean-shaven half, frown with the other. He looked split in two. His eyes were open, but he was not looking anywhere, not at her, not away.

She hustled to the bedroom for the phone, returned to the bathroom and called 911.

After taking Sally's information and dispatching an ambulance, the dispatcher kept Sally on the line. She asked her to ask "the victim" his name. Why had this not occurred to Sally, to ask him his name? He opened his mouth, as if to answer, his tongue poked out a little, then he closed his mouth as if he were done. *Asked and answered, Counselor*, as he sometimes said.

"He cannot seem to talk," she said.

"Okay," the dispatcher said calmly. "Ask him to grasp your finger in his hand. Do this on both sides, the right and the left."

Sally had an impulse to hang up, to call someone who could help her rather than have her play these silly games.

"This is extremely helpful, Mrs. Levlovic," said the dispatcher. "I'm talking to your boys now. They'll be there in a matter of minutes."

For a moment, Sally thought the dispatcher meant Blake and Byron, wondered how on earth the young woman on the other end of the phone knew about her sons, where they were or how to reach them. It restored her confidence in the dispatcher.

But the dispatcher meant the EMTs. The ambulance was on the way. The more information she and the dispatcher were able to exchange before the ambulance arrived, Sally was told, the better the prognosis.

She paced the hospital waiting room, looking at her cell phone's unlit face and willing it to ring. She had left messages for Blake at home, work and cell, and for Bianca and Byron at the new house. Then she surprised herself with a ritual she had drilled into her muscle memory many years ago. She dialed 274-4220, which she had first learned as AShley4-4220. As a young mother, she had decided (in her mercifully unneeded mental list) that if she ever had a life-and-death emergency, she'd call Pete Hotten, a volunteer EMT and an all-around highly competent man.

One of the Margolis twins answered. "Is your father there?" Sally asked.

It was not the memory of Pete Hotten she was after. It was his son-in-law, Keith Margolis. And it couldn't have been more than fifteen minutes later when Keith greeted Sally in the waiting room, apologizing for Jen's absence. She wanted to come, but someone had to stay with the kids.

Shortly after, Billy arrived. Keith had called him, thought he'd want to know.

Sally was grateful and apologetic. Only immediate family members were allowed in the ICU, so the neighbors couldn't see Janic. Never mind that, they told her. They were here for *her*. Did she want anything? Food? Crossword puzzles? Clothes from home?

She didn't need anything, except maybe to talk. She told them how she'd found Janic half lathered, half shaven on the bathroom floor. How the trickle of blood was what had initially scared her, although it was just an untended nick from shaving. She told how the ambulance arrived almost immediately, and she would pay her local taxes with a debt of gratitude from now on. How she hadn't yet been able to reach her sons. She was of course desperate for them to know, for them to come see their father and be with her. But part of her was relieved that they had a little more time on this earth thinking all was fine with Pop and Mom.

She told the diagnosis: stroke, too early to pinpoint location and severity. They were working on him now. That's what one of the doctors, the young, officious one, had said. *We're working on him now.* Like he was a car. Or a work-in-progress, which was just the opposite of what Janic Levlovic was. Early indications showed right-brain stroke, which apparently could affect his ability to sequence details. This was what she was most worried about—the possible interruption of Janic's brain.

"That won't happen," Billy Cane reassured her. "Not that brain."

In a surprising but not awkward moment, Billy embraced her. She put her hand on his neck, touching his shaggy, collar-length hair.

"He's a fighter," Billy whispered into Sally's ear. "And you are too, my dear."

He patted her back and released her, stronger. Billy Cane's effect indeed ran deeper than she had given him credit for. She felt thankful to have him here, this lovely, generous man.

She told more about the prognosis. They were hopeful that she'd gotten him here within the three-hour window. Apparently, there was a sacrosanct three hours in which a person can be saved intact from certain strokes. If she had known that, she told her neighbors, it could have been a principle to live by. For all married couples: don't leave each other for more than three hours. Why didn't anyone tell you that?

She had done errands that morning, lingered, dawdled. Who in heaven's name knew how long she'd been gone? Who in heaven's name knew how long her husband had been lying on the floor, blood clotting and plotting? While she was sitting outside blaming Janic for all she'd missed in life, an embolism was lodging itself firmly in his brain. While she was surveying her tidy lot, placing imaginary Japanese maples, Janic's brain cells were—

Billy and Keith implored her not to blame herself, assured her that no one was more devoted to a husband than she. That Janic was a lucky man, and thank God she *did* find him. Why not focus on that?

At the first sign of Sally's tears, Keith and Billy, God bless them, fiddled in their pockets. Cell phones, keys, wallets. They were casting about for something to do to help, rather than all this standing around and talking. Keith announced he'd drive over to River Rise, see if he could find anyone there—maybe Byron and his family were outside, or maybe something was wrong with their phone. Billy volunteered to make more phone calls, an offer made all the more appealing by the fact that he had to go downstairs to the hospital lobby to do it.

From the depths of her waiting room chair, Sally pictured returning home with Janic—lighter now, old and porous; or would he be heavier, essentially dead weight?—hoisting him somehow, or pushing a wheelchair. Planting him somewhere or other, where he would stay until she upped and replanted him somewhere else. *What do you want for dinner?* she'd ask, and answer herself. *We'll have chicken tonight.* Or, *What do you want to do today?* And she'd come up with something. For a while, a week, a month, she'd keep up the charade. Then she'd stop asking. She'd do occasional commentary. *Salmon for dinner! Let's go to Riverview Park today!* But that, too, would only last for so long. Conversation would drain out of their marriage. *Finally, Janic,* she thought, *silence. What you've always wanted.*

What would she have to do to keep herself from drowning in loneliness? She would insistently invite the children over, make a schedule if she had to. Byron and Bianca and the kids Tuesdays and Saturdays. Blake Thursdays and Sundays. She would even encourage him to bring his family. Liz and Lila would be better than no one.

She closed her eyes, slumped into her chair. Already she was thinking of Janic as *no one*.

Two hundred feet away, he lay in a medically induced coma, in his "Hudson Valley Stroke Center of Excellence" gown. She hated that they put him in such a thing, more false assurance. Center of Excellence. Center of Mediocrity. Either way, Janic looked so vulnerable, slight and shriveled. Gone was her lanky, satisfyingly tall husband of forty-four years.

How could that be, gone so quickly? Gone to the vanishing point. Vanishing right into the horizon of the past.

Before Janic was only one other. Salvatore Spinelli. Three dates. *Sal Spinelli!* When had she last thought about him?

She and Sal Spinelli had joked from the start about having the same name, although that was about all they'd had in common. Where she and Janic were virtually one and the same person, she and Sal were different in just about every way.

She met Salvatore Spinelli on the Long Island Rail Road. She was headed home from the city with a friend, Annemarie Something, after seeing *My Fair Lady* on Broadway, and made eye contact with the young man across the aisle. He was so handsome, if short, as she noticed when he stood to introduce himself. How she'd wished she had a slender waist. He held his hand to his heart and told them his name. She and Annemarie both giggled when he said, "Sal." To Sally, it sounded like he had already internalized her, had mixed them up, himself and her, so intertwined were they. "Sal Spinelli."

"Sal," she said, her hand, too, feathering at the heart. "Sally Bank."

"Like the bank?" he said, wagging his eyebrows like a vaude-villian.

They both laughed nervously at the unfunny joke.

He was more than handsome. He was raffish and exhilarating. He was coming home from a job interview in the city, he'd said, although she never did find out what kind of job it was or why it put him on an eleven o'clock train.

They went out exactly three times. Once to dinner, once to dinner and a movie and once to dinner and ostensibly a movie, but instead of the movie, he drove her to a lovers' lane and they necked—and more—in his father's car. It was all fumbling and headlong. She no longer remembered what the sex felt like—her first time, of course—only that it was like nothing else she'd ever experienced, in both good and bad ways. Afterward, he had stroked and petted her, pressed his lips to her naked chest and neck in a raft of unformed kisses. He told her how much he loved her, how good her skin felt, how he just wanted to stay like this, skin to skin, forever. She learned later that such a thing was foreplay, and it seemed sweet and mixed up that Sal committed himself to this *afterward*.

Her parents forbade her to see him again, the timing of which—after the third date—felt particularly cruel, right in the flush of it. The prohibition had to do with how late she came back, and in an apparent state of disarray, and with the fact that she wasn't able to say what he did for a living or what he intended to do, beyond that vague job interview in the city.

Every time she asked him, she got a different answer, this great idea or that, this invention or that, a hundred possible businesses that couldn't fail.

She wondered why she was thinking about him now, which seemed like exactly the wrong time to think about him, a betrayal of her lifelong husband, whose brain—the engine that had essentially powered the course of her life—had just been attacked by his own bloodstream.

That was how Dr. Penrose had explained it. "A stroke is an attack on the brain, a blood clot forming somewhere deep in the body and laying siege to the resilient yet delicate brain."

"Which is it?" she demanded. The pompous, too-young doctor brought out the contrarian in her. "Resilient or delicate? My überlogical husband would make you pick one."

"It's both, Mrs. Levlovic," he said, mispronouncing her name "*Lev*-lo-vick," as more people did than did not.

Maybe Bianca was right to take mispronunciation seriously and to do something about it, although Sally couldn't see telling this puffed-up doctor with the colorless reddish hair, cropped aggressively short, "Call me Mrs. Love."

Call me Mrs. Spinelli. She couldn't see that, either. Couldn't see entwining her life around someone like Sal Spinelli. Although—if she remembered correctly, in the dimmed sensual part of her brain—there was a time when all she could think about was entwining her body around his.

What would her life be like if she had taken Sal's path rather than Janic's? Everything would have been different, every last shred of her daily life. She looked down at her shoes. She'd dared to wear the olive green Keen sandals that were so popular in this part of the world. Surely she wouldn't be wearing these now if she'd married Sal Spinelli. Nor her white button-down short-sleeved shirt or loose linen jeans with two hundred-dollar bills in the pocket. She wouldn't be living in this pretty Hudson Valley village laced with abandoned rock walls through roadside woods. She was sure they wouldn't have left Long Island. Or maybe she would have followed him on one failed adventure after another. That was probably what life with Sal Spinelli would have amounted to. They'd be destitute in a place like Las Vegas, him still talking a big, romantic game and her still believing him, her mind not having been honed by Janic Levlovic. She wouldn't have a bag of money behind the washing machine, and she wouldn't be wondering how to pay the uncovered hospital bills—not to mention private rehab, which she was sure Blake would suggest—with cash from that bag.

She wouldn't be sitting in a hospital waiting room, waiting to make contact with her sons. Oh, Blake. Byron. This line of thinking became more than she could bear. That her sons would have never been born was too much for her brain. Resilient up to a point; beyond that, her mind was too delicate for even a single thought. That damn Dr. Penrose was right.

33

The Death of Richard

Billy didn't have to wait long before April fell asleep. They were fifteen minutes outside the airport, not yet on the Whitestone Bridge. "That was fast," Maggie said, craning her head to see the sleeping body in the backseat.

"You wore her out, huh?" Billy said.

When he found them at baggage claim, there seemed to be an awkwardness between his wife and April, which he ascribed to the intimacy of travel dislocated by the return home.

"I'm afraid I have some bad news for you," he said.

"No," she said. "Not Janic."

"Oh, no, status quo on Janic." Billy'd told her over the phone about the stroke. "Your uncle Richard."

She closed her eyes and crossed herself, which made her look, for a moment, like a stranger to him, a religious visitor he'd just picked up at the airport. "When?" she said.

"I got the call last night," he said. "Couldn't call you then, with the time thing, so I figured I'd wait until I picked you up."

Maggie nodded. "Uncle Richard," she said. "My favorite grown-up."

"The funeral's this afternoon at five, up there, if you think you can swing it."

"Of course," Maggie said, blinking sleepily.

"We'll drop April off, change and keep going?"

"Of course, of course, of course . . ." She closed her eyes and drifted off, *of course*–ing herself right to sleep, a reassuring enough mantra with which to cross over.

Driving two softly snoring women up the coursing New York State Thruway, Billy pictured Uncle Richard soaring along with them above the car, winged now and visible only to the faithful.

We're trying. When had Billy told Uncle Richard that? Six, nine months ago? Now that Richard had the omniscience of death, Billy would have to come clean. *It's trying,* he'd say. *There's something between us, all the weight of kids without the joy of them.*

Billy looked over at his wife, her head resting on the window, neck bent like a broken stem. He moved to wake her—*you'll hurt your neck*—but he stopped. He had nothing better to offer her. No pillow, no fold-down seat. No business class. Hopefully, sleep would be worth the price of a stiff neck.

April stirred. One leg dropped off the seat. She shifted. Why on earth had April Margolis just gone to Paris with his wife? Maybe for the same reason that the late Richard Stoughton was Billy's heavenly companion up the New York State Thruway. We take our angels where we can.

What were Billy and Maggie doing wrong? Everything had been fine until they'd started trying—rather, until they started trying and failing. Was it her long-abandoned Catholicism rearing its ugly head? Could you call it procreational sex if they couldn't conceive? *In any case, Maggie McKenzie, exquisite sadness after sex is surely more punishment than God intended.*

They had both "tested" fine, but as far as he could tell that meant nothing. One doctor, whom they ditched promptly thereafter, had said, "You're incompatible. Your particular sperm just don't care for her particular eggs. Or vice versa. It's much more common than you'd think." Maggie had cried on the spot. Billy wanted to slug the idiot, although the idiot was quite possibly right.

Billy dropped Maggie off at the house, then drove another 150 yards down Sylvan Street to drop off April.

"What's this?" she asked, as they pulled behind two construction trucks.

"Your pool," Billy said.

"They really did that?" She rubbed her eyes. "I can never tell if they're just talking about something or if they actually mean it. Like, my dad has been promising my mom he's going to take her to Cabo San Lucas since as long as I can remember."

"Looks like they mean business now," Billy said.

He had given up caring whether Margolis bought a Porsche, built a pool, moved to a mansion. He didn't care if Margolis brought down the whole operation. Billy would be relieved. His recent sale of two big-ticket commissions would seem less trivial. What did a $150,000 sale—seventy-five to him, seventy-five to Christian Gray—mean when Billy had $190,000 in cash in a briefcase under the sink?

The idea was starting to take shape. Scrap it all, give it up, give it away, the whole damn lot of it, and go back to a cabin in the woods, back to his childhood, which, unlike Maggie's, was idyllic. He'd had such a sure sense of his surroundings, of his sister as a loyal coexplorer, of his parents always home in the cabin, in their designated spaces, his mother creating clothes and household objects out of recycled materials, his father tending the extensive indoor and outdoor gardens on which they partially subsisted. His father also worked part-time as a CPA, just enough to support their "whole nutty operation," as his mother called it.

Though he loved it, Billy outgrew the nutty operation as soon as he went away to college. His first trip back home from the Oregon College of Art and Craft had him feeling too close, embarrassed that each member of the family always knew what the other was doing, including spending time in the bathroom, a thin-walled structure in the middle of the house. That all they had was each other came to feel like punishment instead of comfort.

"Hey, man." Here was Keith Margolis, clapping him on the shoulder. "Thanks for everything."

"Yes, um, thank you very much for the trip." April turned shy with Keith around.

"Go say hi to your mother. She's inside with Tigey." Keith kissed her on the forehead and took her bags. "And be nice," he called after her.

To Billy, he said, "Are we square?"

"What?"

"What do we owe you for the trip?"

"Oh, please," Billy said, waving his palms. "Done deal." The last thing he wanted to do was talk to Keith Margolis about money. Maggie had told him that April's parents had given her a huge wad of cash to bring to Paris. A dangerous amount, Maggie'd said—she wouldn't even say how much over the phone—which of course she made April pack right back in her suitcase with a vow to hand it to her parents the instant she got home.

"So we're covered?" Keith said.

Billy made a mental note that April had not turned over the money *the instant* she got home.

"We want to do our part. Or more." Keith leaned in, practically on his tiptoes to offer his share.

"How's the pool going?" Billy said.

"Something's wrong with the gunite, apparently. Reshoot, recure," Keith said, wincing. "We'll probably miss the season. So what do I have? A giant hole in the ground and a lot of money out the window."

"They say you can never count on season one with a pool," Billy said.

"They say a lot of things, buddy. But that doesn't change anything."

Billy was surprised to find Maggie in the bathtub.

"I know we're in a hurry to get on the road," she said, "but the whole plane ride I was just dying for a bath."

"We'll get there when we get there," Billy said. "I'm sure Uncle Richard won't mind. He's not dying to go anywhere."

She slipped under the water, resurfaced sleek-headed and small. He pictured her as a little girl, taking on the cold, rocky Maine Atlantic, which he knew her to do have done, swimming to a small island her family owned across the bay from their house. Her mother would drink all morning, starting with something sharp and sweet in her coffee, then by noon she would shut all the shades in the house. As soon as May came, barely spring in Maine, Maggie would put on her wet suit and head out to Blueberry Island, which had nothing on it but a sprawling tangle of blueberry bushes and a giant flat rock on which to lay out her wet suit.

Some of this she'd told him, some he'd imagined. He'd imagined, for instance, that while her wet suit warmed up on the sunny rock, she waited with a mixture of dread and longing. She was alone on a desert island, a strong girl who could take care of herself. Thanks to a summer outdoor-survival program, she even knew what leaves and bugs to eat if she had to stay here forever. But, at the same time, she was lonely and missed her family. She missed her father, who wouldn't be home for hours, and even then, he'd check in first with her mother, which could have him disappearing upstairs for an hour. Maggie missed her mother, too, although what she missed wasn't really *her mother* at all. She missed the idea of a mother. Glacia, who fed and cared for the girl, was the closest Maggie had. Maggie missed her sister, Catherine, in a jumble of secrecy, shame and confusion, something that had never really settled and never really would.

Even now, Billy thought, she's missing those things, longing for a home where everyone's waiting for her, where she's embraced fully. He did his best, but he was only one person. A limited person. Barclay was the expansive one in the family, the real hugger. Oh, how Barclay tried. But now, with arthritis in his back legs and cataracts in his eyes, his displays of affection were inefficient and inexact.

"It's not going to get any more interesting," Maggie said.

"What?" Back to the moment at hand.

"You're staring at me in the bath," she said, "like you're expecting a show."

He wagged his eyebrows, trying to conjure up lasciviousness rather than reveal what he was really feeling—pity.

"Do you think I need a suit?" he said. "Or can I do the jeans-and-a-tie thing?"

"You're a hotshot artist," she said. "I think you can wear whatever you'd like."

"Come get me in the studio when you're ready."

"Look what happened while I was away," she said. "Now you're going to the studio even in the, *gasp*, daytime."

"*C'est ça,*" he said, with a little salute.

The studio had not yet come into its best light. That would happen midafternoon, which had always suited Billy's habit—late to bed, late to rise. He didn't even want to think about how little he used to work. Since he met Christian Gray, he had reported for work every day. Ash Flemming would probably see right through this. Cane didn't do anything unless someone was looking, while Ash, the real artist, labored away in obscurity, not caring about the paint-by-number patron, the galleries, the $150,000 someone had bet on his ability to make something more meaningful and beautiful than original earth-dug rock. Any day now, Christian was due to send Billy his check for half—$75,000, the first money he had made for himself in about ten years.

Just as the cash in the case made Billy's earnings look meager, so did Maggie's trust fund render $190,000 finite. Well invested by her other maternal uncle, Richard's brother Allen, Maggie's family money flooded back at them every quarter. *For the next generation's college fund,* or some such, Allen would handwrite on the statement. *Should cover a Harvard semester—or Brown, if you must.* Recent returns were down by some twenty percent, but Allen still attached a hopeful note. *Back up by the time the kids get to college!* (Did he not know them at all?)

Instead of a secret combination and a bomb-proof safe, Billy had good old-fashioned Hudson Valley humidity to guard his money. Lift the cabinet door a quarter inch and pull it just so. Up and out at the same time, and a little to the left.

In the moment-longer-than-it-should that it took him to wrestle with the door, he wondered what would have happened if he'd found the briefcase on a different day, or at a different time. If it had been just him and Maggie at the pool, they surely would have made a different decision. Turned it in to the police, most likely, or dumped the whole thing in the trash.

What if Billy had found it by himself? *What if . . . what if . . . ?* He would have kept it—and kept it to himself. If only to have a whopping secret. A reserve that was all his own. *Mad money.*

Up and out at the same time, and a little to the left. Lean with a knee, pull with body weight.

He fell back a step, so suddenly did it give way.

No briefcase.

He squatted down, reached in, reached around. There was

hardly anything in this cabinet to begin with. A bucket and an old bottle of Drano. And nothing else.

He pressed his fingers to his eyelids. *Think, think.* Had he moved it? He searched his brain.

Then he searched the studio. There was a lot of *behind, under* and *over*; there were a hundred places it could be. Had Maggie moved it? She claimed not to know where it was, but how hard would it have been to find if she wanted to? How hard would it have been for *anyone* to find? *Not in the pool shed? How about the one other outbuilding on the property? Let's see, let's start under the sink . . .*

His neighbors. Keith came to mind first. The guy wanted a Porsche and a pool, and his wife was after plenty of things that money could buy. How long would it be before they exhausted their own 240 grand? And that wasn't even considering college, food on the table and all the other things he imagined parents had to worry about. How about the Levs? After working hard all their lives, why shouldn't they want an easy retirement, which would come easier with four hundred thousand dollars than with two hundred thousand? And now, the stroke—medical bills, rehab bills. Wouldn't more money mean less worry?

How about the new neighbors? No one knew too much about them. Guy tried to disclaim his Porsche, but who knew? Maybe Daniel Hansen was as greedy as any other working stiff. Another couple hundred thousand couldn't hurt. Especially if he was one of these guys who believed money makes money. Or Flemming. That would be just like him. Not to take it for himself—poverty being the coin of the realm for real artists—but to take it away from Billy, to hit him where he, Ash, assumed it would hurt most.

How about April Margolis, the constant houseguest? He was sure he had track of the money before Maggie and April left for Paris. No, he wasn't sure. Couldn't be sure of anything, once that thread started unraveling. *Had he found anything at all?* Maybe the whole thing had never happened. He'd made a break with reality somewhere along the line. He would check down the street and see if those construction vehicles were really in front of the Margolises' house.

A knock, a peeking head. "No suit?" Maggie said.

"I lost track of time," he said, looking around him, as if time were around here *somewhere*.

"Are you cleaning up?" she said. "You pick the strangest times to do the strangest things."

"You look dressed for a funeral," he said, trying to cover his nerves.

She curtsied.

Again, a stranger. A *McKenzie.* She wore a short-sleeved black jacket with big gold buttons and a short but dowdy black skirt. It looked lined, heavy, made of some old-fashioned, old-lady material, the way it stood separate from her, didn't move as she moved. She wore pearls and pink lipstick.

He somehow got his breath, then he struggled for his courage. All he needed was a casual, "Hey, did you by any chance move the money?" And in the same casual vein he'd probably get a perfectly reasonable explanation. *God, I forgot to tell you. I brought it inside—the humidity!* Or, *On second thought, the front closet is a better place.* Or, *I went to the police after all.*

"You okay?" she said.

He nodded. "I guess the Richard thing finally caught up with me." To his surprise, he teared up.

He conjured Richard's image, walking the grounds in December, half hearty, halfway dead. Could Richard have somehow come back for the money, knowing his last day was near?

"I know," Maggie said. "I was going to say he was like a father to me. But my *father* was really like a father to me. Richard wasn't really like a mother to me, either. No one was. But he was like a, like a . . . well, like a favorite uncle to me."

"Imagine that," Billy said, still trying to get his head in the conversation. Good thing he and Maggie were used to this, being strangers to one another, having conversations that were not remotely about what was on their minds. "Let me grab a tie, and we can go."

Maggie fell asleep before they reached the town limits, five minutes from the house. When she woke up, he would tell her about the money.

They would have a full-blown conversation. About everything. He would ask her about Paris. Then about April Margolis. Then about children. That's what everything was always leading to—or away from, so it wouldn't lead *to*.

Did she want to get started again? At least the Pill, prepare for another round? Their doctor would go over forty, drawing the line at forty-three. So they had more time. Or adopt? Domestic or international, he didn't care. They had the money for surrogacy, although she'd said that would make her feel inadequate, and he hadn't wanted to pry. But now maybe he would. He would come clean, ask her to come clean, and they would make plans together.

For years, he had wondered if he could keep going through

what they apparently needed to go through to have a child. Now he was beginning to wonder if he could go through what he would need to go through to make up for not having a child.

Nothing like a death in the family, he would say, to put things into perspective. They would smile about it, carry that goodwill throughout the funeral, taking care to circulate to the casket and thank Richard for going ahead and dying so they could put things into perspective.

Billy was living half a life. Had been since he met Maggie— since she'd "rescued him," as a friend of his once said derisively. That friend, Ivan, wasn't much of a friend. He was a loser whom Billy was just as happy to stop hanging out with, as he'd stopped hanging out with most of his friends. Billy had also stopped living in his beloved Red Hook studio, which was one of the biggest New York City apartments he'd ever been in. He used to marvel that it was his, that he paid only nine hundred dollars a month, a steal, even if the neighborhood was pretty scary at night (and sometimes during the day). So he'd take a cab home or spend the night at a buddy's in Manhattan if that's where he ended up. So he'd break up with girls who didn't like it, or, or, or . . . Anything, to stay in that apartment. Which he gave up for Maggie.

He found himself driving fast, speeding north on I-91 to Vermont. He just wanted to get there, wanted Maggie to wake up so he could come clean, wanted to be at a funeral so he could put things into perspective.

He was ready to give up his old life when he met her. Timing was everything. With the way Red Hook was changing, that apartment was probably long gone, or long renovated and renting at thirty-five hundred a month. Ten years later.

Ten years! What did he have to show for himself? The biggest thing he'd ever accomplished in his life was finding a briefcase with a million dollars—granted, that was big—splitting it with his neighbors and somehow winding up with nothing. Except a creeping sense of acrimony up and down the street. It occurred to him that there had not been, not from a single soul, anything even resembling gratitude.

Just past Springfield, Massachusetts, traffic slowed to a crawl. In the distance, Billy could see the flashing lights of emergency vehicles.

Maggie blinked awake as the traffic turned stop-and-go. "What is it?"

"Accident," he said.

She nodded, then nodded back to sleep.

There, I told her, he joked to himself. If she asked him later why he didn't tell her right away that the money was gone, he would say, *I did. Right outside Springfield on the way to the funeral. I told you everything. "Accident," I said. What did you think I was talking about?*

34

All Hail

"The sky is falling," Shoshanna said.

Daniel and Shoshanna huddled in the open doorway, bracing to run to the car amid pebble-sized hailstones.

"All hail the end of summer," Daniel said.

The formal end to summer: driving to Connecticut to pick up the kids from a week with their cousins at Shoshanna's brother's seaside house.

"Here goes nothing." Shoshanna charged out to the driveway with her hand over her head.

The childlike optimism of his wife's gesture—a naked hand could protect her from exactly nothing—made Daniel unaccountably sad.

He grew sadder when he couldn't leave the doorway . . . couldn't leave . . . and again he couldn't leave. He was like a kid trying to jump off the high dive on the count of three. *One . . . two . . . three . . .* And there he stood.

Inside the car, Shoshanna shook her hair and brushed at her shoulders. She looked over at him and waved.

The sky had been a monolithic charcoal all morning. But in the distance, a discrete cloud was limned in gold. A break in the mass. Hail was a short-lived rarity in this part of the world, wasn't it? It would stop any minute, wouldn't it?

Shoshanna's wave grew more insistent, turned to a beckon. *Come on. What are you doing?*

The pelting hail was dissipating. A rational person would wait in the doorway another moment for it to be over.

She honked the horn. One, two, three angry blasts.

Which somehow brought an end to the hail. More golden light shouldered into the sky. Daniel patted himself down, pretending to double-check for keys although he could feel them in the front pocket of his jeans, digging into his leg.

Finally, he left the house. "Sorry," he said, getting into the car.

"What were you waiting for?" she said.

He gestured to the sky, which was brightening with a vengeance. "I knew it was almost over."

"Why didn't you tell me that before I ran out into a hailstorm?"

"Honestly," he said, starting up the car, "I didn't know you were going to run out into a hailstorm."

"Wasn't that what we were doing, running to the car? Why were we standing in the doorway with the door open if we were waiting for the storm to pass? Why weren't we sitting at the table with a cup of coffee, saying, 'Let's wait for this thing to blow over'?"

He shrugged. The fresh-washed silence and light-pierced

sky were recriminating, as if it had been a perfectly beautiful day all along and Daniel Hansen had simply stayed put in the doorway.

"Since when are you a chicken?" she said.

"Just started," he said. "Just now."

He knew that on another day, or even another moment in this day, he might have been the one running to the car while Shoshanna stood in the doorway. It wasn't as if Shoshanna was the brave one and Daniel the timid one. It wasn't as if she was careless and he, cautious. It was just that they were making decisions separately now. There was no telling—even if they actually told one another—who'd be still standing on the high dive and who'd be in the water below.

His mind kept running to bold red lines of marching dialogue. *My husband doesn't understand me. . . I'm here, always here.*

Michelle had not committed to anything. Why had he felt such complicity? Her utter responsiveness was just the nature of instant messaging.

"How are the roads?" he heard his wife say.

The roads . . . the roads . . . Driving. Here. Now. Wife. Kids.

"The roads?" she said. *"Terra mater?"*

"Mmmmm." He bit the inside of his cheek. "I'm trying to decide."

"It's more of a 'yes' or 'no' question than a 'deciding' question," she said.

"Okay, then—yes."

"I guess I mean more of a one-word-answer kind of question," she said. "Some examples would be *slippery, fine, unpredictable, not bad,* which is technically two words but in this case functions as one."

"Ah, semiotics."

"Something," she said. "Otherwise I think we might not talk the entire drive."

"It's only forty-five minutes."

"That's your take?" she said. "That's your whole take on the fact that we haven't really talked to each other in months?"

"No," he said. "That's my take on how long the drive is to Etan's house. I didn't know we were having a conversation about whether we have or haven't talked in months."

"Haven't," she said.

"So I hear."

She went through her pocketbook, zipping it, unzipping and rezipping it. She put it on the floor of the backseat.

After a minute, she asked, "How much money do you have in your wallet right now?"

"No idea," he said. "Why?"

"I went to the ATM yesterday for cash," she said. "I had honestly forgotten, then I remembered. And I thought it was funny to be going to the ATM."

He nodded, paused, waited.

"I haven't even opened the trunk," she said. "You?"

He shook his head.

Since he left his job, Daniel had been depositing Zayde's cash (which was how he thought of it) each week into their bank account to mimic his paycheck. So far, the trunk was down about twenty-two thousand dollars, which did little to change the bills' high-water mark at first glance.

He'd been in charge of dividing up the money. Why hadn't he foreseen this, that he and his wife would go down entirely separate paths? He could have written that into the formula.

Couples acting together get a certain figure; couples acting apart get double.

The car lost its footing through a curve. Just a little, just enough for him to tighten his grip on the steering wheel. If asked about the roads again, he'd have something to say. *Slippery*, he'd say, *especially the curves.*

She settled into her silence. He concentrated on driving. He heeded the lowered speed limit on the ample "curvy road" signs, but he ramped back up to highway speed between curves.

"What's the matter with you?" Shoshanna asked after about ten minutes of silence.

"What do you mean? I'm driving," he said.

"You never talk about work anymore. How is work?"

"It's fine," he said.

"How come you never talk about it?"

"It's so banal, it doesn't bear retelling."

"We used to share our days, no matter how banal," she said. "Which most everything is, anyway. That's life."

"You want me to let you know every day that nothing's changed?"

"Nothing's changed *so much* that I can't help thinking that something's changed. You come home at the exact same time every day."

"It's called a train schedule."

"But for, like, a month and a half, not a single variant. You used to work late at least once a week. And you'd go in early now and then, like before the Tuesday staff meeting. And late, too, for those midmorning client meetings you love to schedule so you can go in late."

"Things are so uneventful, barely a dull meeting to tell you about." He took this curve too fast. He knew it as soon as it was too late.

"Slow down." Shoshanna grabbed his leg.

The car kicked out of its arc.

He touched the accelerator and turned with the fishtail. With it, with it.

"You're speeding up," she shouted.

They straightened out. He tapped the brake, reclaimed his lane. Mercifully, there was no one else on the road, midmorning Saturday, middle of the woods in the middle of Connecticut.

"What were you doing?" she said. "You sped up. Were you trying to kill us?"

"You can't brake in the middle of a curve. Even if your wife shouts at you. If you can bear the counterintuitiveness, you're supposed to speed up a little. Counter the centrifugal force. But you don't brake. That makes it worse. You asked about the roads—there's your answer."

"You could have said 'slippery,' " she said, "instead of almost killing us."

He wished he had his keyboard. Then he might be able to talk to her.

White clapboard and shingle houses grew bigger the closer they got to the shore. Slow down to a strictly enforced fifteen miles an hour, Main Street, a sharp right at the end of town, then 1.4 miles to the Yanivs' unmarked street. "Cousins' Camp" at the beach house was Shoshanna's sister-in-law's idea. Leslie and Etan had four kids, including a boy Caleb's age, and Leslie thought Caleb and Allie would love staying for a week without their parents. Maybe you'll love it, too, without the kids, she'd said to Shoshanna and Daniel.

Without the kids, he and Shoshanna drifted to TV, Sudoku, e-mail, which would take Daniel into another world entirely. If they were still in the city and without the kids for a week, they could have gone out to eat, gone to a movie, seen one of Daniel's coworkers in a band, play or reading. Gone out for a drink, walked the Promenade. Now, they couldn't seem to find anything to do alone together.

If he had his keyboard, he would have typed, *Why did we move to Ashley-on-Hudson?*

He would have typed, *Just when I think I'm starting to understand the rules, you change them.*

Or he would type, *Just when I think I'm starting to understand the rules, my wife changes them.* And Michelle would bring her own marital discord to the fore, telling him again how little attention her husband paid to her.

Shoshanna touched his leg. Daniel jumped.

"Don't look at me like that," she said. "I'm not going to yell at you. I just want to stop and pick up a cup of coffee before we get there. Do you want anything?"

He shook his head, pulled up in front of Hill of Beans and let her out. He could see from here that there was a line inside. He picked up his cell phone out of habit—wait in the car, check voice mail, check e-mail, check on work, check on something, anything.

He'd gotten Michelle's number from her e-mail and stored it in his phone under the name "Bud."

"Hello," she whispered.

"Did I wake you up?"

"Who is this?" she said.

"Daniel."

"Oh, my God. Are we calling each other now?"

"Apparently," he said.

"I don't know if I'm ready for that," she said. "I mean, my God, what are we doing?"

"I'm sorry," he said. "I'm sorry. I just needed, wanted, needed to make sure you were real."

She laughed. "Sometimes I wonder myself."

"I can't even talk now," he said. "I'm waiting in the car for someone—"

"Your wife," she said. "You can say you're waiting for your wife. Who else are you going to be waiting for in the car on a Saturday morning?"

"Is your husband there, is he home?"

"Saturday morning squash. To be followed tomorrow by Sunday morning squash. It's just me and Peyton. Oh, and his spit-up."

Daniel looked inside the coffee place. Shoshanna was nearing the front of the line already.

"I should go," he said. "I'm sorry to call, especially if I woke someone up. Especially if you didn't want me to call."

She breathed audibly into the phone. He couldn't tell if it was meant for him, something intimate, or if she was simply breathing.

"I don't mind," she said.

"I love you," he said.

"I should go," she said. "You should remember that you don't even know me."

* * *

"Who were you talking to back there?" Shoshanna asked as they pulled into Leslie and Etan's long white gravel-and-seashell driveway.

"Voice mail."

"You were *talking*."

"Can't get anything by you," he said. "You and your X-ray vision."

She mock-widened her eyes, as if to see through him. Playful like this, she was pretty and familiar. *His*.

"So who were you talking to?"

"Practicing," he said. The alibi came to him fully formed. "I got a message from this client who's being really difficult. I was practicing what I was going to say."

"You have to practice?" she said. "You always seem to know just what to say. I thought that came naturally."

He had no idea she thought this about him. She kissed him lightly on the cheek.

"What's that about?" he said.

"I don't know," she said. "You. You, who always seems to know what to say. When you want to, that is." She touched—almost touched—the hair graying at his temples. "Very distinguished."

"Great," he said. "Now I'm officially old."

As they got out of the car, crunching onto the pebbles and shells, Shoshanna said, "How do you think I look?"

It took him a minute to make sense of the question, which was so out of context and out of character.

"Never mind," she said, "if you have to think about it for so long." She started walking down the sandy path to the house.

"Great," he said, catching up. "To me, you always look great."

"How come you took so long to answer?"

He shook his head. "There's no way I can win here. Tell me what to say and I'll say it."

"Too late," she said.

"You're my wife. I love you. You look great to me. What more do you want me to say?"

"Nothing," she said.

Into this would come the kids, and the four of them would be right back to their daily lives.

35

Break in Patterns

Over the course of the summer, Keith watched the daily logs for units near Rippeskill, looking for any break in patterns. Here were the patterns: B&E, noise complaints, domestic disputes, graffiti, broken windows, violations of court-issued restraining orders, drunk and disorderlies. There was the occasional twist, nudity during a B&E, graffiti on the mayor's roof. Over the summer, there was a series of school break-ins a couple towns over. That stood out. Stolen computers and science equipment, including sanctioned chemicals.

Now, end of summer, another break in patterns: undocumented alien found beaten to death in a Rippeskill parking lot where day laborers were known to gather. The department, like others up and down the Hudson Valley, had been cracking down, trying to clear illegals from town parking lots. Earlier this year, a few towns over from Ashley, cops had shot and killed an undocumented day laborer who they said threatened them when they tried to move him.

Keith hoped that this upstate homicide, an illegal Haitian named Jean Adnet Batista, wasn't cops. And he hoped it wasn't Nishal Tamobour, formerly of 7047 Palisades Boulevard.

36

Talisman

Something was different today. Cooler air sweeping through. Seasons changing. Getting closer to something. He could feel it. Couldn't name it, but could feel it.

Four times during the hot summer, when Charysse worked a double shift at the hospital, Nishal had pointed his car toward a dream of a pool in a town called Ashley-on-Hudson. Same pattern each time. He would pull just beyond the big white house, into a crooked elbow of the road (shitty paving job). He could see a big quadrant of pool and fence, enough to imagine the whole sparkling thing. Enough to forget that in his real life, he was sleeping outside on cement steps for their whisper of cool. Here, in his head, he was diving into the water, swimming a length, another. Holding his breath the whole time. He was good at this. He and his brothers used to see who could frog-swim the farthest underwater. The winner was always Nishal.

Had his *titi* given him a dream to follow, with this house, this pool, this promise of money? Or a glimpse of yet another thing he would never have?

Today, as he sat waiting in his spot, a long-legged guy, white guy, jogged past him. Right up to the front of the big house. And right inside! So that's who lived here? Shaggy-haired, not very old. Wearing a wool *tope* like Toomer. Nishal's *jai-titi*, in another chance at life.

Nishal's chest clenched with trespass.

In his earlier visits, he hadn't seen anyone come or go from the house. He'd begun to think that no one lived here. That little by little, he could take root. Bring his one box of stuff. Then bring Charysse. And her boxes, three or four. Nothing big, nothing heavy. Even from the car, he could see through the house—window to window, front to back—enough to know that it had plenty of furniture, probably very nice.

He had a plan to get closer to the house today. As he left Charysse's this morning, on the way to his car, he'd tripped on a leaf blower someone had left on the sidewalk. He cursed it, kicked its nose. Then grabbed it. A brown man with a leaf blower prowling a suburban yard? Perfect camouflage. Perfect start.

A small boy without pants ran up S-y-l-v-a-n Street.

Mother ran up the street after him.

The long-legged white guy came back outside, headed to the driveway. He called down the street, to the mother and boy.

—I'm off to the airport.

The mother came up the street.—Thanks again for picking her up. And for Paris!

—No problem. Want to hang here? By the pool?

Kid pissed an arc on the lawn.

—Oh, baby, stop that. We better get home.

—No worries. See you in a couple three hours.

Guy got in the car. Mother collected the kid and headed back down the street.

Nishal hauled the leaf blower around his neck and got to work. Waved the thing around in front of him, aiming at the few leaves on the ground. The blower was surprisingly violent, big gun against these thin leaves. He *whooooshed* his way to the pool, the shed. He could only hope no one else was home. Easily, they could be. But he had his talisman *11 Hill Road* scrap of paper in his pocket. *Baka* handyman. Blowing leaves at the wrong address. Not to mention wrong time of the year. Barely fall.

THREE

37

Fire Drill

"Oh, my," Daniel said. In the doorway stood a mirage.

No. A very real incarnation of his fantasy—projected and remembered—as well as a flesh-and-blood young mother, someone he had never known. Her face and neck were mottled with sleeplessness and her eyes were on the brink of tearing over.

She turned away. "I shouldn't have come. I feel horrible, and I look worse."

"Oh, no," he whispered. "That's not it at all. It's just that I've been thinking about this so much . . . It's kind of surreal."

"No," she said. "*That* was surreal. The e-mails, the calls, the thing in my apartment a hundred years ago. All that you're remembering. That was surreal. This right here"—she stamped her foot, which echoed surely more than she'd intended on the wide pine plank floors—"this is real."

"You look beautiful," Daniel said. "Stunning. It's just

shocking to square image with reality. Honestly, I've been doing a lot of imagining."

She brushed her hand roughly over her hair, to indicate, he assumed, how messy she looked. But the way her hair fell, off her neck, a few loose strands onto her face, was incredibly sexy.

He grabbed her, ran his fingers into her hair. He kissed her neck, and her head went right onto his shoulder.

"Mmmm," she hummed. "This is so nice I could fall asleep right here and now."

"Not exactly the response I was after."

She popped her head up. "I just dropped the baby off at my mother-in-law's house, and she said the same thing you did. 'Oh, you look terrible, poor thing.'"

"I never said that," he protested.

"You indicated it," she said. "With your eyes. Deer in headlights." She touched his cheekbone. "In any case, it's not what you want to hear when you're going off to have an affair."

"In fairness," he said, "your mother-in-law probably didn't know that's where you were going."

The tears that had been gathering in her eyes spilled over, rolled down her face. She didn't seem to realize it right away, didn't know she was crying until she felt at the damp neck of her shirt. The darkening of the heather blue T-shirt made him lick her salty neck, kiss her mouth, pry with his tongue.

Her fragility was making him desperate for her. It was part remembered fragility—they had met on a tightrope between life and death—but here it was anew, an entirely different fragility, that of a new mother. That of an unloved woman.

Arm around her back, he led her to the bed. In a shared joke, she pretended to need help, to be so exhausted, or hurt, that he had to support most of her body weight. It was a big room—this was the third-floor garret but a hell of a garret, as it had once been the focal point of this early-nineteenth-century painter's grand home. Over the traverse of the room, they fell into a mutual rhythm, as though they'd been walking together for years.

They sat on the edge of the bed. The last time, he hadn't even seen the bed, never saw any more of that railroad apartment than the hallway. He hadn't even gone into the kitchen for a glass of much-needed water.

She exhaled heavily and deeply, in a way that suggested sleep. He felt tired, too, catching the contagion.

It was exhausting to lead a double life. And he'd only just started. He was balanced on the cliff's edge of cheating on his wife, as this inn was balanced on a cliff overlooking the Hudson. Well. It had been balanced this way for more than a hundred years and didn't seem any worse for the peril.

He kissed her at the hairline, which seemed to rouse her. And him. He kissed her face, which brightened her. She had looked so . . . so wrecked. Beautiful, but wrecked. That was part of what his *Oh, my,* at the door had been about.

Once again, he noticed what he'd first noticed—her rare combination of fragility and wholesomeness. That was what had made him grab her hand and run down thirty-eight flights of stairs with her, had kept him holding as they walked from Manhattan to Brooklyn.

But the lit-from-within quality was missing, the thing that had made him look at her on the corner of Fort Greene Park and Something and think with absolute certainty that she was the most beautiful woman in the world. Or perhaps the quality had been lit-from-without—the sun, that September eleventh sun, that crystal clear early autumn day, that heightened experience. Of course. It had been the sheer height, or *depth*, of the experience that drew such profound contours.

And now here they were, in soft, forgiving light—light of the Hudson River School—in the middle of an Everyafternoon, in a rented room whose deep history threw into relief the shallowness of theirs.

"I miss him," she murmured.

"Tomas?" It was hard to say the name without mocking it. *Toh-mahs.*

"Peyton," she said. "I haven't been away from him for more than five minutes his whole life."

"But not *your* whole life," Daniel said.

She shook her head fitfully. "How about your babies?" she said. "Do you miss them? Twins, are they?"

Babies? Twins? He was suddenly relieved that he didn't have twin babies, but why on earth had she thought he did?

"You said you had two babies," she said. "I just assumed they were twins."

He laughed. "Caleb's eight and Allie's seven." Had he not included his children's ages? Had he been covering up from the very beginning?

Michelle laughed, too, harder and harder, until it turned to crying. "What am I doing?" she said.

He kissed her again, kissed her neck, down her chest. Reached the Maginot Line of the breasts and stopped. She was a nursing mother. What *was* she doing?

"Let's not do this," he said. "You're right. This is ridiculous."

Michelle stretched out on the bed, buried her face in the pillow. "This," she said sleepily, "*this* feels illicit. What I want to do more than anything else right now is lie here and sleep."

This was his affair? Served him right.

He stood. The absence of his weight made her turn over. "And hold on to you," she said. She pouted her lips. He couldn't tell if she was mocking seduction or meaning it. "There it is—the limitation of my fantasies. But I do want you badly. To hold on to."

He lay down next to her, arms around her. They both struggled to get comfortable.

"Ah, eighth grade," he said as they settled in chastely. "I remember it well."

They must have drifted off because it took them each a moment—her, several—to come to when the noise started. It was loud, like a foghorn, and seemed to be coming from all directions, from each of the four walls, from each of the four winds.

Daniel went to the window, saw a small clutch of people milling around on the back lawn. "Fire drill?" he said, shaking his head.

As if in answer, one of the men down on the lawn spoke out of a bullhorn, "Ladies and gentlemen, this is the fire alarm that you're hearing. All rooms must proceed down the stairs and onto the Great Lawn."

Once more, they held hands and marched together down flights of stairs, in this case two inside the house and the final grand staircase off the porch, leading to the Hudson River.

They skirted the small crowd, and he led her to the lawn's edge, to a flat picniclike rock where he'd sat many times before and looked over the river.

Distant sirens grew closer and closer. Two fire trucks pulled up in quick succession. Two hale crews piled off. They were greeted calmly by staff, who explained that the alarms had gone off but there didn't seem to be an actual fire. Assurance all around, and the firemen lumbered up the grand central staircase, bulls in a china shop shaking the porch up to its ornamented railings.

"We have to stop meeting like this," Daniel whispered. "Alarms, firemen." He put his arm around her and directed her gaze out to the river, while behind them firefighters continued their heroic march.

Today was a bleached summer day, Indian summer, hot and hazy even on this cliff. Fall had started to creep in in the last couple weeks, straw-scented chill in the air. But today, no crisp snatches of fall. Time was no longer marching forward but slipping backward.

Michelle slouched into him again. He was not sure what in this coupling was about lust and what was about sheer exhaustion, what was about desire and what was about physical collapse. He remembered feeling on 9/11, *Please, God, don't let me have to take care of this woman right now.* He was relieved when Michelle (Dineen, he would learn later) turned out to be strong. Strong *and* beautiful. That day—day? was it only a day?—had upended everything, revealing character like dust under a sofa. Who helped others, who ran for their own lives? Who was strong, who was not? (Strong's opposite, in this case, was not *weak*; there was no weak on that day; you did what you had to do to keep moving forward, even the unhealthy, the out-of-shape, the poorly shod, the mentally or morally unhinged, the emotionally needy, the professionally questionable; everyone moved forward, weakness crowded out by smoke and the singular urgency of getting downstairs; when there was one direction to go, everyone went one direction; the only ones who went in the opposite direction were the firemen, the heroes; but heroism met no villainy on the ground that day; the heroes had arrived too late to slay the villains.)

"This is pretty," she said, looking up and down the Hudson. "How do you know about this place?"

"I come here sometimes," he said.

"With your family?" she asked matter-of-factly, perhaps forgetting what they were doing here.

"By myself."

"Really?" she said. "You just say, what, 'Gotta go look at the river, back by dinner'?"

His confession lodged in his throat. "Something like that."

"I'll have to try that," she said. "My husband heads out every chance *he* gets. 'Gotta go whack a hard little ball around a white court with another asshole who's as angry as I am.'"

She looked startled, and a little amused. "Wow," she said, biting her lip. "I didn't know I felt that way about him."

"Live and learn," Daniel said.

"Live and loathe, apparently," she said.

"I'm sorry," he said. Then, after a minute: "Actually, I come here to work on my novel. I'm writing a novel."

She cocked her head, interested. She didn't know that this was the first time he had told anybody, the first time he'd uttered it out loud. She didn't know that he had quit his job, had written fifty pages, thought it might be good, might be worth pursuing. She didn't know that he had no idea who in the world he was, that he had blacked out the first eight years of his life. She didn't know that she was about to have an affair with someone whose father had been a small-town, small-time embezzler, which Daniel had come to believe was the worst kind—all the pain and little of the gain. She had no idea that her potential lover and his wife had taken a couple hundred thousand dollars that the wife thought was immoral but the husband didn't. Daniel realized only now that he had been thinking of the source of the money as some penny-ante swindler, some loser who deserved to lose his money. Hell, the guy had actually lost the money. Can't be any more of a loser than that.

That the money had found a better home on Sylvan Street, among deserving people, seemed all right to Daniel, although his wife, and, he gathered, other neighbors, had turned it into some kind of morality play, though just who the enemy was no one knew. Everything was black and white with Shoshanna. With him, it was all gray. How could their marriage survive?

He threw Michelle back on the rock, kissed her, sucked her neck, fingered the button of her jeans. Behind them, engines started up again. He glanced over, watched people walking back up the stairs.

"Come on," he whispered. "Come upstairs to my garret."

Mounting the stairs with this woman—*that* was the 9/11 feeling he was after. Again they found themselves groping each other on an old wooden floor. Guilt, exhaustion and desperation, in equal measures, found a single united form that couldn't even wait the traverse of the room, to the bed.

38

The Brothers Grim

Chapter 3: Robbie, Run

You cannot believe what you've done. You cannot square it with all that you meant, all that you hoped.

You have left a woman at the altar.

On the rare occasions that you have heard about some Neanderthal who did such a thing, you've always thought it was the lowest form of cowardice.

You started the journey to the altar with such hope and promise. You had a newfound appreciation of all living things, your family, past, present and future. Your girlfriend, soon to be your wife. Your imperfect, felonious, generous parents. Your stiff brother, who was generous in his own stiff way. His growing inability to forgive your parents has made it easier for you to forgive everyone everything.

In fairness to you (oh, why not?), extenuating circumstances intervened between your popping the question and your getting out of Dodge. Extenuating circumstance #1: your father died.

Extenuating circumstance #2: Charles refused to take any of his money and gave most of it to you. Not all. He donated a small amount to a charity for victims of handgun violence.

These factors should have made it easier, not harder, for you to get married, to start your new life in peace and prosperity.

Instead, they made you run. Again.

Habit, yes. But hadn't Rebekah become habit, too? You were starting to relax into this life—"throwing in with someone," as she delightfully put it. Discovering things together, having someone to debrief, and debrief to, at the end of the day. Staying in bed on Sundays, doing the *Times* crossword puzzle. Making love in the middle of the night, the middle of the week, the middle of the day. How surprisingly satisfying to have someone around all the time who loves you and wants to fuck you, or at least doesn't mind it.

You still took off now and then, but your trips—at first—had a different character, a more wholesome, promising feel, since you had someone to call home to. These trips were even productive, perish the thought, as you investigated the possibility of buying a small-town newspaper, newspaper group or other modest media opportunity.

Your mind wanders—it's *your* mind, after all, so it is on the run, too—to these media opportunities. You're heading toward a newspaper chain in North Platte, Nebraska. Ostensibly. And another opportunity out in Montrose, Colorado, a newspaper/television partnership seeking to take advantage of newly relaxed FCC regulations. On the way, you plan to stop in Denver to visit Claire Littlefield, a former college housemate to whom you drift when you're running away. After all these years, she still holds a candle. She will take you in, she will feed you and sleep with you, stroke your ego, make you feel good for as long as any synthetic high lasts.

You think about how buoyantly Claire Littlefield is cleaning her small duplex right now in anticipation of your visit, how she is grooming herself more thoroughly than she has in months, how she is trying desperately to lose a few pounds in these few days, which will only make her famished and more susceptible to getting drunk on the first glass of wine once you arrive. You know you never should have taken the friendship here. You genuinely care about her. She was the one you liked best in the house full of women—and one man, sensitive Robbie Wills, who pulled his weight doing the cooking, cleaning and other house chores. Claire understood you, or so you thought, until her crush took her down the wrong road, the road of getting blowsy around you, drinking too much (or, worse, pretending she had), letting her knee fall against your leg at a movie, letting her hip or buttocks brush cruelly close to your crotch as you two moved around each other to cook together in the tiny house kitchen.

Maybe you'll call her and tell her you broke down. Leave another woman at another threshold.

Please, let you stop thinking about Claire Littlefield.

You pass a sign that says I-80, NORTH PLATTE, CHEYENNE. Which makes you think of Macky Fine. You wonder whether he's dead or alive, what name he chose, where he might be if he's still walking this earth. Does he ever think of your parents?

You think a lot of random things because you have a lot of time to think. *On the run* is a bit of a misnomer. It's more like being *on the think*. You are, first of all, not running. You sit in a car all day every day. It's the opposite of running. You do not

move a single muscle. You feel your strength and vitality drain-
ing away by the day. You deserve it. You deserve for all your
manly qualities to desert you. You should grow fat, out of shape,
bald. Your mother used to say, with that famous glint in her
eye—at once sly and genuine—You get the face you deserve. She
would say this after receiving a compliment on how great she
looked in her latter years. Which she did, and people frequently
told her. That steel gray braid, steely constitution, strong nose,
bright eyes.

You didn't know then, of course, how fraught, perhaps ironic,
it was for her to say that, *You get the face you deserve.* You
thought she meant: by putting up with your father, by playing
second fiddle all these years, by caring for everyone else around
her so they could shine while she flickered on untended, year
after year. You didn't think she meant: by committing and then
running from a violent federal crime, although she thought with
all her moral fiber that it was the right thing to do at the time.

Mother gone, father gone. Technically, you are an orphan,
although you hardly want to take any deserved sympathy from
the real orphans, the poor, parentless little children of the world.
At some point, most of us become orphans. Those who don't—
that's where the real tragedy lies.

Your father has essentially been gone for about a year. Cruelty of Alzheimer's. But now he is actually gone. He died two
weeks ago. Passed, Charles said, as he spread the news, phone
call after phone call, to those in Dad's address book.

First, and quite possibly not in Dad's address book,
was you.

"Robert," Charles said. So you knew either it was something
to do with money or Dad died.

Charles left the details of planning the funeral to you (of all people). Calling the funeral home, greeting people at the door. Flanked by your fiancée, you rose to the challenge. You were a normal person for a little while, beloved and responsible, knowing you owed your father your life. Whatever he did in his did not negate that.

Charles, seething, feels otherwise. The secret revealed has divided your brother's life, gave him a *self he knew* and a *self he no longer knows*. He is on the run, too, although he won't dare leave town. His wife has called you a few times over the past year, since your father confessed his secret, and asked if you knew what was wrong with Charles. "He's completely shut down," she said.

"How can you tell?" you asked.

Thankfully, she took that the right way, the way you actually meant it, rather than the way someone could have taken it, given Charles.

They came to the funeral, Charles and Tricia, but just barely. They didn't bring their kids, which seemed terribly unfair to your father. To your mother, too, and to the children, who, until a short time ago, loved their grandparents. Charles and Tricia sat in the back of the room. They left right after the service.

"He's dead to me," Charles whispered as he walked out the door.

This was all the more devastating with your father at the front of the room in a coffin.

You are in the middle of Nebraska. That's where your drive has taken you. One thing you don't think about is how long it will take you to get anywhere. The newspaper in North Platte, the media opportunity in Colorado—they'll be there whenever you get there. And if they're not, just as well. Then they weren't for you anyway.

Another thing you don't think about—okay, now you are— is the woman you are leaving at the altar. She would be glorious on the day itself. *Shit, today.* You would surely be walking down the aisle thinking, *I don't deserve her.* Rebekah has a way of dressing up that catapults her way out of your league. She has a glamour to her that, if properly attended, makes her look old-time rich, Upper East Side. Or, as you and Charles used to say when you were teenagers, "dripping with it." She has deep chestnut hair, porcelain skin (shockingly white, actually), high cheekbones, a fine-boned nose—a look that at first, out of habit and loyalty to Flatbush, turned you off, then, out of a more primordial habit, turned you on.

She would have gone all out (or should you say, out on a limb?) for this day, which she agreed to with great trepidation. "With your history of taking off?" she had said. "I would be crazy to say yes."

You learned your lesson, you changed, you loved commitment now because you loved her. You said this every way you could think of. Indignantly, desperately, lightly, gravely, angrily and even, if it came across the way you hoped, spiritually.

Then, it was as if you'd used up every available ounce of your convincing powers and had none left for yourself.

You make yourself stare at the image of her at the altar, standing under the chuppah at the temple, looking around with a dawning panic. *He better not . . .* You have to use your imagination because she did not let you see the dress, the veil or her bouquet beforehand. How puny superstition is under the brutal steamroller of destiny. You imagine the details you know. Her rich brown hair swept up into the complicated knot she wears for special occasions (none so special as this), the heart-shaped neckline of the dress (she told you this one detail, perhaps to grant you a lust-provoking image in the long weeks leading up to the wedding), alabaster skin that makes you touch your hand to your own face right now just to be touching skin, just to ground—however imperfectly—that image of her skin. Otherwise, you imagine, the charge will kill you. You concentrate on these details, squint even, to conjure up your would-be bride, knowing—hoping—it will burn out your corneas as surely as if you were staring at the sun.

39

The Birds and the Bees

It was only the third week of school, and April was already seeing a boy. When she was home at all, she was on her cell phone, talking to or about this Tucker (first name or last, Jen did not know). The twins trilled *Tucker, Tucker,* making kissy lips, whenever April's phone rang a particularly appalling ringtone, a catcall whistle.

"April," Jen said in a rare moment between phone calls, catching her daughter in the doorway, on her way out. "You can be really dense for a know-it-all. That's a pretty sexist ringtone for someone who purports to be your boyfriend."

"What do you mean, 'purports'?" April said. "And what do you mean, 'know-it-all'?"

"How about, What do you mean, 'sexist'?" Jen said. "If he's your boyfriend, he should treat you with more respect than that whistle."

"Don't be dense, Mother," April said. "*You* set someone's ringtone. *They* don't set it for themselves."

"That's even worse."

"What do you want me to give him, Mozart?"

"That would be classy, Margolis," Jen said. "I bet you don't have it in you."

April opened the screen door but didn't leave right away. She stared at her phone. Jen was hopeful that the mother, for once, had won, that her daughter would rise (sink?) to the reverse psychology, show her mother a thing or two by going to her new computer and downloading a Mozart ringtone.

"Damn," April said. "I missed a call." The screen door sprung shut behind her. If only she were just going to the Manor House. What used to seem so worrisome—April spending every afternoon with Maggie Cane—was now a distant memory of easier, more innocent times when April was not angry and spiteful and off with a boy.

Jen knew that she, of all people, should have the Talk with her sixteen-year-old daughter. Be careful with a boy. Sex is special and should wait until you're old enough to know what you're doing. Don't let what happened to me happen to you.

In the middle of the lecture-in-Jen's-head, April ducked back inside. "Forgot my hoodie."

Jen took a breath, took April by the wrist and sat her down on the couch. *Now or never.* "We need to have a little talk," Jen said.

Jen sat inches away from her daughter, even though Jen knew full well that with a teenager, the maternal magnetic field repelled rather than attracted.

"I need to talk to you about boys and . . . and all the things that that means. Sex, birth control, respecting yourself."

Tiger streaked through the room and leapt onto the couch, the mother-toddler magnetic field all attractant.

"Go upstairs, sweetie," she said, hoisting him to the floor. "Go find your sisters.

"Brit, Beth," she hollered at the ceiling, "please watch your brother. He's coming up."

"How come they don't have to listen to this?" April said.

"They're twelve, and you're sixteen," Jen said. "So let's focus on you. You and me, to be exact. Here it is: sex has consequences. I'm living proof, and so are you. You were the best baby ever, and I wouldn't trade you for the world. But sixteen is no time to take care of another human being. I didn't go to college, didn't go out and do all the things kids are supposed to do before they have to be grown-ups."

April fidgeted into every position possible, tucking one foot under her, two feet, pulling one back out, kicking the floor. She stared alternately at the couch arm and at her phone. But she stayed, and that was all you could ask from a teenager.

"The only thing that made it okay was your dad," Jen said, modulating her voice as carefully as she ever had. *Don't cry. Don't sound desperate. Don't lose her.* "He rescued us. He went to work right away to support us. He and Grandma and Grandpa made it possible. But it was crazy hard, and I didn't know what I was doing, and the last thing in the world I want is for you to end up how I ended up."

"In this dump," April muttered.

"Excuse me, I misspoke," Jenny said, breathing to the count

of three. "I, we, *ended up* fine. What I mean is I would hate for you to start out how I started out."

Keith strolled into the room. "Hi, girls." He plopped into his chair and took off his windbreaker, as if the weather were calmer inside.

"Dad," April said, "make her stop yelling at me when I haven't even done anything."

Keith looked to Jen, back to April. "I doubt she's doing that, Ape. What's going on, Jen?"

"We have a *teenager* on our hands," Jen said. "And there are things she has to know."

Keith gave her the half-dope, whatever-you-say look.

"Don't look at me like that," Jen said. "The birds and the frigging bees."

He stood, took a step.

"Don't you dare," said Jen. "You're here. You help."

"Oh, come on, Jen," he said. "I'm terrible at this. I'll strong-arm the boyfriend if you want, or disable his car so he can't get anywhere. I'll put a dead bolt on my baby girl's bedroom door. But please don't make me stay for this."

April, at least, was smiling. "Yeah, me neither."

"Oh, go. Both of you," Jen said. Alone, she was weak. "Don't do anything stupid. Either of you."

April slipped out the door. Keith ducked into the kitchen.

"I should have known something was up," he said when he came back with a beer. "The two of you sitting on the couch like that. *Boxers, take your corners.*"

Over the course of the brief lecture, she and April had inched away from each other until they were practically hugging opposite arms of the couch.

"Thanks for the support," Jen said.

"Live to serve, ma'am," Keith said, clicking his heels and squaring his shoulders.

"What do you think happened on that trip to Paris?" Jen asked.

"What do you mean?"

"She seems different. More . . . more angry at us."

"I think she turned sixteen is what happened," Keith said. "I don't think it had anything to do with the trip. Or maybe it opened her eyes, one thing in a long line of things that are going to show her all there is in the world, how small she is, how small—smaller—we her parents are. How much there is to *want*. She's a teenager. That's what happens."

"Since when did you become a philosopher?"

"Always have been," he said. "I just keep it well hid."

"*Very*," she said.

Keith came over to the couch. He kissed her neck, pressed himself against her.

"What are you doing?" she said.

"Making a pass at my wife," he murmured into her hair. "There are no kids around, for a change."

"Are you trying to demonstrate exhibit A, case in point?" She squirmed away.

He went after her, though halfheartedly. "I'm just being friendly."

"It's four o'clock in the afternoon." She stood up.

He exaggerated his fall off the couch, landing on one knee. "Gee, thanks a lot."

"Come on," she said. "I just barely got finished saying no sex, and . . ."

"You were talking to the teenager," he said. "I, on the other hand, am a consenting adult."

"Sometimes I wonder, Keith, if you're with me or against me."

His ears reddened. She didn't know why she'd said it. It wasn't true, never had been.

His face tightened, and his shoulders. "I've been with you from the beginning," he said, "since you were Jenny Hot'n'Heavy."

"Screw you," she said. "Don't say that name."

"And you know what?" Keith said. "I married you anyway."

"That's *why* you married me. Don't make yourself out to be Mr. Virtuous."

"I married you and took on a baby when I was eighteen years old because I wanted to sleep with a hot chick?" He was bouncing on the balls of his feet. "Think about it, Jen. The minute I married you, my teenager fantasy days were over. Since we've been married, I've slept with you, my *wife*, about—how many kids do we have together?—three times, counting the twins as one."

"Is that all you think about? How disappointed you are because we don't have sex all the time?"

"Forget all the time. How about *any* of the time?"

"If you make me, I'll count. It's about every two weeks, which I'm sure if you take a poll of American couples is right about average."

"Is that all you want to be, average?"

"In this particular case, yes, I would settle for that."

He deflated into his chair. "I don't know when it started. With the money, I think. You doubt everything I do and say."

"That's not true," she said.

But he was right. The money was supposed to make every-thing better, easier. A pool, a Porsche, a giant flat-screen and another, smaller, in their bedroom. *Yes* to a follow-up appoint-ment with the orthodontist. *Yes* to the pediatric optometrist. *Yes* to the Abercrombie hoodies and Mad Milo jeans, instead of *no* to everything. Even the trip to Cabo seemed possible. They were talking about Christmas, the whole family, at a resort that had activities for the kids while the parents lay by the pool with umbrella drinks. *My, my, look how far the Margolises have come.*

"I want to tell her," Keith said.

"Tell who? What?"

"Tell April," he said. "Tell her everything."

"Why on earth would you do that?"

"It's the truth."

"It's *our* truth," Jen said, her heart beating across her voice. "It's not *her* truth."

Now Jen was the one fidgeting on the couch. "We'd be send-ing her so many wrong messages," she said. "First, she'll won-der why we lied to her all these years. Second, she'll wonder what that makes you if you're not—" She lowered her voice to a harsh whisper, in case other kids were in earshot. "She'll won-der what the hell that makes you if you're not her father. And her, too, if she's not your daughter—"

"She's my daughter in every way," Keith interrupted, "includ-ing in the eyes of the law."

"Another great message you'll be sending," Jen said, "is that her mother's a slut. Which is a wonderful thing for a teenager to think about when she's all hopped up with hormones."

"I'm still her father," Keith said, eerily calm, sounding like a stranger. "And you're not a slut. I just want to stop having a secret from my daughter."

Jen squeezed the heels of her hands to her temples, giving herself an instant headache. "You're on your own with this one," she said.

"Good," he said. "I'm sure it will be easier that way."

She watched out the front window as he walked up the street, looking for his daughter.

Seventeen years ago, Will "Two-Timer" Glendenning was co-captain of the high school football team and All-State lacrosse. Jenny Hotten was a fifteen-year-old girl who had no idea you could actually talk to a boy, especially a boy like Will Glendenning. And then there they were, drinking beer at a party, standing next to each other, and before she knew what had happened—*nothing*, most likely—they were swaying to a slow song. He was getting hard against her, possibly not even knowing who she was, and leading her to a darkened, coat-strewn bedroom. They had sex a total of six times over the next couple months. He was still going out with Beth Frankle, but Jenny knew they were going to break up because Beth thought she was too good for him. *Imagine*, thinking you were too good for Will Glendenning. Jen learned later, too late, that that was a boy's code for complaining that a girl wouldn't sleep with him.

For about a semester, she went to the smaller, invitation-only jock parties, rather than the huge "open parties" everyone else went to. Sometimes the parents were even home at these smaller parties, and there was actual food out on the counter, crackers and cheese, mixed nuts, carrots and dip.

She knew that it was only a matter of time before Will broke up with her, or whatever you wanted to call it, since they were not really dating. She cushioned herself against this inevitability by sleeping with the other guys who wanted to sleep with her because they knew she was sleeping with Will. Stockie Stockwell, Terry Calloway, Sascha Goldsmith. She knew people called her Jenny Hot'n'Heavy behind her back.

Sascha was the only one she really wished was her boyfriend. He was the only one who noticed things about her. That she was good in math and in an advanced math class, that when she didn't understand something she wrinkled her nose—he touched it, called it cute—that her hair was really very pretty, especially with this new haircut.

The guys used condoms most of the time. They did not want to ruin their chances for college by getting a girl pregnant. When she missed two periods, bought herself a pregnancy test, and with a dizzying sense of loneliness and confusion did the two-pink-lines math, she determined that it could have been Terry or Sascha, neither of whom she was still sleeping with by then or even, really, running into at the parties she was only dwindlingly invited to. She called Sascha and had to say "Jenny Hotten" twice before it registered.

He didn't think it was him, he said, since they hadn't slept together for, like, two months, and he had heard she slept with a lot of guys. But once she broke down crying, he volunteered to come over with some money off his parents' ATM card and take her to get an abortion.

"I'm not getting an abortion," she said. "It's a baby. *My* baby."

"Well, it's not mine," he said, "and if you want to screw up your chance at college and the rest of your life, I can't stop you. You're a good kid, but I can't help you if you're going to sleep with a lot of guys and not be prepared to have an abortion."

"I never asked for you to *help* me," she said.

"Then what did you call for?"

She hung up.

"I thought you'd want to know," she said into the dead phone.

Then she called Keith Margolis, who she knew had a huge crush on her. Everyone knew. Keith made sure of that. He sent flowers to her in homeroom when they sold them in the gym on Valentine's Day, maneuvered his way none too subtly to walk out of math class with her, complimented her if she'd asked or answered a question, no matter how small or dumb. She wondered why he didn't know that the more he embarrassed her—flowers!—the less likely she was to go out with him. Was he really that thick?

Smart, it turned out. Keith Margolis knew what most guys in high school did not know. Nice guys do *not* finish last. You can, in fact, make a girl like you by public displays of kindness.

After Sascha, she called Keith under some pretense—missing homework assignment or missing notes. She was surprised how good it felt to talk to him, and she told him what had happened. "You're the first person I've told," she said, and she didn't feel like she was lying because Sascha Goldsmith had, over the course of this conversation, become *no one* to her.

They stayed on the phone for almost an hour. Then he asked her if she was dating anyone right now or if she might want to go to his senior prom with him.

She cried, which later became a joke in their marriage. "My loving wife," he'd say. "I ask her to my senior prom, and what does she do? Bursts into tears."

40

Friend or Foe?

Dinner came and went with no phone call from April, which was the first rule she broke. She was about to break the second: back by ten on a school night. Bedtimes had descended on the house. Keith, too, was in bed, watching TV. Jen was watching TV on the living room couch, trying to figure out how much to worry.

Keith had told April.

He'd felt good about what he was telling her, he told Jen. The truth. A truth that changed nothing between him and his daughter. "I told her it's just a formality, like checking a different box on your driver's license."

"Checking a box on your license?" Jen had said. "Oh, come on."

"If you're going to judge me," Keith said, "I'll stop. I've already told April, so my work is done, as far as I'm concerned.

But if you want to know more and can bear to withhold your judgment, I can go on."

He had delivered all this with an eerie calm, which, if Jen were to admit it, meant he was doing the right thing for his own peace of mind.

April didn't seem shocked or crushed, Keith reported. "She was very mellow. She said, 'I guess it makes a certain kind of sense.'"

"What on earth does *that* mean?" Jen said. "It's definitely an insult."

"No judgment, please." Keith held up his hand.

April apparently hadn't had many questions. She took Keith at his word, that it didn't mean anything, that it was little more than a formality. She hadn't asked why they'd kept it a secret from her all these years. "Frankly," Keith told Jen, "she acted like it was none of her business. Like it was a problem with the taxes or the mortgage, grown-up stuff that I was bringing to her."

The more he had tried to explain, or apologize, the more April was full of mercy. "God, Dad," she finally said, "it was so long ago, I wonder how you can even remember."

Then her friends drove up. "I love you, Dad," she said as she got in the car. "Not to worry."

When April didn't come home by dinner, Jen started calling April's friends, who were ridiculously wise and comforting, as mature and responsible as April used to be. No, April was not with them. She was probably with Tucker, at his house watching TV or something. If she and Jen had had a fight (which was how Jen had put it), she would probably break curfew to punish her mother. "Sorry, Jen, we all do it," said little four-and-a-half-foot-tall Katie Forbes, speaking for her generation. "We're *juniors* now."

Jen learned the boyfriend's full name, Tucker McMurtry—"He's a good kid," Katie assured her—and found the McMurtrys' number in the Ashley phone book. She copied it onto a scrap of paper, which she placed by the phone and hoped not to need. It seemed like a bad omen to introduce herself to April's boyfriend's parents this way.

She went outside just to be moving, to be doing something. Maybe April was sitting cross-legged at the foot of the driveway, talking on the phone, hugging her knees, calculating how long she'd have to stay outside on a chilly September evening to properly punish her mother. Jen reached back inside to turn off the floodlight. Forget "keeping the home fires burning."

Keith said something very smart tonight, about April growing up enough to feel small and alone in the universe. When had she, Jen, last felt alone in the universe? Probably not since she was sixteen and pregnant with a virtual stranger's baby. Ever after, there was Keith. Then April. Then the rest of the kids, *boom . . . boom . . . boom . . . boom.*

She sat down at the end of the driveway, cross-legged and hugging her knees. She thought of that night in June when everyone came out to watch the lunar eclipse. April, Jen remembered, had made a beeline for Maggie Cane. It seemed weird, but Jen couldn't say why. The twins had enlisted Allie Hansen in their flashlight-waving game, until Allie's mother told her not to waste light. Her father, Daniel, pointed out that she was wasting batteries, not light, but Shoshanna said that there was such a thing as light pollution and it was encroaching on our ability to see the stars, something we should all be acutely aware of on a night like tonight. That was when Jen's hopes diminished that she and Shoshanna would become fast friends, new neighbors with children about the same age.

Daniel seemed to know a thing or two about the eclipse, as did Janic. Jen was thankful that Keith, who knew nothing about an eclipse, had kept his mouth shut for a change. Billy Cane was quiet, too. Wouldn't it be funny, Jen thought, if Maggie had been thinking the same thing as Jen. *I hope my husband doesn't say something stupid.*

Jen had stayed out later than everyone else that night. She and Janic. Janic told Sally that he wanted to time the eclipse, or gauge it, somehow monitor it to see if the news reports had predicted correctly. For her part, Jen had been enjoying the night air and the sense that something new was possible in the largely unchanging world, the moon being erased, turning red, darkening in shadow then reappearing again, all back to normal. Unchanged.

Up the street now, the beam of a flashlight appeared. April? She had gotten in the habit of being dropped off at the corner rather than at the house, a teenage amnesty for her accomplices. Did she have a flashlight? Jen didn't know.

Shuffling and jingling. Barclay. And Maggie, who didn't see Jen until she swept her beam up the Margolises' driveway.

"Oh!" Maggie flinched. "You scared me."

Barclay raised a laryngitic bark. "Poor boy," Maggie said. "Still wants to say hello, even though he can barely talk."

Jen stood, patted his head. "Friend, not foe," she said.

Barclay nosed up the driveway.

"No, you don't live here," Maggie said, tugging at the leash. "Jen does."

"For better or for worse, Barclay," Jen said.

"Well," Maggie said into a purgatorial moment—would they linger, or would they get on with their respective evenings?—"I better get going. Lest things go from better to worse on me."

Jen put on her best false smile. *Tell me how to hold on to my daughter.*

"Onward, trusty steed," Maggie said, directing her flashlight down the street.

If Jen wasn't mistaken, Maggie was nervous, or trying to impress. *Lest? Onward, trusty steed?* Funny, Maggie nervous around *her*. *If it was about the money*, Jen thought, *Maggie was right*. Pool, Porsche, new dishwasher, new TVs. Doing exactly what they'd been asked not to do.

Maybe Maggie's nervousness had nothing to do with Jen. Maggie always seemed out of place in her own life, which felt to Jen like a luxury you couldn't afford if you had kids. She looked back at her house, windows checkered light and dark for the asleep, the awake and the awaiting.

Would April tell her siblings? Every morning that April woke up earlier than Jen and got cereal or toast for her little sisters and brother, every afternoon that the twins trailed April up the street where she would wait for a ride, every evening that the kids trampled down to the basement to watch TV, Jen would wonder. *Was she telling them now? How about now?* Maybe April would keep the secret for two more years, then head off to college. Still, every time she came home, every Thanksgiving or Christmas, every time the twins visited their big sister and stayed in her dorm room, Jen would wonder.

Keith had gone upstairs right after dinner. He was probably surfing news shows, reality shows, cop shows, baseball, football, staying on nothing for longer than thirty seconds, which Jen hated. For Keith, it was a way of watching everything. For Jen, it was watching nothing.

Let him stay up there. Let him not come downstairs looking for her, whether to apologize or be apologized to, then come outside in his underwear, thinking no one was watching. She should head him off at the pass, let him know that Maggie Cane was outside, let him know to act civilized, *please*. Which would rub him the wrong way, as everything seemed to do these days, and he would be sure not to come downstairs, which he probably hadn't been planning to do, anyway.

Boxers, take your corners. She wished he hadn't given her that image. Now she could picture everyone in the family that way.

"Still here?" Maggie said, her flashlight politely downcast this time.

"That was fast," Jen said.

"He's getting old," Maggie said. "We both are. We spend a few minutes in the woods, then back home. It's past our bedtimes."

Barclay nosed back up the driveway again. "I think he's looking for April," Maggie said.

"Join the club," Jen said. "You don't by any chance know where she is, do you?"

Maggie shook her head. "She's not home?"

"She has a boyfriend now," Jen said. "So she's hardly ever home."

"Oh," Maggie said. "I didn't know that."

Who was April to Maggie Cane?

"You think that's where she is?" Maggie asked. She let go of Barclay's leash and sat down with Jen on the driveway.

"Will he run away without the leash?" Jen wondered.

"Watch," Maggie said.

The dog turned a few stiff circles, then lowered himself to the driveway in arthritic collapse.

"Where would he go that's better than this?" Maggie said.

"You're lucky," Jen said. "I wish I could say that about my sixteen-year-old. *Where would she go that's better than this?* Just about anywhere, if you ask her. Your house, for one."

"That's only because I'm not her mother," Maggie said.

What was it like, Jen wondered, to have no children? What would she have done with her life? She was good at math. She could have gone into business with Ken Beckman, their accountant. *Her* accountant, as Keith had it. Imagine, spending her nine-to-five day with Ken, discussing investment strategies and politics, rather than chasing Tiger around trying to put pants on him, constantly searching for Kelli, arguing with April or trying to curb the twins' affluenza.

What if she just had a dog to walk three times a day, an ancient, crippled one who wouldn't even run off?

"What happened in Paris?" Jen asked, night bringing out the boldness in her.

Maggie reached for Barclay and pet—shook?—his back. "What do you mean, what happened? *Nothing* happened."

"I don't mean 'happened' like that, like something was wrong," Jen said. "She just seems more distant, angrier. Keith says it's part of growing up, of turning sixteen, of seeing the world. Then again, what the hell do I know about turning

[307]

sixteen and seeing the world? Know what I was doing when I was sixteen?"

"Actually, I do. April told me." After a long pause, Maggie added, "Pretty heavy."

"About forty pounds," Jen said. "So you can see why I'm nervous that she's off with a boy."

Jen should have pressed Keith for more information about April's tone of voice when she got in her friend's car and said, "I love you, Dad. Not to worry." *Did it sound haunting and ominous, like in a movie? Did it sound like that was the last time you were ever going to see her?*

"For what it's worth," Maggie said, "I think she'll be very careful. I know she thinks about it, and I know she doesn't want to end up—"

"In this dump," Jen said.

"That not what I was going to say," Maggie said. "You have a nice house, a robust family—"

"*Robust?*" Jen said. "That's a good euphemism."

"I mean it as a compliment."

The floodlight went on behind them. "Damn it," Jen said. "I'm being summoned. Tiger's up. Or Kelli can't be found. Or Keith's going to sleep and wants to let me know. That's my robust family. I'm going to try to ignore it."

"Can I tell you something?" Maggie's voice was quivering.

Jen concentrated on her seated shadow, double-cast in the man-made light. She imagined it anchoring her to the ground.

Maggie was looking at Jen expectantly, squinting one eye against the floodlight.

"Of course," Jen said.

"We've been trying to have a baby for years," Maggie said.

Jen had no idea what to say. "Are you doing things," she tried, "you know, fertility things?"

"I'm doing one right now," Maggie said, tearing up. "Crying at the drop of a hat is about the only fertility thing everyone agrees on."

"I'm sorry," Jen said. "Must be hard."

"Excruciating. Constant." Maggie looked off in the distance, off to the woods. "You have no idea."

The floodlight went off, as though it had been illuminated for the sole purpose of extracting a confession from Maggie Cane.

Jen and Maggie were released back into semidarkness, semisilence, another purgatorial moment, one in which Jen, mother of five, could reach out or, embarrassed and having so little margin for generosity lately, could reach back in, collect and hold what was hers.

"I'm sorry," Jen said, looking back at the mostly dark house. She realized what had probably happened with the floodlight. Keith, hearing his wife outside, turned it on to make her life easier, then remembered he was mad at her and turned it off. "I should go. I should call that boyfriend before it's really too late."

Maggie stood, too. "If you don't mind, I'll stick around, to make sure April's okay."

As they walked up the driveway, Jen took care to match her step to Maggie's, in case proximity could be taken as sympathy.

"I can just wait outside on the steps," Maggie said when they arrived at the front stoop.

"Please," Jen said, sounding, she feared, sarcastic, "come in."

"Barc." Maggie snapped her fingers and pointed to the

ground. Barclay, who'd been walking behind them, struggled to lie down. "Try doing that with a kid."

Jen glanced at the kitchen clock, 10:35, and dialed the McMurtrys'. The woman who answered sounded perfectly awake. Jen introduced herself as April Margolis's mother and apologized for calling so late on a weeknight. "I just wanted to know if April was over there, if I could talk to her."

"I'm sorry," said the mother. "I'm not sure I know April."

Jen took a sharp breath, regained her composure. "I believe she's dating your son, Tucker," she managed to say.

No glimmer of recognition. "I'm afraid Tucker's not here. He's at band practice."

"I'm sorry to bother you," Jen said. Stupidly. She had nothing to say, no orientation. She circled back to Maggie, sitting on a stool at the counter.

"She didn't even know who April was," Jen said after she hung up. "Is she blind? Or dumb? Am I? Is my daughter a pathological liar? All I see is April on her cell phone every minute of every day, going out the door, out and out and out—how is that even physically possible, to keep going out but never, it seems, come back in?"

When Jen was dating boys, if you could call it that, they never talked on the phone, hung out with friends, went to movies or dinner. They only had sex. And always in some marginal space that wasn't theirs—someone's brother's room at a party, someone's father's car, someone's neighbor's back woods.

She had imagined it was different with April. She'd pictured April doing homework with this boy or watching television on the couch with him, his parents in the room, too, asking April about her classes. But instead, Mother McMurtry had never met

April, didn't know she existed, which meant her daughter was prowling the teenage margins as well. Basement, car, woods.

"Did you call her friends?" Maggie asked.

Jen nodded, feeling sorry for Maggie, who could offer only the most rudimentary parental advice.

"Listen," Jen said. "About what you told me, about trying to have kids, I don't really know what to say—"

"I'm sorry," Maggie said. "You can forget I brought it up."

"No, of course not," Jen said. "I wish there was something I could say or do."

"We all do," Maggie said. "Billy. My doctor. Barclay. God."

"Mrs. Cane." Here was Keith in the doorway, pretending to tip a hat—to cover, Jen suspected, for his childish inability to call Maggie by her first name.

"Sergeant Margolis," Maggie said, rising to the occasion.

"April back?" Keith asked.

"No," both women said.

"Jenny called the boyfriend," Maggie reported, "to no avail."

Jen was more than happy to stay out of it as Keith and Maggie, to Jen's surprise, exchanged small talk. Jen unloaded the dishwasher, glad to be doing tomorrow morning's chore tonight.

After who knew how long, they heard Billy on the street. "Maggie?" he was calling. "Barclay?"

Maggie hid her face in her hands.

"Barc!" Billy was in the driveway. "Where's your mother?"

"That would be me," Maggie whispered, making no move to get up.

"I'll go outside and tell him you're here, if you'd like," Keith said.

"Ask him to take Barclay home, will you?" Maggie said.

Was she going to spend the night?

"I'll go," Jen said, hoping neither of them could hear her eagerness to get out of this kitchen, to leave Keith and Maggie with their secrets and their small talk.

Outside, the night was equal parts summer and fall, with lake-like pockets of warmth and chill. It was pleasantly dark and quiet until Keith, always trying to help, flipped on the flood-light.

Billy, gathering Barclay's leash, turned around and stuck up his hands—*freeze.* "Caught me stealing my dog." He bent down to scratch Barclay's ears. "Hey, have you seen my wife?"

"Actually, I have," Jen said. "She's inside."

"Kind of late, isn't it?" He rubbed his hat back and forth on his head. It was too warm, still, for wool, but Billy seemed to wear a ski hat as often as not.

"She's helping me out, I guess," Jen said. "April hasn't come home. Teenager stuff, new boyfriend, fight with the parents. You know . . ."

Billy nodded skeptically. *No, I don't know,* Jen imagined him thinking.

"She said you could take Barclay home," Jen said. "I guess she wants to stay until we get hold of April. Just to, you know, be sure."

"Couldn't you give Mag a call when you find out?" Skeptical again, as in, *Why does my wife care so much about your daughter?*

The hedges shook. It was Sally, warning them of her approach. "William? Jennifer?"

"Everything all right?" Billy said.

"Mmmm," Sally said. "I couldn't sleep. I saw lights on and heard voices."

"Just us chickens," Billy said. "How's our professor?"

"Those rehab people make the doctors look decisive," Sally said. "No one can say anything about anything, apparently."

"Probably afraid of being sued," Billy said.

"I'd sign a waiver," Sally said. "I don't even care if what they tell me is true. I just want to hear *something*."

Janic, she explained, was due to stay in the Jeannine M. Sparkes Rehabilitation Center until certain measurements were attained and milestones reached, but no one could, or would, tell her anything about his chances of reaching them.

"And honestly," she said, out into the night, "I'm going to be paying my above-Medicare share in cash. So I'd like to know what I'm in for."

Billy rubbed his hat again, so hard that Sally said, "Careful, don't catch fire."

Jen swallowed. The confessional spirit of the evening finally caught up to her. "Speaking of cash," she said, "I suppose now is as good a time as any to apologize for breaking the very first rule we made. About, you know, not going out and buying a lot of conspicuous *stuff*." She gestured up the driveway. "Porsche, in case you haven't seen it, and pool, although it's getting delayed and might stay a hole all winter. So feel free to say 'I told you so.' "

"My goodness," Sally said. "I don't think we're an 'I told you so' bunch, are we, William? Guess what? We bought a house. What could be more conspicuous than that?"

"Are you moving?" Jen said. All her life, *14 Sylvan Street* had meant the Levlovices.

"No, the kids' new house," Sally said. "On River Rise. We covered a fifty-percent down payment, although they don't know the source of their, shall we say, *good fortune*. As far as they know, it's a lifetime of their parents' good work as civil servants."

The conversation lulled. The women, separately, turned to Billy.

He threw up his hands again. *Freeze.* "Not guilty," he said. "Whatever it is you two are about to accuse me of."

"What are you guys doing with it, if we may ask?" Jen asked.

"We're doing the most ridiculous thing of all," he said.

"What's that?" Sally said.

He laughed nervously, took a pack of cigarettes from his jeans pocket and tapped one free. "This is why I came outside in the first place. Not allowed to smoke in my own house."

He offered cigarettes to the women, clearly as a joke. Surprises all around; they both took him up on it. He lit cigarettes for them with exaggerated gallantry.

"So what are we doing with the money?" he said, in a puff of smoke. "Absolutely nothing. It's like it's not even there."

Sally inhaled, closed her eyes. "When we were very young," she exhaled.

Jen, too, smoked herself back in time. After April and before the twins, the new Jennifer Margolis had briefly taken up smoking, trying to look like the adult she'd suddenly become, already on her way to—what did Maggie call it?—her robust family.

Billy whistled smoke through his teeth like a real smoker. Jen would have to tell Keith that Billy seemed awfully nervous tonight, that the Canes seemed to be cracking up. Then again, maybe she wouldn't. The Margolises could rise above the poor Canes tonight, couldn't they?

"It's *exactly* like the money's not even there," Billy said. Long inhale, long exhale. "Fuck me," he said. "It's gone. The whole case. Weeks ago, and I haven't told my wife."

Jen shivered. It had finally happened. Someone was coming back for the money. As soon as April came home, Jen would collect her robust family and rise above everything and everyone.

41

Something for Nothing

Nishal waited, as usual, until the needle—never very far from *E*—dipped under the line. He stopped at the next gas station, unholstered the nozzle. Let the dial run wild. Past ten dollars. Felt like he was holding a gun. White-knuckled (common beginner's mistake), jazzed and powerful. Past twenty. Let it go without even looking, until it stopped, with a click and a dare, at forty-four dollars, thirty-eight cents.

He hoped his *titi* was watching. Knew he was. Had been all along. Might as well have been Toomer waving that leaf blower around this afternoon. A divining rod like Nishal's father, desperate, used to use on the beach. In his father's case, it had led him to nothing. Again and again. In Nishal's case, it led him right to that sweet workshop. He could see rocks inside, and tools. He let himself in. *Couple three hours*, the long-legged guy had said. Place was his. Simple thumb latch on the door put up no resistance. As always, he was welcome.

Not *his* rocks and tools. Not the mind-numbing and back-breaking work. Jackhammer, wedge, feather. These rocks, beautiful and graceful, were already slabbed, sheeted, split. Prizes. Pirates' gold. Retrieved from someone else's hard work.

Small tub of silicone tipped over. On its own. Out of nowhere.

No. Not on its own. Not out of nowhere. The hand of his *titi*. The silicone drew Nishal to clean it up. Then drew him to the sink to wash his hands. And drew him under the sink for a towel. Not without a fight; finally, a door resisted him. But he worked it. Up and out, a little to the left.

His *titi* had it right. There *are* riches in rocks. If only you know where to look.

Nishal went to the trunk of his car. Opened the case slowly, as if the money would jump out. Like a cat. In the shed, he'd opened the case just an inch. Just opened one clip. Enough to see money. Enough to see that he wanted to be on his own turf before he opened it fully, counted it. Dreamed.

Had to admit that this bleak upstate gas station was his turf. Popped open both clips. *Shit*. Money. But a shitload of folded brown paper bags, too. Fools' money. Still, more money than he'd ever seen in his life. He knocked like a *linja* ball—small, hard and excitable—back and forth between glee and stiffed.

Could this be a message from Toomer? Or a trap? Maybe his *titi* was alive, fine, trolling the country with the other half of this money. Or back home. Rich boy. *Rey de la montaña.*

Or had those *baka* runners planned the stiff all along? Planned to set up his *jai-titi*. Clever little mouse stiffed right back!

Of course, could have been the long-legged man in the *tope*. Nishal imagined the guy using the money to buy his whole spread. House, pool. Corner lot. If only Nishal had come earlier, come right away, right when his *titi* called, he, Nishal, could have been the one living there! (Logic abandons the head of a man staring at so much cash.)

Nishal went into the convenience store. He had no idea what one hundred dollars—minus the gas, so $55.62—would buy. He blurred his eyes, and the bright, plasticky food looked like the bright, useless things the *chucochas* sell on the corner. He grabbed. Doughnuts, corn chips. Flashlight, beef jerky, little fudge squares, two dollars a square. Could all this nothing really add up to something? He felt more foolish than rich.

The young kid at the register punched his keys as he combed through Nishal's mountain of nothing. "With the gas . . . ninety-two ninety-two." He smiled at Nishal. "That's a funny one."

Nishal wanted to get even closer. Without going over. He scanned the counter, behind the counter. Panicky. Like he was going to rob the place.

"I'll take that red box there." Pointed to cigarettes.

Kid rang it up. "With tax . . . now that'll be a hundred two fourteen."

"Nah, wait." Scanned again. His eye landed on a small maroon bag with bright orange writing. *CIGAR-ets*. "Let me see that."

Picture on the front showed small cigars, eight lined up in a neat row. Nishal pictured his grandfather. Always puffing a small, sweet-smelling cigar, telling stories in a dialect that the kids couldn't understand. Nishal and his brothers stole cigars from their *avabe* and smoked behind the church, behind school. He couldn't have been older than seven or eight. His *titi* was there, too, smoking away. Couldn't have been more than three or four years old.

Nishal slid the *CIGAR-ets* back across the counter to seal the deal.

"Ninety-six eleven." Kid looked down at the bag, then up at Nishal. "Cheap shit." Smiled again.

"No shit." Nishal smiled back. Liked this kid.

He reached into his pocket. Carefully separated one bill from the rest. Then separated another one. Slid them as a pair of aces over the counter and took his three bags of loot with him before the kid turned back from the register.

42

Cause of Death

Labyrinth, Virginia, 525 miles south of Ashley-on-Hudson, New York, another cop ran another plate: 1999 Ford Fiesta, forest green. Registered to Alejandro Barba, twenty-seven, Kingston, New York. Kid had a record (using, running, dealing, jacking) a mile long. Which was how they knew the DOA in the car was not Alejandro Barba, twenty-seven, Kingston, New York.

Report said DOA. But inside the sheriff's department, they called it a DOF. *Dead on finding.* In the sticks, aka Labyrinth, Virginia, a dead body can go a long time without notice. Especially one in a 1999 Ford Fiesta registered to a twenty-seven-year-old New York fuck-up. Left to rot under a highway overpass. Not even a real road under there. Barely wide enough for a Ford Fiesta.

Not unheard of for high school kids with toy cars like that to snake their way down to the river. Smoke pot or drink beer. This was not that. *Hispanic male between eighteen and thirty; cause of death: generalized sepsis.* Traces of you-name-it in the trunk. Must have been a real pharmacy at one time. Not now, though. No pharma itself. No explosives, no visible blood. Quite possible the DOF had been running the familiar path overhead. Highway from Florida to New York was full of runners of all kinds. This one pulled off long enough to die.

In the morgue, lab technician and cop traded details. For weeks, regular patrol missed it; car's the same color as that shit-swamp down there. Probably undocumented. No ID, no nothing. Wounds from an old injury. Pretty extensive beating, looks like.

—Fuck anybody's grandmother's *generalized sepsis.* What do you think he really died of?

—Being at the bottom of the food chain.

43

The Adirondack

Daniel first thought he would take the car rather than the train. Shouldn't a guy ride off into the sunset in a Porsche? But having shed morality and logic, he was leaning heavily on superstition. Didn't want to change a thing for fear of everything unraveling. So Amtrak it was. The overnight 9:57 Adirondack to Montreal, via Saratoga Springs, Whitehall, Ticonderoga, Rouses Point, St-Lambert, place-names that captured the imagination.

He was staring down the barrel of ten o'clock. Nine fifty-seven had come and gone with an announcement that the train would be ten minutes late. Maybe Michelle was the kind of person who checked the status of trains and planes, so she knew she had an extra ten minutes to get to the station. Travel with babies was so unpredictable, especially at night. You hoped against hope that she would not bring the baby, but honestly, you couldn't imagine her leaving him. Leaving the husband, the awful Tomas, yes. But you were quite sure that if you had this woman and the road—the border!—in your future, you had little Peyton and his spit-up in your future, too.

44

An Ordinary Moon

Three months ago, on the night of the partial eclipse of the moon, Jen had talked Keith into coming outside with her. She loved celestial drama—falling stars, rainbows, fireworks, even a good harvest moon—and the kids would take any excuse to extend bedtime.

Sally had been invited outside by Janic. She grabbed her spring jacket, delighted that he was the one initiating the companionship for a change.

Maggie and Billy had been on their way home from walking Barclay when they came upon their milling neighbors. The marginal time before bed was always the hardest for the Canes. When they were feeling particularly close or dangerously distant, and when the weather was agreeable, Billy would join his wife on her evening dog walk. At least he could help with his only as-yet-extant progeny.

Allie Yaniv-Hansen had been the first in her house to notice a crowd down the street. She'd asked her mother if they could go outside and see what everybody was doing. Shoshanna assumed just the girls would go, the boys being wholly uninterested in their new neighbors. But after a few minutes with nothing to do, Daniel and Caleb looked at each other, shrugged and went outside to see what was going on.

Ash had been the only one, the only adult, who hadn't wandered onto the street the night of the eclipse. Tonight would be a different story. Washing his brushes at the end of a now-rare good night of painting, he noticed his neighbors milling around on the Margolises' front lawn. Late. Midnight.

This time, he had a stake in his neighbors' assembly.

Clouds floated willy-nilly in front of the gibbous moon. For a moment, a particularly crisp, reddish cloud looked like it could be the earth's shadow sitting in front of the moon, as it had in June. Individually, then together, they began to wonder if they were due for another eclipse.

"Could it happen again so quickly?" Jen wondered, taking a swig of her who-knew-how-manyeth cup of white wine.

"I don't think it's even a full moon tonight, a fully full moon," Maggie said. "If that has anything to do with it."

Maggie offered Ash, newly arrived, a Dixie cup of red wine, which would save her from drinking the entire bottle herself. Keith had given her the most expensive-looking (silver-edged label; what more did he know?) of the three bottles standing on his kitchen counter. The Dixie cups had been Maggie's idea. "So we won't break your good wineglasses," she'd said. Keith had been a little thrilled by the raucous premise.

"Janie would know whether or not we're in for another eclipse," Billy said.

Sally had no particular reaction to the mention of her husband's name. She didn't seem to be listening to the conversation. She'd turn her head now and then to look at one of her neighbors, but never the one who was speaking. She was, in fact, a couple of sea breezes to the wind.

Earlier, when Keith had offered her beer or wine, she'd asked if he had anything stronger. "What would you like?" he'd asked.

"Bartender's choice," she'd said. "As long as it's flammable."

If Janic had been there, he might have explained how the ancient Babylonians had discovered that any particular eclipse was not to be repeated for another eighteen years, eleven days and eight hours. The Saros cycle. And he could have, if anyone was interested, gone inside to retrieve a lengthy chart mapping the geocoordinates of not only the particular eclipse they'd intersected in June but the eclipse cycle's entire duration, beginning in 1427 and due to complete in 2707. They would have taken a look at the dates and wondered about Sylvan Street so far into the past and future. Sally might have joked that the Levlovices still remembered that February eclipse in 1535; Jen might have joked that she hoped Tiger would be potty-trained by the eclipse of November 2562.

"I think we would have heard if there was going to be another eclipse," Jen said.

"That's right," Maggie said. "We heard so much on the news before the spring one."

"It's just a cloud," Keith said, lacking the women's constitution for charade. Tonight, Sylvan Street had gathered to bear witness not to celestial wonder but to potential tragedy, domestic drama, family scandal: a child was missing. It was midnight, and, as everyone knew, April Margolis had not yet come home.

"Mag, I have a confession," Billy Cane said, taking a step closer to his wife.

She fanned her hand in front of her nose. "Smoking?"

"Only out in the wide world," he said. Then, to the assembled: "I'm not allowed to smoke in the house. In my own house."

"For the good of our future children," she said, in an odd, accented voice. She might have been imitating a movie, but if she was no one got the reference.

"Our money's gone," he said. "As in stolen."

"Stolen?" Maggie blew into the bottle she was holding and covered it, which Billy knew was her superstition: wishing on a spent wine bottle. Then she went over to the front stairs and laid the bottle on its side, carefully, as if it contained a ship. Perhaps she was gathering her thoughts; perhaps she was drunk. In either case, her response was beyond subdued.

Keith Margolis took up the charge. "What the—? Where'd you put it? Did you see anyone? Anything out of the ordinary? What kind of safe was it in?"

Ash, too, snapped to attention, probably wondering what it meant for him, for his money. He always seemed to be looking to get gypped, and this might be another opportunity.

"Not a safe, exactly," Billy said. "I locked it in my workshop, locked it in a cabinet in the locked shop." He had everyone's attention now, which was the last thing he wanted. It occurred to him that he could ask for all the money back. He didn't have to have given it away in the first place.

"Who knew it was there?" Margolis said. "Anyone besides you and your wife?"

"*I* didn't know it was there," Maggie said.

"You didn't tell your wife?" Margolis said.

"That was *her* choice," Billy said.

"Why?" Jen said.

Maggie squinted, as though she was thinking about this for the very first time. "I was afraid of what I'd do with it."

"Maybe your daughter," Billy said. All night he'd been feeling it: there was some other shoe with April Margolis, and it might as well drop now. "Not a bad sum to run away from home with."

Jen, who'd been picking up littered Dixie cups, dropped them right out of her hand. "How dare you accuse my daughter of such a thing."

"Billy," Maggie said, wounded. Her precious April, and everyone knew it. "That's a terrible thing to say."

"Listen, Cane—" Keith started. But he stopped talking when he heard a car turn onto the street.

There were no sirens, no flashing lights, but the police car turning onto Sylvan Street woke Shoshanna up as certainly as if there had been. She hurried to the window and watched the car, down the street, turn into the Margolises' driveway. It took her a moment—and the fact that she was fully clothed, the phone in the middle of the bed—to realize why she'd been expecting the police car to turn into her driveway.

She went downstairs for the hundredth time that night, in case Daniel had changed his habits and was making himself a midnight snack in the kitchen, working on his car in the garage, falling asleep in front of the TV in the living room. She had checked the kids' bedrooms a hundred times, too. All was habitual there: Allie asleep on her back, face upturned; Caleb in a different position every time she looked. No father dozing on the floor, as the mother had done years ago (in smaller, creakier Brooklyn bedrooms), having been unable to outlast the child in a race to resist sleep.

It was a little after midnight—*tomorrow already*, which added disproportionately to her anxiety. She searched the kitchen desk for a business card of Daniel's, for his office number. That was how long it had been since she'd called anything but his cell. Which he had not answered all night.

His office extension kicked her to the main number.

"Daniel Hansen?" said the young, impatient guy who answered. "Whoa, he hasn't worked here for, like, two or three months."

What . . . ? When . . . ? Where . . . ? She couldn't even formulate a question.

The guy made it clear that it was midnight, he was on deadline and had no time to spare. She didn't dare say she was Daniel Hansen's wife, which might have elicited more details—but can you imagine? The wife doesn't know! She couldn't bear to admit that to some unknown junior account executive.

Two or three months?

Each step to the basement felt like her last. She'd never walked so slowly in her life, even when she held a tiny hand for its owner's first steps.

She knelt in front of the trunk much as Daniel had, whoever he was then. Whoever she was now. The trunk hadn't changed, banged-up green army thing. Stout, utilitarian. She'd chosen it among all her *zayde*'s things to keep after his death. The trunk had been with her well longer than her husband.

She couldn't get the cash out fast enough. *Forgive me, Zayde.* Eight . . . nine . . . ten . . . eleven. Quick calculation: $110,000. She didn't remember the exact figure, didn't want to remember, but she knew it was over two hundred thousand.

She went into the laundry room, found a clean, dry pillow-case. *Goddamn him.* She threw the bills in there, one packet after another. She gathered the pillowcase by the neck. Wrung it until her fingers burned, as though she could seal it for good this way. As though she could seal anything for good.

She heaved it over her shoulder like Santa Claus, went outside and locked her sleeping children in their parentless house for the few minutes it would take her to walk down the street. At the end of the cul-de-sac, there were two cops on hand and a second chance to do the right thing. To return the money, return her family to before. Such as it was, but at least as it was before.

April, in the back of the police car, tugged her hood over her eyes. She was jumpy in a way that was familiar to Keith, that catlike way of bad teenagers, whether from drugs, a bad home or a guilty conscience. Whenever he dropped off a bad kid, a repeat offender, he wondered what must be going through the minds of the parents—at least the parents who were home and sober and pronouncing dismay. What would it be like, he'd wondered, to have lost your child so thoroughly that he or she is coming home in a cop car? Does it happen a little every day, so you don't notice until it's too late, like the proverbial frog in hot water?

The squad car's gold and black lettering—ASHLEY POLICE: WE CARE—shone like a false promise under the harsh floodlight. In the front seat was Mac Tannenhaus, an old-timer. Was this official transport or a ride home for Margolis's kid?

Mac got out of the car, shook Keith's hand, Jen's.

Turned out that April had been at the Pinnacle with Tucker McMurtry. "All clothed, Mother," Mac said, sotto voce. "Cigarettes and beer cans, but those were probably not theirs. They were just sitting there together, the two of them. She had her head on his shoulder—just waiting to go home, I think. Sweet, really."

April tried three times in quick succession to open the disabled back door, like any passenger for whom this was the first trip in a cop car. (Let's hope, Keith thought, that he never had to see her waiting patiently for a cop to come around and open the childproofed door for her, as did anyone who'd ridden in a cop car more than once or twice.)

"Ready for her?" Mac said.

"Keep her in there a little longer," Jen said. "At least we'll know where she is."

Mac surveyed the crowd of adults on the lawn.

"Neighbors," Keith explained.

"Neighborly," Mac said. "Waiting up for the kid?"

"We're a close street," Keith said. "We look out for each other."

While Keith and Mac exchanged shop talk, Jen opened the squad car door. "After the talk we just had?" she said, trying to block April's egress.

"*You* had the talk, Mother. Not me." She clutched her hoodie around her—as her mother might do with a sweater—and stomped to the front door.

As the police car drove away, Keith watched his daughter's back. After the screen door slammed behind her, he went inside, too. Door slammed again, floodlight cut off.

Maggie and Billy, separately, wondered if he was going to get his gun.

Keith, trash bag in hand, crossed the lawn and dumped the money at Billy's feet. "Here, have ours. What's left of it."

The floodlight was still off, but the ambient heat-light of a gathering of people was enough to see that the cash had dwindled down to ten or a dozen packets.

"Take it," Keith said. "Hell, take the Porsche, too. I don't know what any of it means anymore."

Poor Margolis, Billy thought. He was the last to realize that money had lost its currency on Sylvan Street.

"And wait, this, too." Keith dropped a bulging money belt. "But I'm sure April took *your* money, Cane. Not this twelve thousand dollars that she just handed me, which she had kept under her mattress because she was too embarrassed to tell us you wouldn't accept it."

Then, to Maggie: "You think you can do a better job with April? I'll sure as shit give you a try."

"Keith." Jen whispered something into his ear.

"Right, well, we all have our crosses to bear," Keith said, chastened, though not quite ready to renounce his bluster.

"I think they're feeling sorry for us, Billy," Maggie said. "I told all. Might as well join you in a smoke, since I have nothing to lose." She held two fingers rakishly to her parted lips.

"All right, Mae West." Billy seemed to treasure the lightness of the moment, although he also seemed uncertain of it. He lit a cigarette, took a drag until it glowed then placed it between his wife's lips.

Maggie kept it there for a moment, as if deciding whether or not to smoke it. Whether or not to breathe.

Barclay, the only sober one around, suddenly shook himself awake. Perhaps fleeing a bad dream, he tried to stand himself up. Once, twice, thrice, half rose, stumbled back to the ground.

"Poor thing," Sally whispered. "Poor Janic."

Finally, Barclay got all four legs to work at the same time and shuffle-clicked down the driveway. His leash, dragging audibly, summed it up: where a parent should be.

"Fuck it, Mag," Billy said. "Let's adopt. Let's change everything. Two kids, three. We can talk to Bianca, if you want. I've been thinking about it. We're a good home. Let's give some lucky kids a good home."

Maggie knelt at Billy's feet—an amazing, horrifying act of supplication.

But only in misperception. Actually, Billy's feet were right next to the money. Maggie touched the glowing end of her cigarette to a packet of bills.

Smoke and smolder, despite her patience. Bundled like that, money does its best to defend its value.

Ah, but the bills' wrapper! Flared instantly and, with a whoosh, disappeared. The naked bills fell out of their neat pile and flamed into a beautiful, winged, late-summer, late-night fire. The light was flattering, the glow warm, and everyone stood mesmerized. The flames raged and dimmed, raged and dimmed, as a paper fire does while it seeks something more nourishing.

Billy decided to take his wife's act as one of forgiveness. For his losing the money. For his finding it in the first place. For his being *Billy*, whimsical, lucky and unlucky in about equal measure and, in the end, limited in his power to change her world.

All one-hundred-dollar bills look alike. Staring at the fire, Shoshanna had to concentrate hard in order to keep an accurate picture of her own cash—safe and whole, inside a pillowcase, locked inside her garage. She'd barely gotten past her driveway with it when she realized that if her husband had left his unemployed wife alone with two children, she better not give up a hundred thousand dollars in cash.

Ash squatted, poked the fire with a thick stick. He pushed it deeper, hoping it would catch. He had a visceral urge to feed the flames something lasting. The heavy messenger bag in his basement, densely woven and stuffed with its own self-perpetuating kindling, would have been perfect.

Maybe it was just a coincidence that once he was flooded with money, he felt drained of talent. He'd spent as much as he could on materials, almost a thousand dollars. He'd felt productive, lucky, *ascendant* as he mixed the new malachite, gold leaf and various indigos, cyan blues, grays. But the instant he put brush to canvas, he couldn't paint.

If he was as hard-core as he'd once been, in his twenties and early thirties, he would have gone down to his basement, retrieved his messenger bag and fed it to the fire. But he was older now. He, too, needed something lasting. He would wait out this latest bout of painter's block, and his talent would return. He would wait out this lousy market for art, and his sales, perhaps only occasional but at least trending upward, would return. He was in it for the long haul. Meantime, he was covered. He felt sorry for his younger self, which would right now be watching its daily sustenance go up in flames without knowing better.

Maggie stepped into the crook of Billy's arm. Her face was brighter with reflection than anyone else's. Somehow, this fire knew it was *hers*.

Jen was the first to break the spell. She rushed over and kicked free three packets of yet-unburned bills and April's melting plastic money pouch. She gathered the bills in her arm. She kept a foot on the nape of the pouch, too hot to handle.

Sally leaned in and dropped a hundred-dollar bill. It lofted for a moment, as though the flames were trying to save it from itself, then fluttered back onto the pyre and flared into oblivion.

"Brava," Sally said. "Brilliant show."

A sadness—reality, perhaps—passed over her face. "Well, I need the rest of mine," she said. "That trash bag in my basement is my lifeline now. Janic's, too." A childlike smile, then: "But it sure was fun watching that hundred. I can finally say I had money to burn."

45

The Good Life

Pull up the line. *Nothing*. Nishal didn't care. This fishing wasn't about feeding a small, good wife or hungry, growing sons.

This was pure *being*. Being and waiting.

Wheel in his hand. Poised at Fate's edge. He could go anywhere.

Unlike his father, Nishal had bought his boat outright. Had no liens. Owed no back pay to a crew.

And Nishal had something else. A hundred twenty-five thousand dollars in American cash. Sealed in a waterproof bag, tied and dropped down an abandoned well at the edge of his family's property. At the fallow far south corner, where he and Charysse were building their new cinder-block house, two stories. Had to build fast, before the forest overtook the land.

The well made him nervous. Tricky to get his hands on the bag. But he couldn't very well bury the money in the ground. Can't trust this ground. Floods, mudslides, fires. He had more trust in the sea. But cardinal rule of the sea: bring no more than you need (and be prepared to lose what you bring).

Next to the cinder-block house would go a one-room cinder-block nurse's clinic. Village was starved for it. People worse off than his *titi* got nothing, not even a Band-Aid.

Nishal's mother, ageless, would help take care of the baby. Due in three months. Already named Tasmin.

The baby, the baby. Eased Charysse's mind over leaving Natasha.

—Poor Tasha. First Toomer, then us.

Poor Tasha? *Ha ha*. As soon as Nishal offered—and she grabbed—the ten thousand dollars, she forgot all about them. Just her and her million ideas. She'd buy a house. Go to college. Go back to high school. Get a dog. Or buy lottery tickets.

—If you can win the lottery off of one lousy ticket, brother, think of *my* chances if I buy ten thousand dollars' worth.

That had been Nishal's story. The less Tasha knew, the better. Charysse, too. One day, he would tell her.

He was heading back into harbor now. This warm salt wind could change any subject, could shift any mind. He was remembering, his body was, how to be on the water: be ballast. Move not forward but up and down. Absorb the swells and chucks of the Atlantic. Go with the movement. Give.